the OUTLAW PRINCE™

For Rod and Frank—two English knights.

THE OUTLAW PRINCE™

**Based on the novel *The Outlaw of Torn*,
by Edgar Rice Burroughs**

SCRIPT
Rob Hughes

PENCILS AND INKS
Thomas Yeates

LAYOUTS
Michael Wm. Kaluta

COLOR ARTISTS
**Lori Almeida with Thomas Yeates, Steve Oliff,
and Gloria Vasquez**

LETTERING
Steve Dutro

COVER ARTIST—STANDARD EDITION
Esad Ribic

COVER ARTIST—LIMITED EDITION HARDCOVER
Alan Lathwell

DARK HORSE BOOKS

PUBLISHER
Mike Richardson

EDITOR
Philip R. Simon

ASSISTANT EDITORS
John Schork and Patrick Thorpe

DESIGNER
Amy Arendts

DIGITAL PRODUCTION
Chris Horn

*Special thanks to Danton Burroughs, Sandra Galfas,
James J. Sullos, Jr., and Cathy Wilbanks at Edgar Rice Burroughs, Inc.,
and to Cary Grazzini and Jeff Slemons.*

THE OUTLAW PRINCE

Published by Dark Horse Books
A division of Dark Horse Comics, Inc.
10956 SE Main Street
Milwaukie, OR 97222

DarkHorse.com

To find a comics shop in your area,
call the Comic Shop Locator Service toll-free at 1-888-266-4226.

First edition: April 2011
ISBN 978-1-59582-710-4
Limited Edition ISBN 978-1-59582-721-0

3 5 7 9 10 8 6 4 2

Printed at Midas Printing International, Ltd., Huizhou, China

LOVE and Loyalty

Introduction by Rob Hughes

FEELING A BIT NOSTALGIC THIS bright morning. Sitting here in the quiet solitude of my childhood bedroom, looking up at the Soledad Mountain Cross that dominates the skyline above my window and reflecting back more than thirty years to the day when I discovered a story that would touch me as few ever would during my life. I was around eleven or twelve years old at the time, an avid comic-book reader and collector, but I had never read an actual novel, a book without any pictures, and decided it was about time that I did so. Going to my parents' library, I chose a book, not because of the author (of whom I was somewhat aware as the creator of Tarzan), but because of the tremendous cover it featured by the legendary Frank Frazetta, a painting that was simple in design and yet so potently powerful in its impact upon such a young and impressionable mind. And so, it was here, in this very room, that I was introduced to Edgar Rice Burroughs's second work, *The Outlaw of Torn*.

Some stories resonate down through the years. Always present, never forgotten. They are masterful tales that teach us how we *should* be. They inspire us to reach high and far, with all our might, to become what

we could and *ought* to be. How to think and act, not with selfish desires or design, but with purity of heart. They challenge us to our face to walk in faith toward an unseen and often unknown, yet very real ideal. They strengthen and fortify us, showering bright rays of hope upon our troubled spirits as we walk a very lonely road that would otherwise be unbearably dark. These elite stories possess the power to touch the heart and take up residence in our inner personal and most private sanctum we call the soul. They become part of us! *The Outlaw of Torn* is such a story for me. One of the very finest I have ever read. An immensely rich historic medieval saga with a powerful, heroic figure at its nucleus, around whom revolves a terrific supporting cast, who are all thrust into the tumultuous time of the Second Barons' War. A larger-than-life central character of such vehement noble conviction of heart and soul and indomitable will that he inspires unwavering love and loyalty from friends and followers alike. Two timeless themes that dominate this novel.

Nearly an entire century has passed since Burroughs first wrote this masterpiece. In undertaking the challenge of adapting the novel into a visual medium, it was not my intention to write an exact retelling of the story, but to take the foundation that Burroughs laid down and build upon it by enriching both character development and plot points, yet always remaining true to the spirit and direction of the novel. I was compelled to do so. A truly timeless book that remains, as the great prophet Jeremiah explains, "in mine heart as a burning fire shut up in my bones, and I was weary with forbearing, and I could not [stay]."

It has been my privilege to adapt this wonderful work, an honor to work with the amazing talents in bringing this graphic novel to fruition, and I thank God, first and foremost, for granting me the opportunity. May He guide me in the full completion of this epic saga.

Finally, a heartfelt gratitude to my family and close friends who believed in me and supported me in this project, and to you, the reader, for spending your time with us when the undying legend of Norman of Torn was born.

Rob Hughes
La Jolla, California, Winter 2010

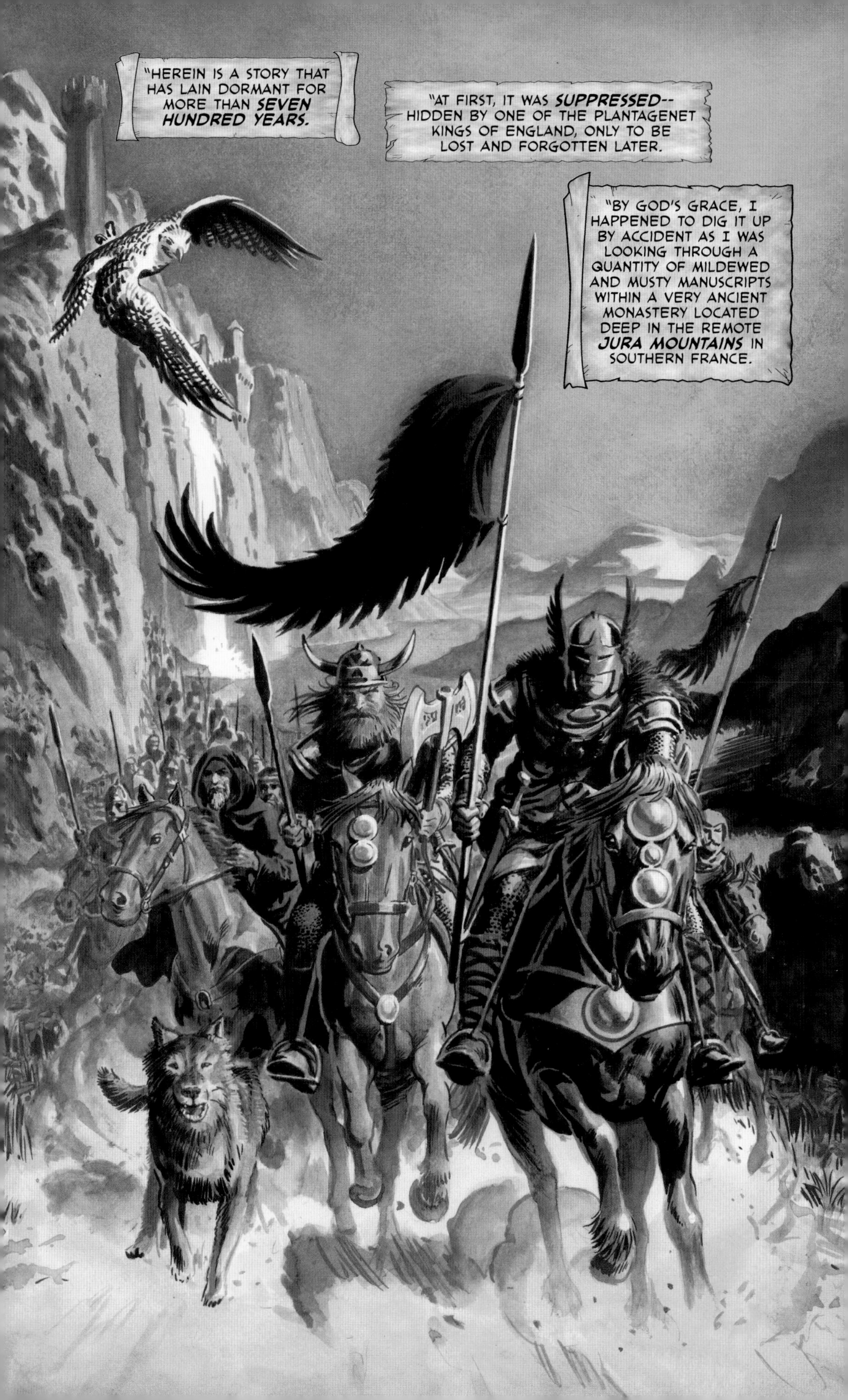
"HEREIN IS A STORY THAT HAS LAIN DORMANT FOR MORE THAN *SEVEN HUNDRED YEARS.*
"AT FIRST, IT WAS *SUPPRESSED*-- HIDDEN BY ONE OF THE PLANTAGENET KINGS OF ENGLAND, ONLY TO BE LOST AND FORGOTTEN LATER.
"BY GOD'S GRACE, I HAPPENED TO DIG IT UP BY ACCIDENT AS I WAS LOOKING THROUGH A QUANTITY OF MILDEWED AND MUSTY MANUSCRIPTS WITHIN A VERY ANCIENT MONASTERY LOCATED DEEP IN THE REMOTE *JURA MOUNTAINS* IN SOUTHERN FRANCE.

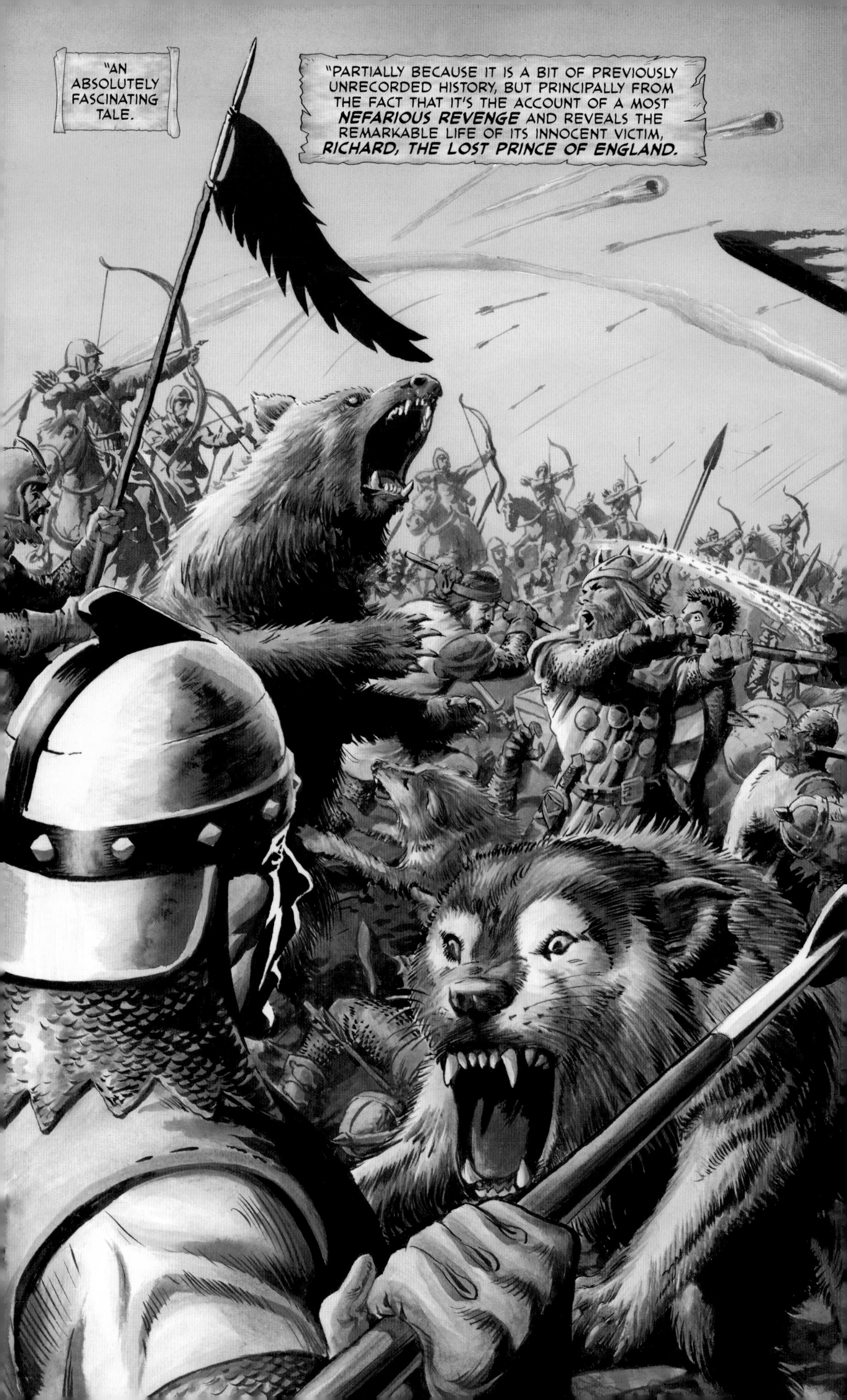
"AN ABSOLUTELY FASCINATING TALE.
"PARTIALLY BECAUSE IT IS A BIT OF PREVIOUSLY UNRECORDED HISTORY, BUT PRINCIPALLY FROM THE FACT THAT IT'S THE ACCOUNT OF A MOST NEFARIOUS REVENGE AND REVEALS THE REMARKABLE LIFE OF ITS INNOCENT VICTIM, RICHARD, THE LOST PRINCE OF ENGLAND.

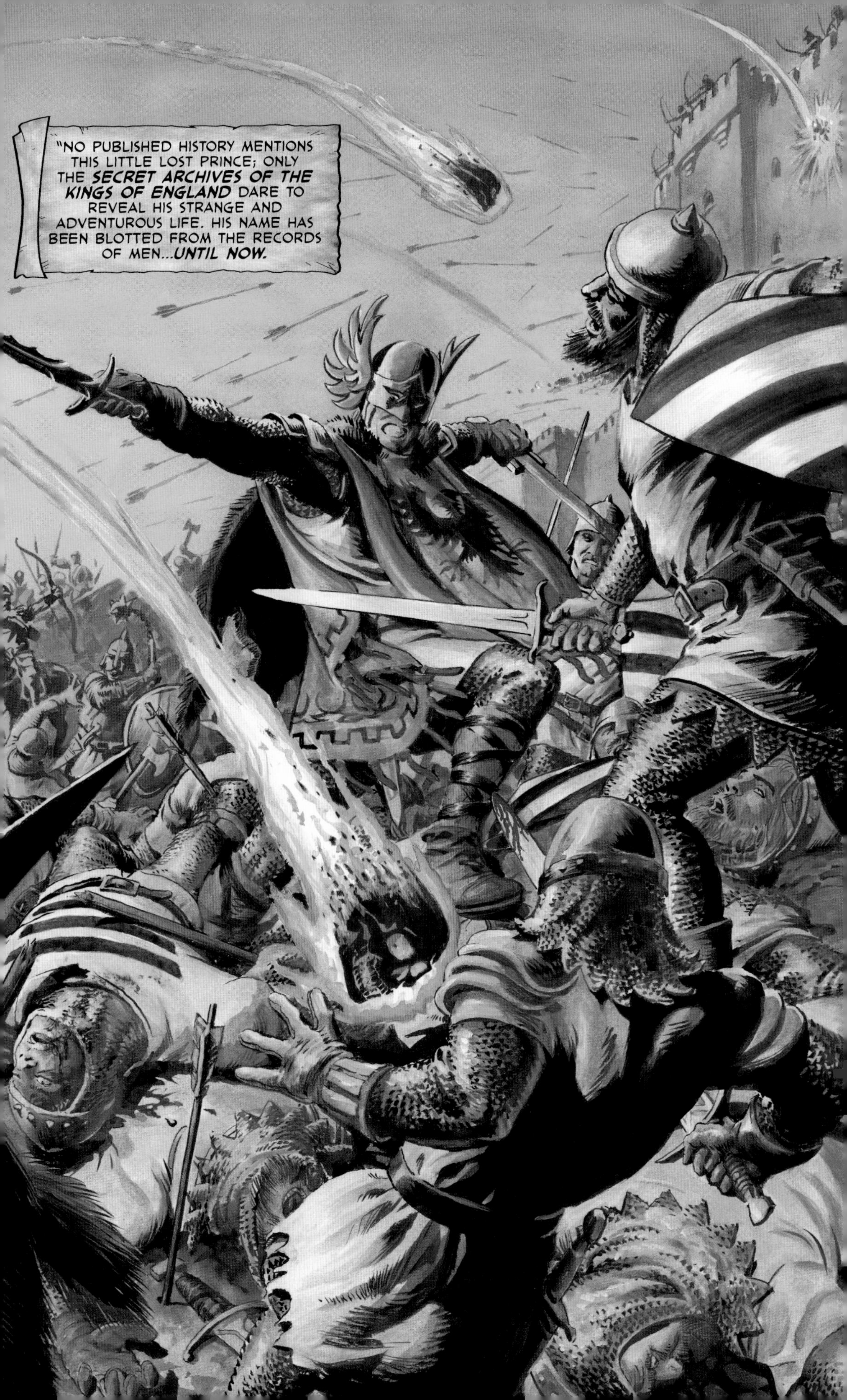
"NO PUBLISHED HISTORY MENTIONS THIS LITTLE LOST PRINCE; ONLY THE ***SECRET ARCHIVES OF THE KINGS OF ENGLAND*** DARE TO REVEAL HIS STRANGE AND ADVENTUROUS LIFE. HIS NAME HAS BEEN BLOTTED FROM THE RECORDS OF MEN...***UNTIL NOW.***

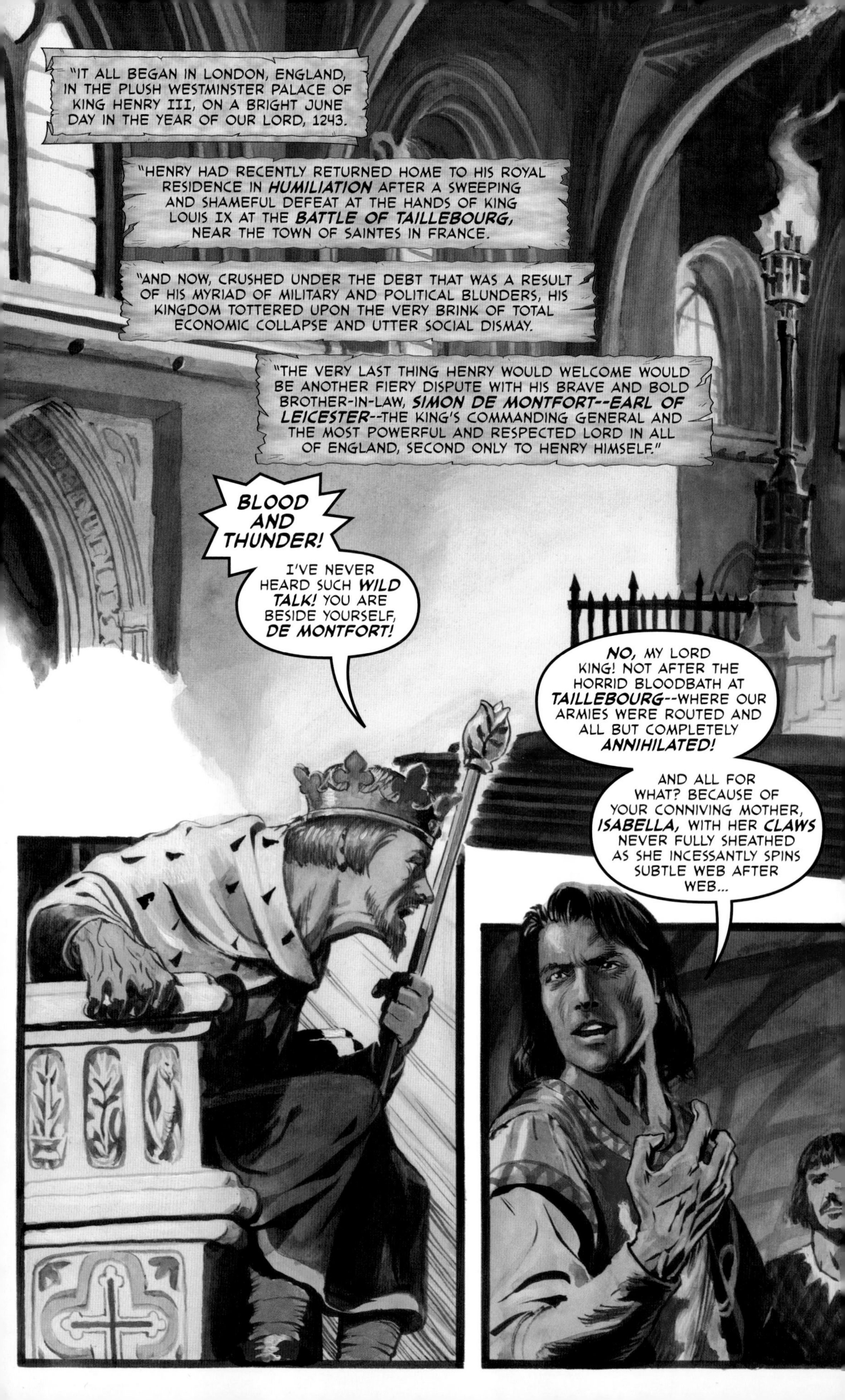
"IT ALL BEGAN IN LONDON, ENGLAND, IN THE PLUSH WESTMINSTER PALACE OF KING HENRY III, ON A BRIGHT JUNE DAY IN THE YEAR OF OUR LORD, 1243.
"HENRY HAD RECENTLY RETURNED HOME TO HIS ROYAL RESIDENCE IN HUMILIATION AFTER A SWEEPING AND SHAMEFUL DEFEAT AT THE HANDS OF KING LOUIS IX AT THE BATTLE OF TAILLEBOURG, NEAR THE TOWN OF SAINTES IN FRANCE.
"AND NOW, CRUSHED UNDER THE DEBT THAT WAS A RESULT OF HIS MYRIAD OF MILITARY AND POLITICAL BLUNDERS, HIS KINGDOM TOTTERED UPON THE VERY BRINK OF TOTAL ECONOMIC COLLAPSE AND UTTER SOCIAL DISMAY.
"THE VERY LAST THING HENRY WOULD WELCOME WOULD BE ANOTHER FIERY DISPUTE WITH HIS BRAVE AND BOLD BROTHER-IN-LAW, SIMON DE MONTFORT--EARL OF LEICESTER--THE KING'S COMMANDING GENERAL AND THE MOST POWERFUL AND RESPECTED LORD IN ALL OF ENGLAND, SECOND ONLY TO HENRY HIMSELF."
BLOOD AND THUNDER!
I'VE NEVER HEARD SUCH WILD TALK! YOU ARE BESIDE YOURSELF, DE MONTFORT!
NO, MY LORD KING! NOT AFTER THE HORRID BLOODBATH AT TAILLEBOURG--WHERE OUR ARMIES WERE ROUTED AND ALL BUT COMPLETELY ANNIHILATED!
AND ALL FOR WHAT? BECAUSE OF YOUR CONNIVING MOTHER, ISABELLA, WITH HER CLAWS NEVER FULLY SHEATHED AS SHE INCESSANTLY SPINS SUBTLE WEB AFTER WEB...

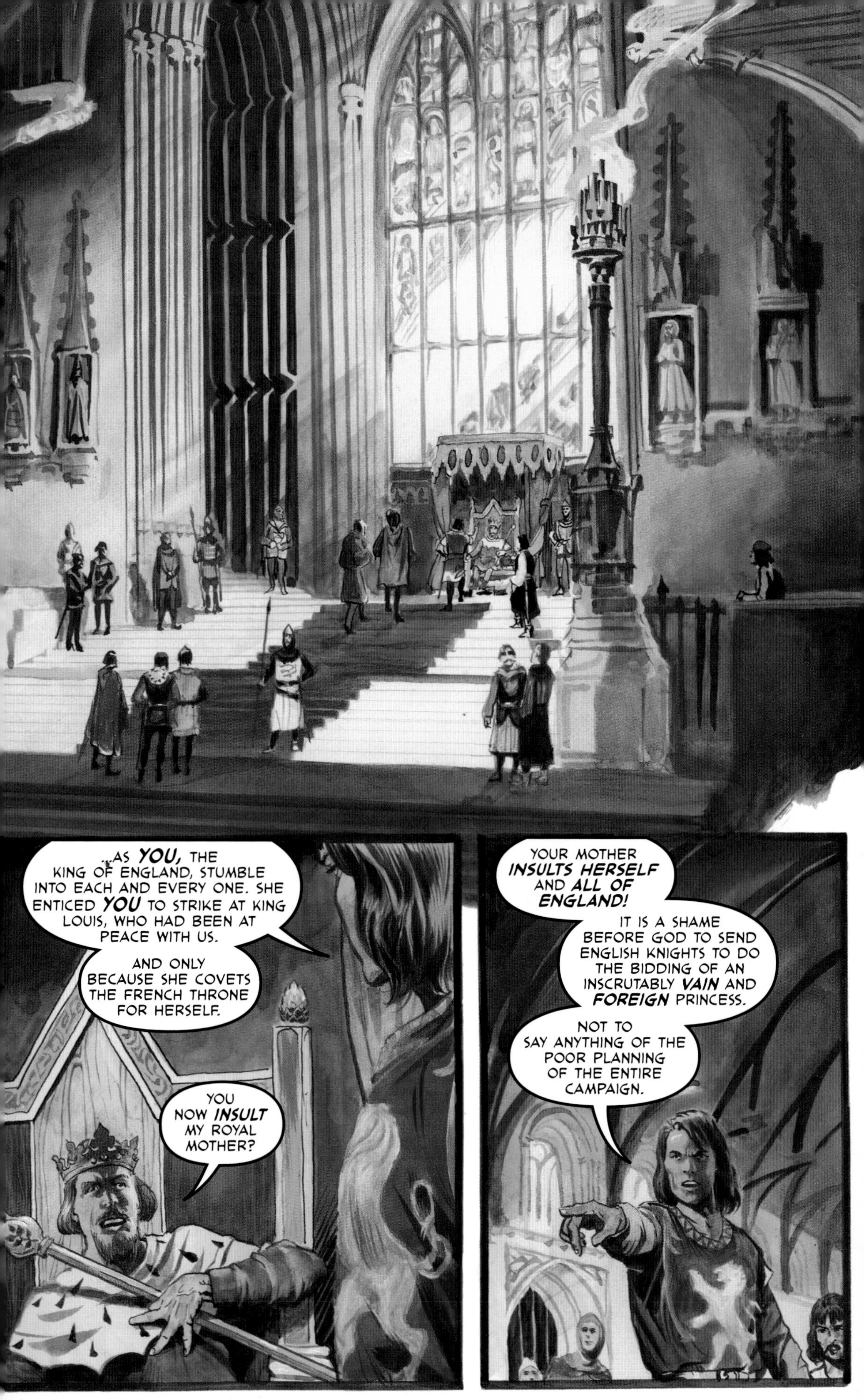
...AS YOU, THE KING OF ENGLAND, STUMBLE INTO EACH AND EVERY ONE. SHE ENTICED YOU TO STRIKE AT KING LOUIS, WHO HAD BEEN AT PEACE WITH US.
AND ONLY BECAUSE SHE COVETS THE FRENCH THRONE FOR HERSELF.
YOU NOW INSULT MY ROYAL MOTHER?
YOUR MOTHER INSULTS HERSELF AND ALL OF ENGLAND!
IT IS A SHAME BEFORE GOD TO SEND ENGLISH KNIGHTS TO DO THE BIDDING OF AN INSCRUTABLY VAIN AND FOREIGN PRINCESS.
NOT TO SAY ANYTHING OF THE POOR PLANNING OF THE ENTIRE CAMPAIGN.

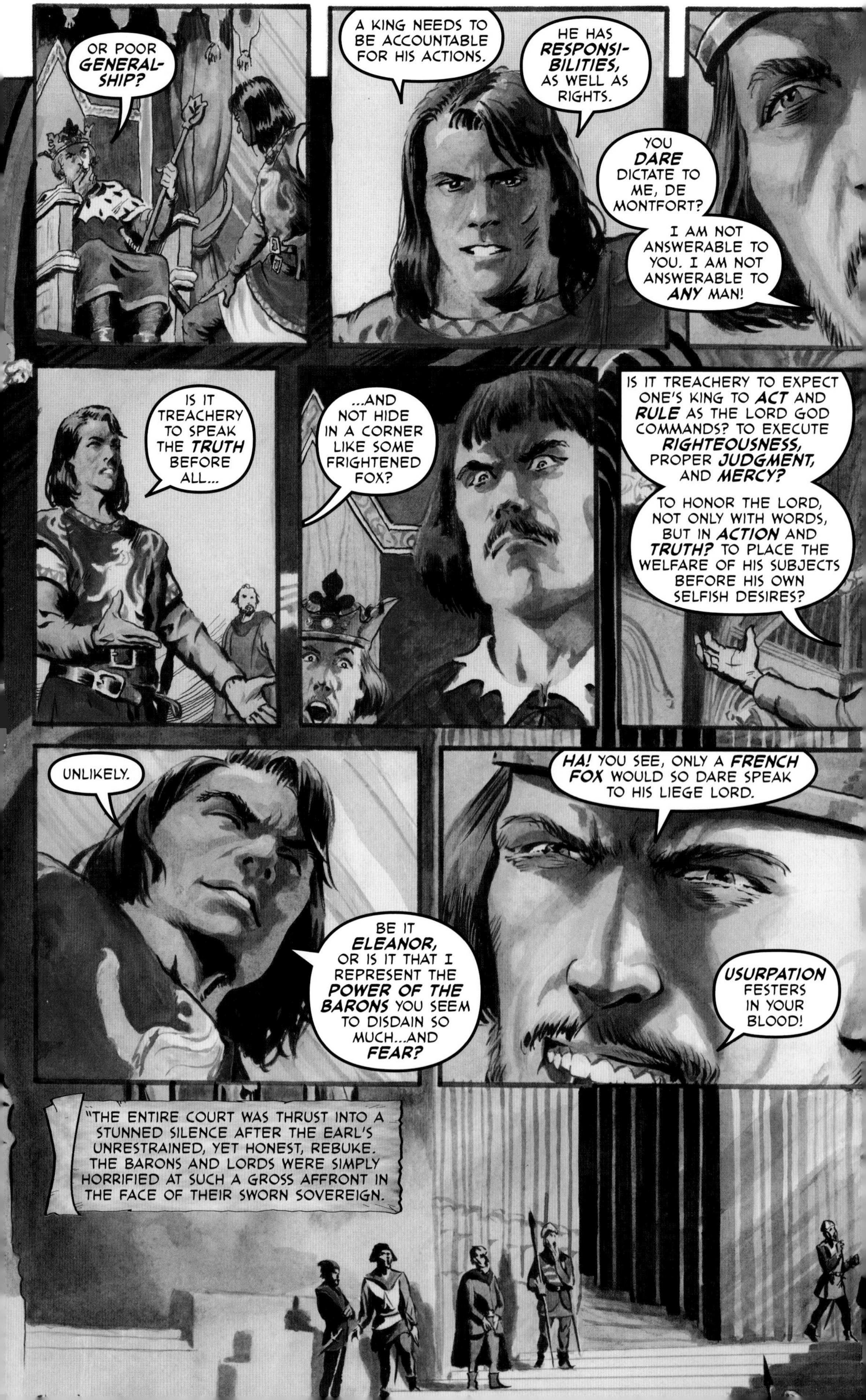
OR POOR GENERAL-SHIP?
A KING NEEDS TO BE ACCOUNTABLE FOR HIS ACTIONS.
HE HAS RESPONSI-BILITIES, AS WELL AS RIGHTS.
YOU DARE DICTATE TO ME, DE MONTFORT?
I AM NOT ANSWERABLE TO YOU. I AM NOT ANSWERABLE TO ANY MAN!
IS IT TREACHERY TO SPEAK THE TRUTH BEFORE ALL...
...AND NOT HIDE IN A CORNER LIKE SOME FRIGHTENED FOX?
IS IT TREACHERY TO EXPECT ONE'S KING TO ACT AND RULE AS THE LORD GOD COMMANDS? TO EXECUTE RIGHTEOUSNESS, PROPER JUDGMENT, AND MERCY?
TO HONOR THE LORD, NOT ONLY WITH WORDS, BUT IN ACTION AND TRUTH? TO PLACE THE WELFARE OF HIS SUBJECTS BEFORE HIS OWN SELFISH DESIRES?
UNLIKELY.
BE IT ELEANOR, OR IS IT THAT I REPRESENT THE POWER OF THE BARONS YOU SEEM TO DISDAIN SO MUCH...AND FEAR?
HA! YOU SEE, ONLY A FRENCH FOX WOULD SO DARE SPEAK TO HIS LIEGE LORD.
USURPATION FESTERS IN YOUR BLOOD!
"THE ENTIRE COURT WAS THRUST INTO A STUNNED SILENCE AFTER THE EARL'S UNRESTRAINED, YET HONEST, REBUKE. THE BARONS AND LORDS WERE SIMPLY HORRIFIED AT SUCH A GROSS AFFRONT IN THE FACE OF THEIR SWORN SOVEREIGN.

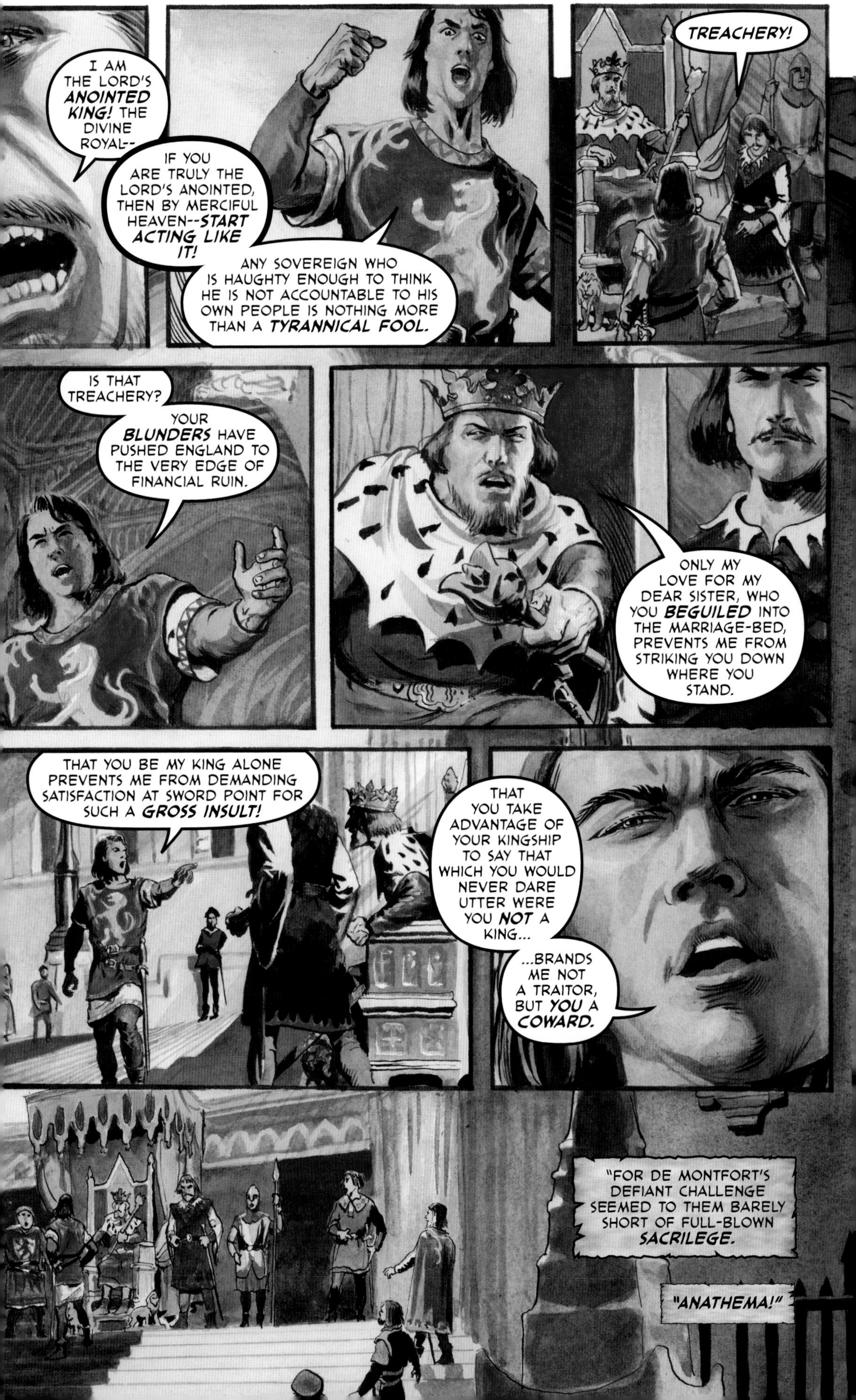
I AM THE LORD'S ANOINTED KING! THE DIVINE ROYAL--
IF YOU ARE TRULY THE LORD'S ANOINTED, THEN BY MERCIFUL HEAVEN--START ACTING LIKE IT!
ANY SOVEREIGN WHO IS HAUGHTY ENOUGH TO THINK HE IS NOT ACCOUNTABLE TO HIS OWN PEOPLE IS NOTHING MORE THAN A TYRANNICAL FOOL.
TREACHERY!
IS THAT TREACHERY?
YOUR BLUNDERS HAVE PUSHED ENGLAND TO THE VERY EDGE OF FINANCIAL RUIN.
ONLY MY LOVE FOR MY DEAR SISTER, WHO YOU BEGUILED INTO THE MARRIAGE-BED, PREVENTS ME FROM STRIKING YOU DOWN WHERE YOU STAND.
THAT YOU BE MY KING ALONE PREVENTS ME FROM DEMANDING SATISFACTION AT SWORD POINT FOR SUCH A GROSS INSULT!
THAT YOU TAKE ADVANTAGE OF YOUR KINGSHIP TO SAY THAT WHICH YOU WOULD NEVER DARE UTTER WERE YOU NOT A KING...
...BRANDS ME NOT A TRAITOR, BUT YOU A COWARD.
"FOR DE MONTFORT'S DEFIANT CHALLENGE SEEMED TO THEM BARELY SHORT OF FULL-BLOWN SACRILEGE.
"ANATHEMA!"

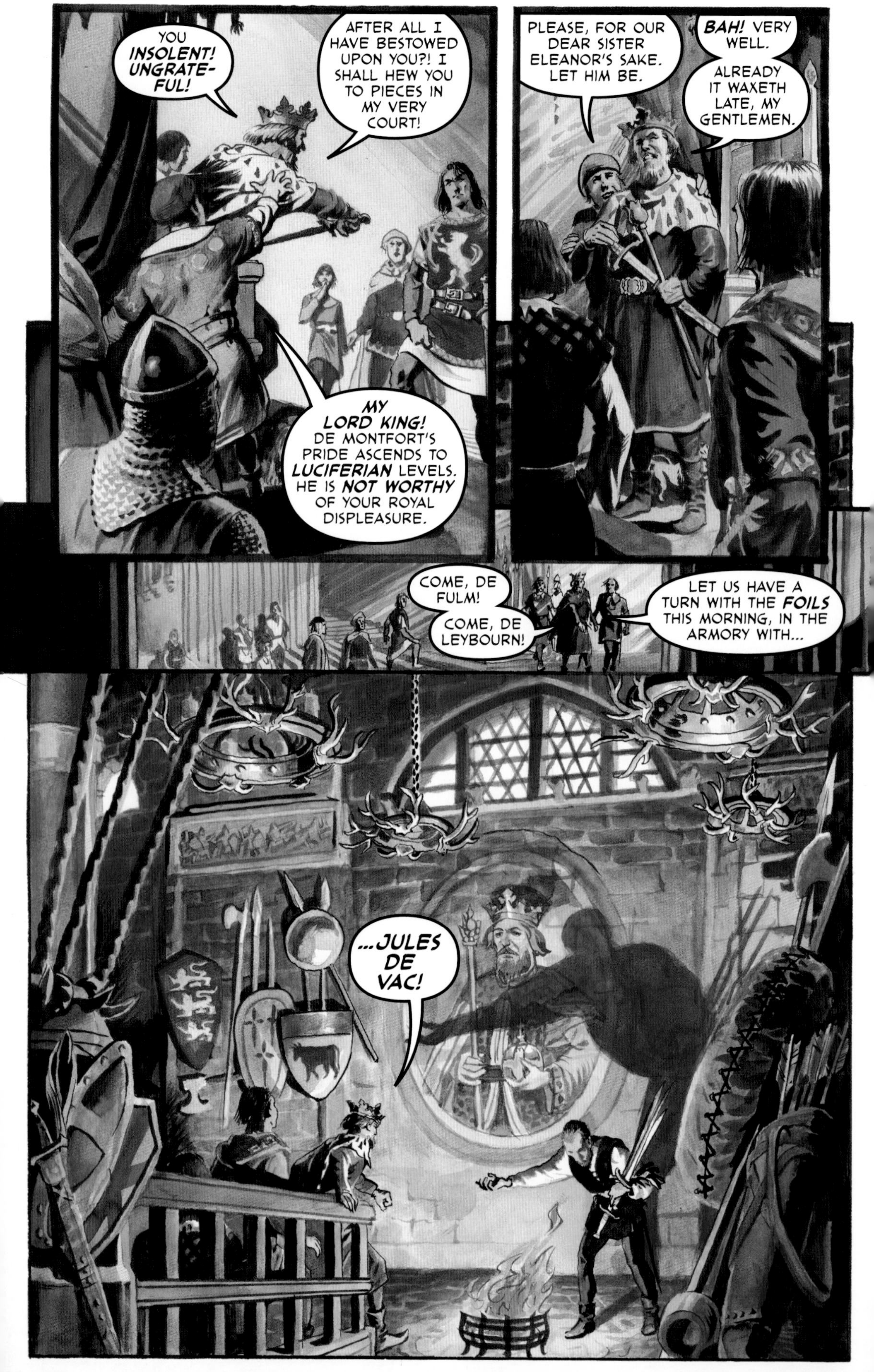

YOU INSOLENT! UNGRATE-FUL!
AFTER ALL I HAVE BESTOWED UPON YOU?! I SHALL HEW YOU TO PIECES IN MY VERY COURT!
MY LORD KING! DE MONTFORT'S PRIDE ASCENDS TO LUCIFERIAN LEVELS. HE IS NOT WORTHY OF YOUR ROYAL DISPLEASURE.
PLEASE, FOR OUR DEAR SISTER ELEANOR'S SAKE. LET HIM BE.
BAH! VERY WELL.
ALREADY IT WAXETH LATE, MY GENTLEMEN.
COME, DE FULM!
COME, DE LEYBOURN!
LET US HAVE A TURN WITH THE FOILS THIS MORNING, IN THE ARMORY WITH...
...JULES DE VAC!

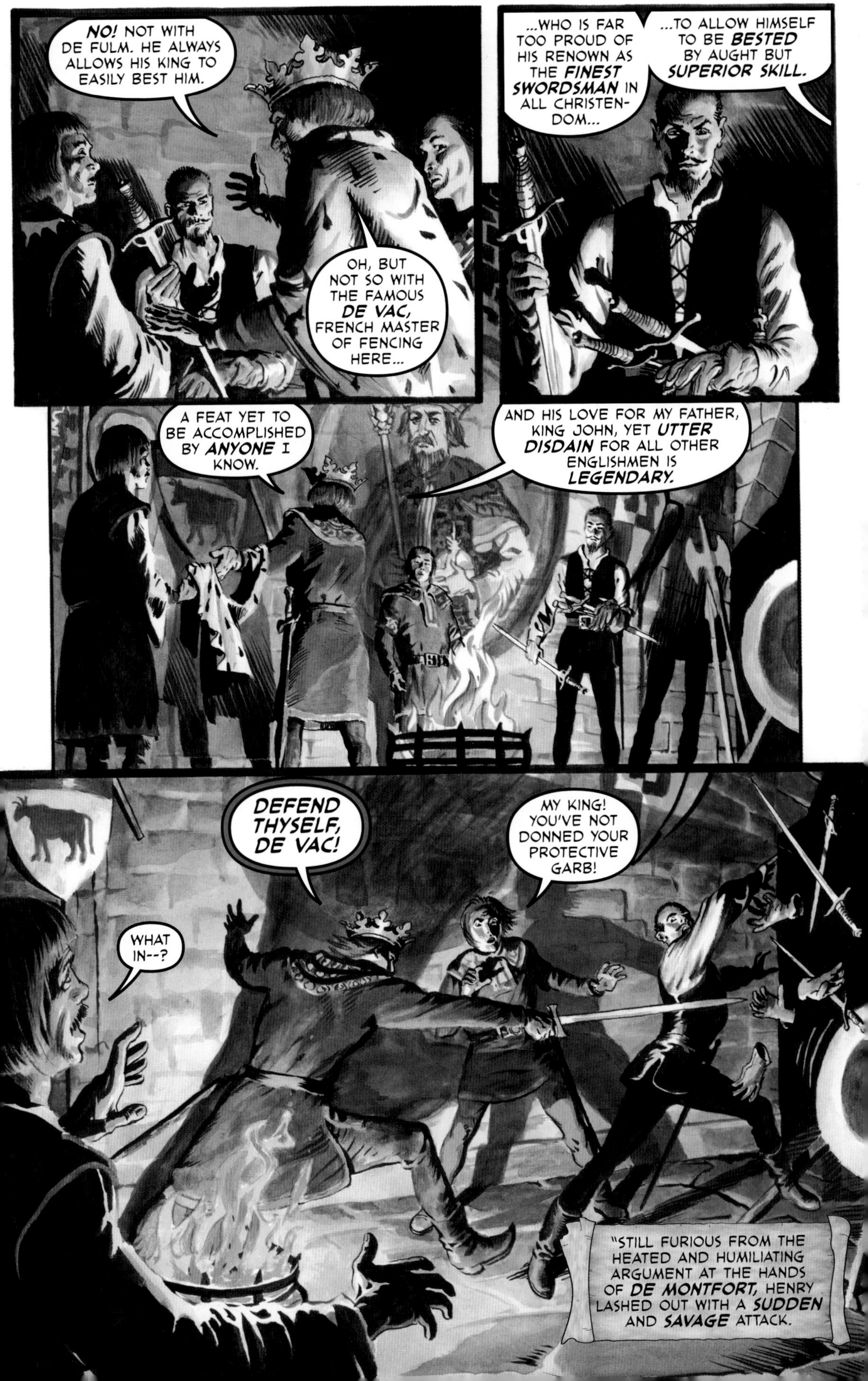

NO! NOT WITH DE FULM. HE ALWAYS ALLOWS HIS KING TO EASILY BEST HIM.
OH, BUT NOT SO WITH THE FAMOUS DE VAC, FRENCH MASTER OF FENCING HERE...
...WHO IS FAR TOO PROUD OF HIS RENOWN AS THE FINEST SWORDSMAN IN ALL CHRISTEN-DOM...
...TO ALLOW HIMSELF TO BE BESTED BY AUGHT BUT SUPERIOR SKILL.
A FEAT YET TO BE ACCOMPLISHED BY ANYONE I KNOW.
AND HIS LOVE FOR MY FATHER, KING JOHN, YET UTTER DISDAIN FOR ALL OTHER ENGLISHMEN IS LEGENDARY.
DEFEND THYSELF, DE VAC!
MY KING! YOU'VE NOT DONNED YOUR PROTECTIVE GARB!
WHAT IN--?
"STILL FURIOUS FROM THE HEATED AND HUMILIATING ARGUMENT AT THE HANDS OF DE MONTFORT, HENRY LASHED OUT WITH A SUDDEN AND SAVAGE ATTACK.

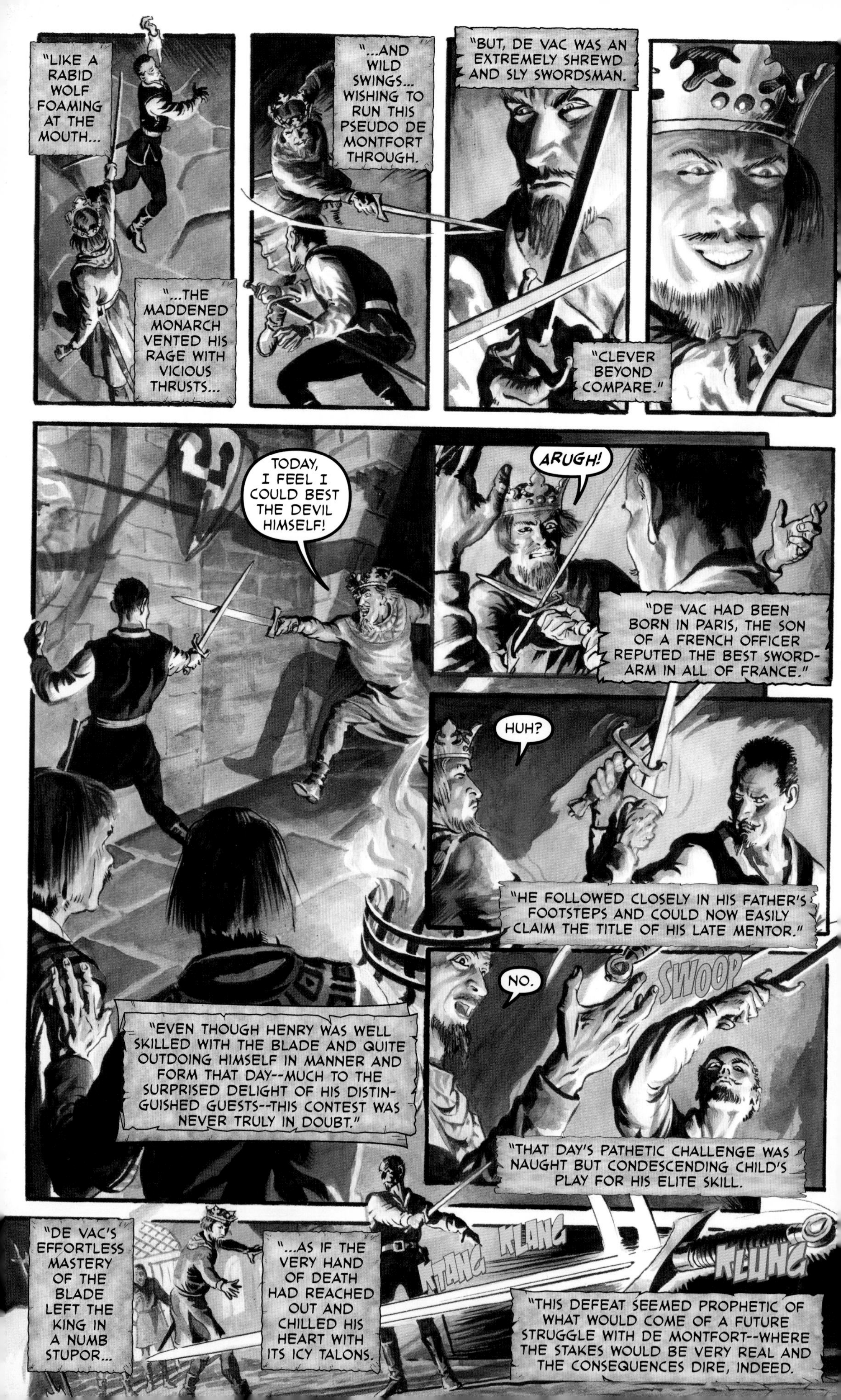
"LIKE A RABID WOLF FOAMING AT THE MOUTH...
"...THE MADDENED MONARCH VENTED HIS RAGE WITH VICIOUS THRUSTS...
"...AND WILD SWINGS... WISHING TO RUN THIS PSEUDO DE MONTFORT THROUGH.
"BUT, DE VAC WAS AN EXTREMELY SHREWD AND SLY SWORDSMAN.
"CLEVER BEYOND COMPARE."
TODAY, I FEEL I COULD BEST THE DEVIL HIMSELF!
"EVEN THOUGH HENRY WAS WELL SKILLED WITH THE BLADE AND QUITE OUTDOING HIMSELF IN MANNER AND FORM THAT DAY--MUCH TO THE SURPRISED DELIGHT OF HIS DISTINGUISHED GUESTS--THIS CONTEST WAS NEVER TRULY IN DOUBT."
ARUGH!
"DE VAC HAD BEEN BORN IN PARIS, THE SON OF A FRENCH OFFICER REPUTED THE BEST SWORD-ARM IN ALL OF FRANCE."
HUH?
"HE FOLLOWED CLOSELY IN HIS FATHER'S FOOTSTEPS AND COULD NOW EASILY CLAIM THE TITLE OF HIS LATE MENTOR."
NO.
SWOOP
"THAT DAY'S PATHETIC CHALLENGE WAS NAUGHT BUT CONDESCENDING CHILD'S PLAY FOR HIS ELITE SKILL.
"DE VAC'S EFFORTLESS MASTERY OF THE BLADE LEFT THE KING IN A NUMB STUPOR...
"...AS IF THE VERY HAND OF DEATH HAD REACHED OUT AND CHILLED HIS HEART WITH ITS ICY TALONS.
KTANG
KLANG
KLUNG
"THIS DEFEAT SEEMED PROPHETIC OF WHAT WOULD COME OF A FUTURE STRUGGLE WITH DE MONTFORT--WHERE THE STAKES WOULD BE VERY REAL AND THE CONSEQUENCES DIRE, INDEED.

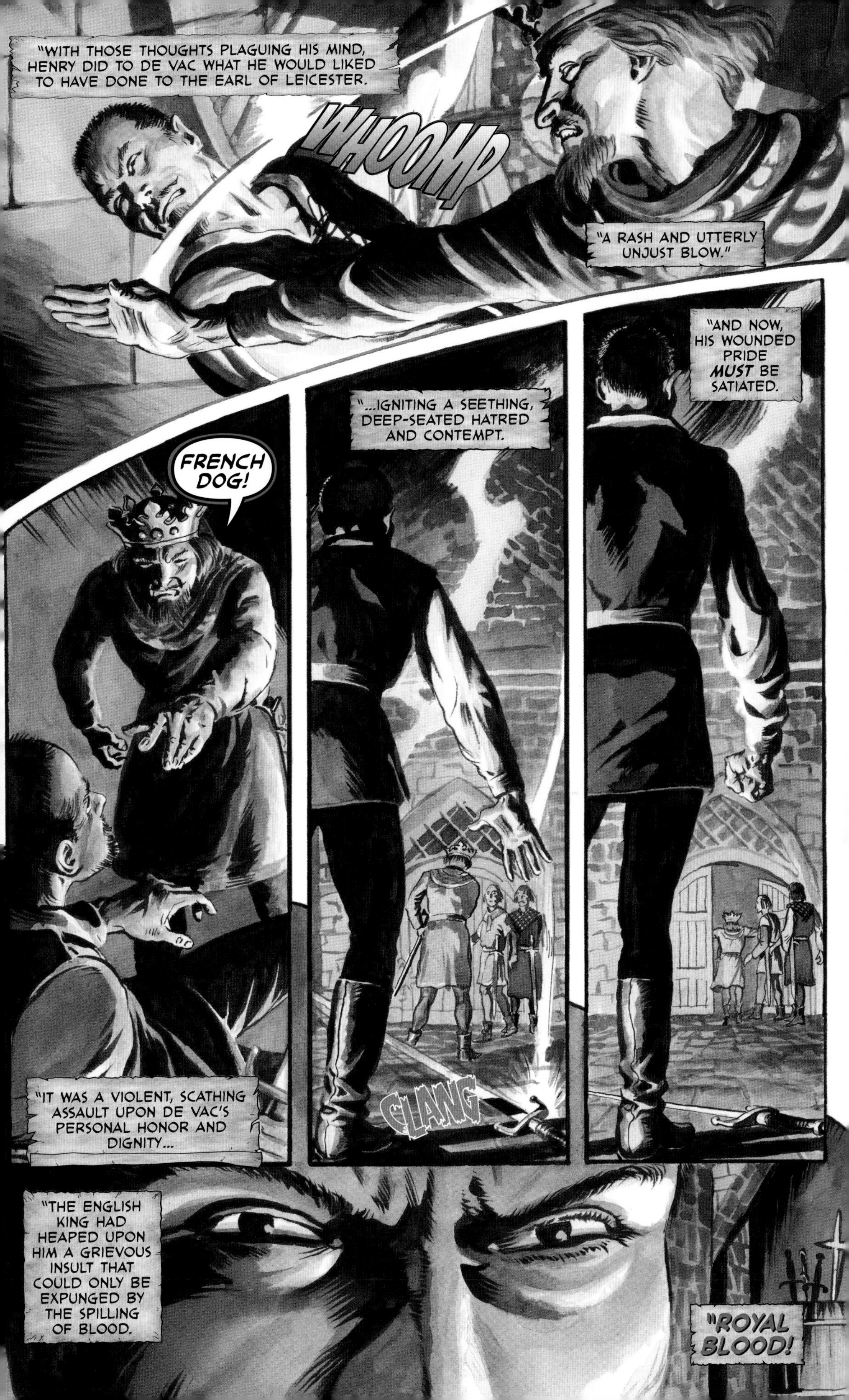

"WITH THOSE THOUGHTS PLAGUING HIS MIND, HENRY DID TO DE VAC WHAT HE WOULD LIKED TO HAVE DONE TO THE EARL OF LEICESTER.
WHOOMP
"A RASH AND UTTERLY UNJUST BLOW."
FRENCH DOG!
"IT WAS A VIOLENT, SCATHING ASSAULT UPON DE VAC'S PERSONAL HONOR AND DIGNITY...
"...IGNITING A SEETHING, DEEP-SEATED HATRED AND CONTEMPT.
CLANG
"AND NOW, HIS WOUNDED PRIDE MUST BE SATIATED.
"THE ENGLISH KING HAD HEAPED UPON HIM A GRIEVOUS INSULT THAT COULD ONLY BE EXPUNGED BY THE SPILLING OF BLOOD.
"ROYAL BLOOD!

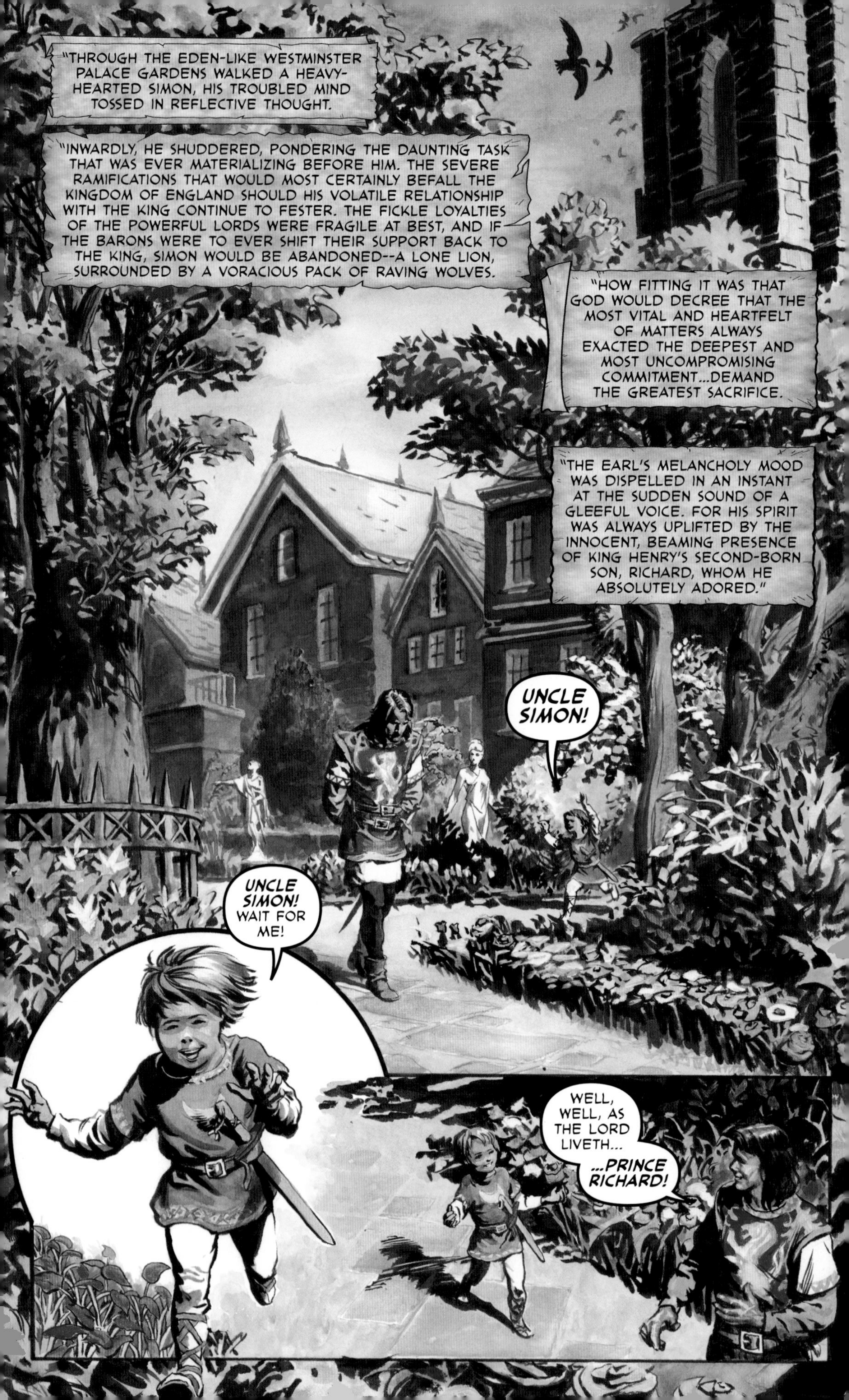

"THROUGH THE EDEN-LIKE WESTMINSTER PALACE GARDENS WALKED A HEAVY-HEARTED SIMON, HIS TROUBLED MIND TOSSED IN REFLECTIVE THOUGHT.
"INWARDLY, HE SHUDDERED, PONDERING THE DAUNTING TASK THAT WAS EVER MATERIALIZING BEFORE HIM. THE SEVERE RAMIFICATIONS THAT WOULD MOST CERTAINLY BEFALL THE KINGDOM OF ENGLAND SHOULD HIS VOLATILE RELATIONSHIP WITH THE KING CONTINUE TO FESTER. THE FICKLE LOYALTIES OF THE POWERFUL LORDS WERE FRAGILE AT BEST, AND IF THE BARONS WERE TO EVER SHIFT THEIR SUPPORT BACK TO THE KING, SIMON WOULD BE ABANDONED--A LONE LION, SURROUNDED BY A VORACIOUS PACK OF RAVING WOLVES.
"HOW FITTING IT WAS THAT GOD WOULD DECREE THAT THE MOST VITAL AND HEARTFELT OF MATTERS ALWAYS EXACTED THE DEEPEST AND MOST UNCOMPROMISING COMMITMENT...DEMAND THE GREATEST SACRIFICE.
"THE EARL'S MELANCHOLY MOOD WAS DISPELLED IN AN INSTANT AT THE SUDDEN SOUND OF A GLEEFUL VOICE. FOR HIS SPIRIT WAS ALWAYS UPLIFTED BY THE INNOCENT, BEAMING PRESENCE OF KING HENRY'S SECOND-BORN SON, RICHARD, WHOM HE ABSOLUTELY ADORED."
UNCLE SIMON!
UNCLE SIMON! WAIT FOR ME!
WELL, WELL, AS THE LORD LIVETH...
...PRINCE RICHARD!

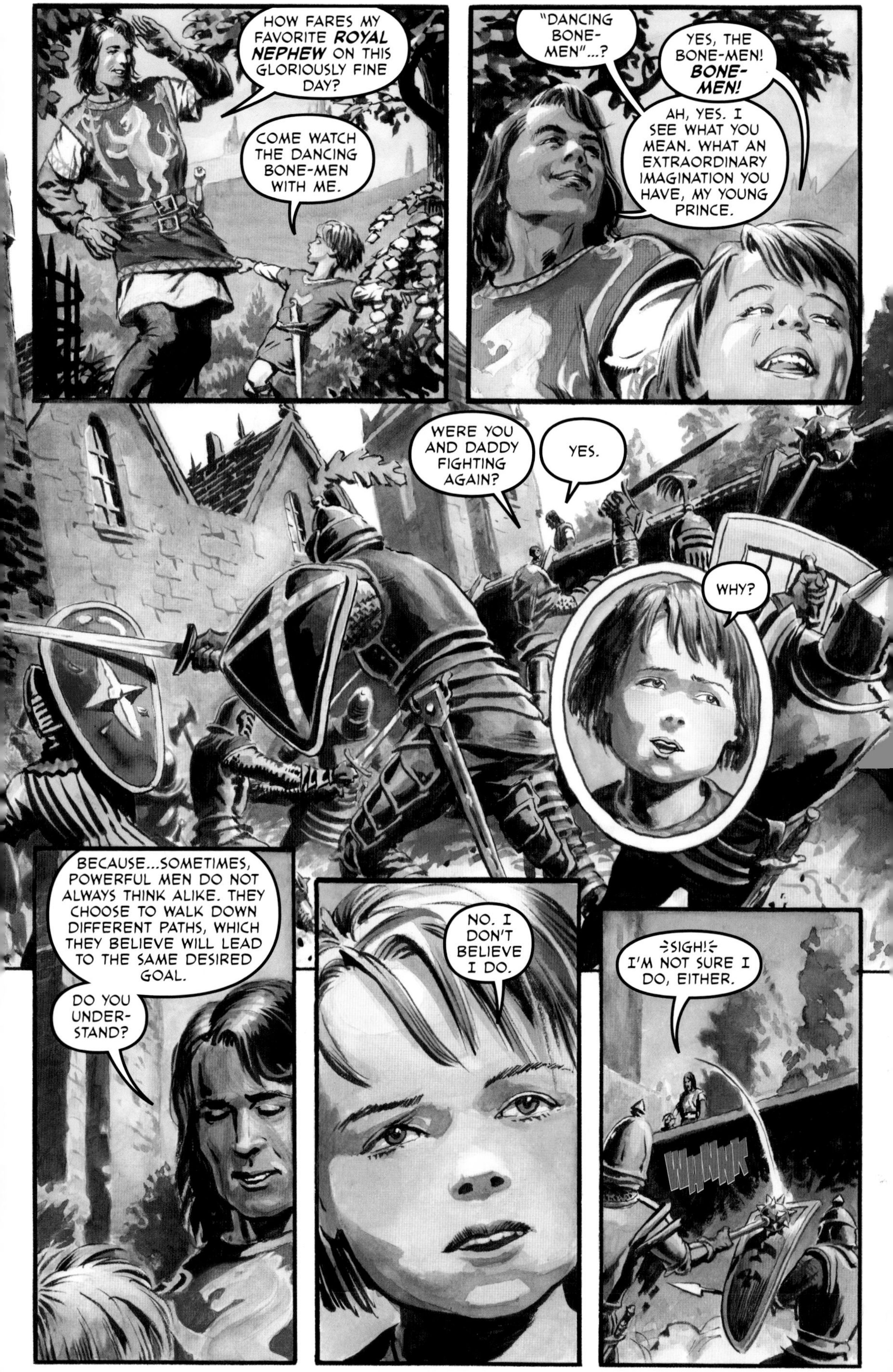
HOW FARES MY FAVORITE ROYAL NEPHEW ON THIS GLORIOUSLY FINE DAY?
COME WATCH THE DANCING BONE-MEN WITH ME.
"DANCING BONE-MEN"...?
YES, THE BONE-MEN! BONE-MEN!
AH, YES. I SEE WHAT YOU MEAN. WHAT AN EXTRAORDINARY IMAGINATION YOU HAVE, MY YOUNG PRINCE.
WERE YOU AND DADDY FIGHTING AGAIN?
YES.
WHY?
BECAUSE...SOMETIMES, POWERFUL MEN DO NOT ALWAYS THINK ALIKE. THEY CHOOSE TO WALK DOWN DIFFERENT PATHS, WHICH THEY BELIEVE WILL LEAD TO THE SAME DESIRED GOAL.
DO YOU UNDER-STAND?
NO. I DON'T BELIEVE I DO.
SIGH! I'M NOT SURE I DO, EITHER.
WHANK

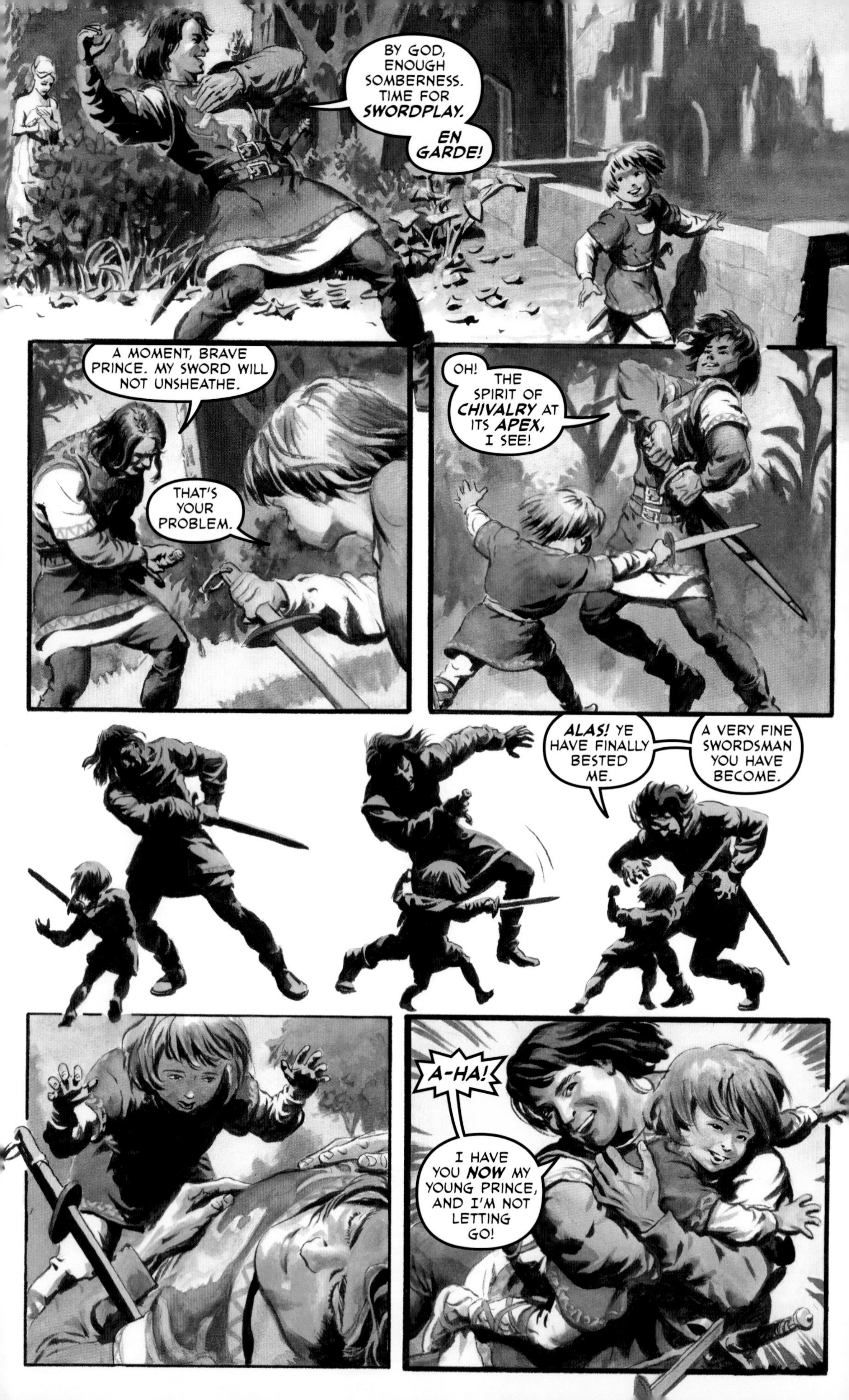

BY GOD, ENOUGH SOMBERNESS. TIME FOR **SWORDPLAY.**
EN GARDE!
A MOMENT, BRAVE PRINCE. MY SWORD WILL NOT UNSHEATHE.
THAT'S YOUR PROBLEM.
OH!
THE SPIRIT OF ***CHIVALRY*** AT ITS ***APEX,*** I SEE!
ALAS! YE HAVE FINALLY BESTED ME.
A VERY FINE SWORDSMAN YOU HAVE BECOME.
A-HA!
I HAVE YOU ***NOW*** MY YOUNG PRINCE, AND I'M NOT LETTING GO!

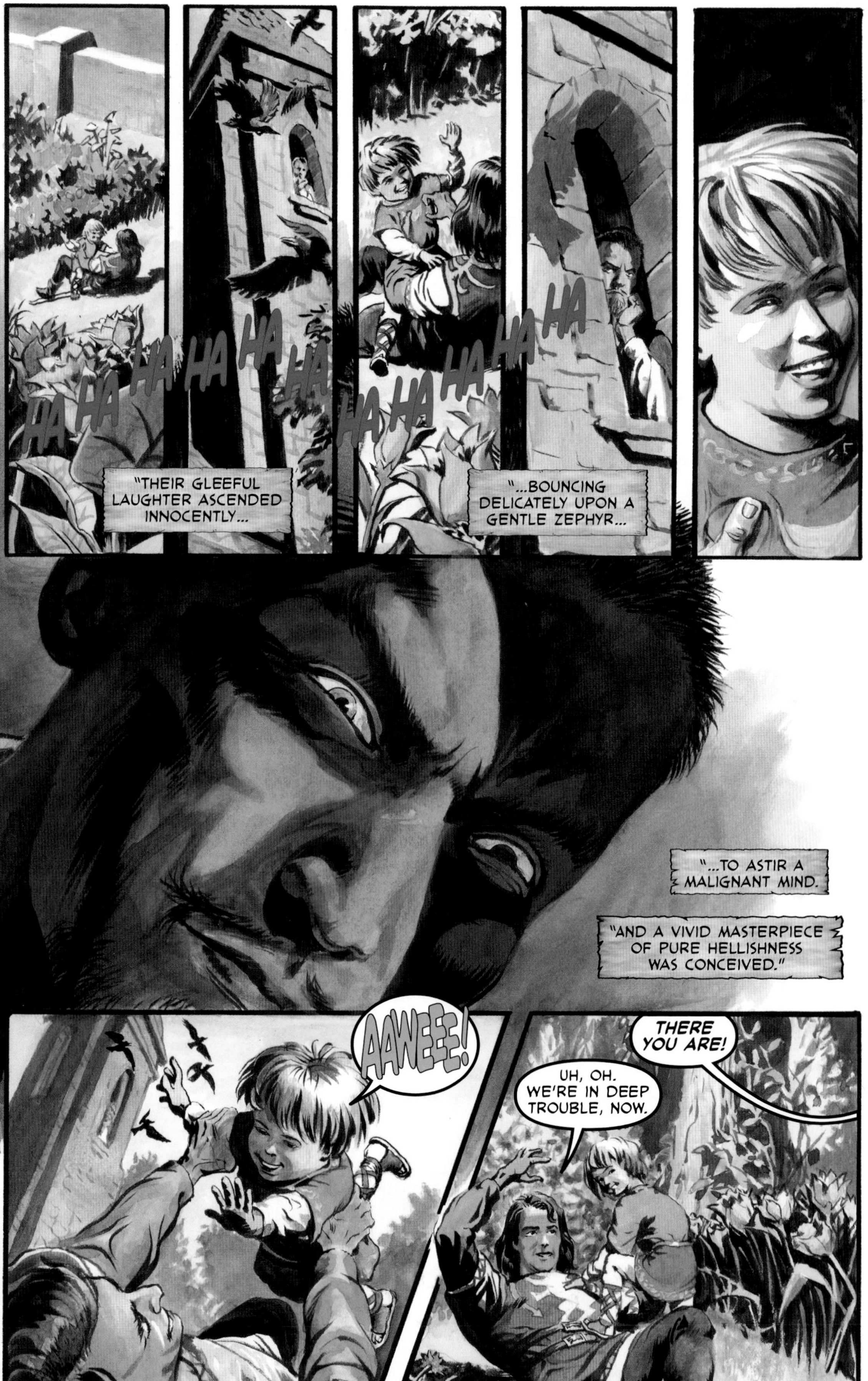
HA HA HA HA HA HA HA HA HA HA HA HA
"THEIR GLEEFUL LAUGHTER ASCENDED INNOCENTLY...
"...BOUNCING DELICATELY UPON A GENTLE ZEPHYR...
"...TO ASTIR A MALIGNANT MIND.
"AND A VIVID MASTERPIECE OF PURE HELLISHNESS WAS CONCEIVED."
AAWEEE!
THERE YOU ARE!
UH, OH. WE'RE IN DEEP TROUBLE, NOW.

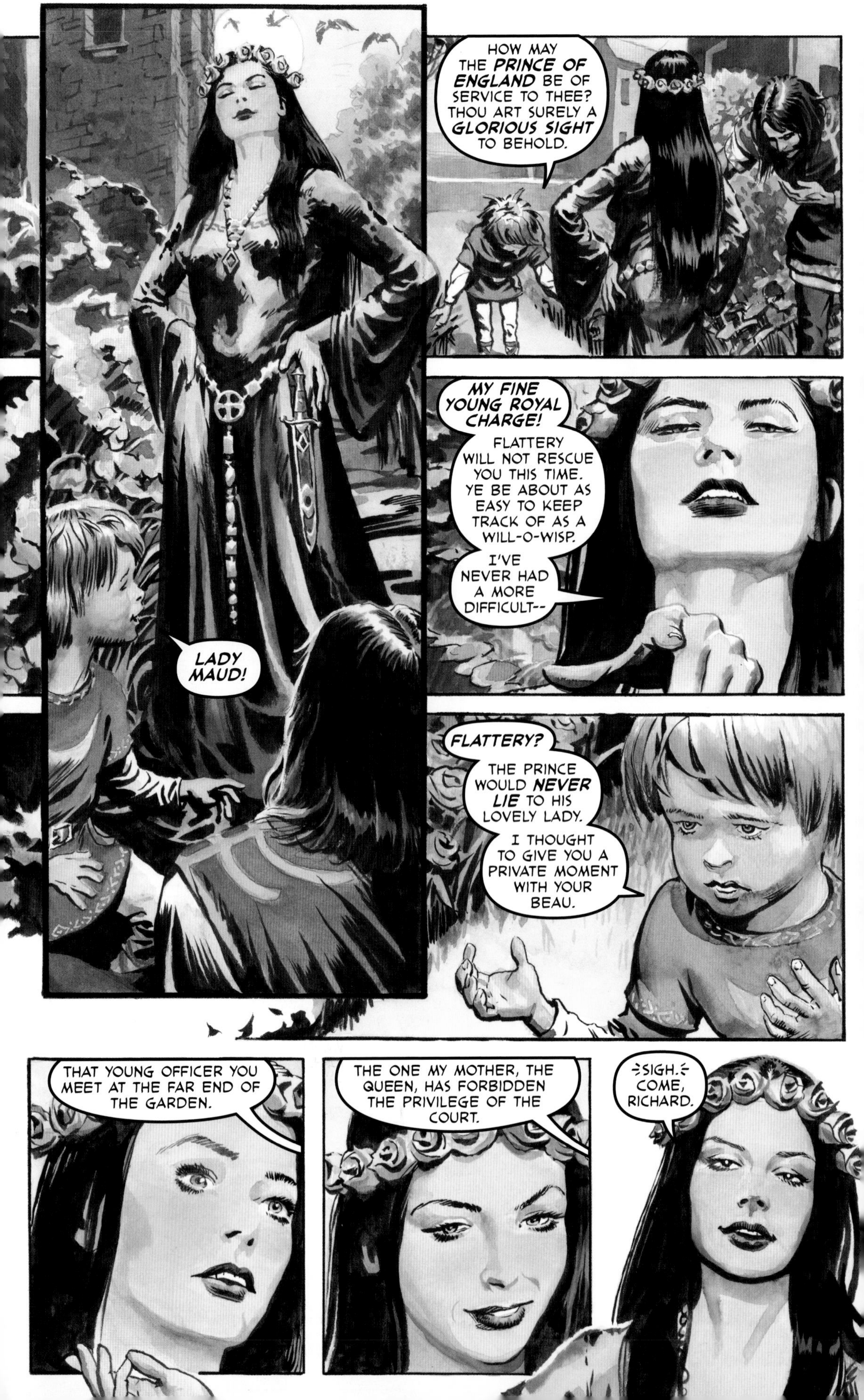
LADY MAUD!
HOW MAY THE PRINCE OF ENGLAND BE OF SERVICE TO THEE? THOU ART SURELY A GLORIOUS SIGHT TO BEHOLD.
MY FINE YOUNG ROYAL CHARGE!
FLATTERY WILL NOT RESCUE YOU THIS TIME. YE BE ABOUT AS EASY TO KEEP TRACK OF AS A WILL-O-WISP.
I'VE NEVER HAD A MORE DIFFICULT--
FLATTERY?
THE PRINCE WOULD NEVER LIE TO HIS LOVELY LADY.
I THOUGHT TO GIVE YOU A PRIVATE MOMENT WITH YOUR BEAU.
THAT YOUNG OFFICER YOU MEET AT THE FAR END OF THE GARDEN.
THE ONE MY MOTHER, THE QUEEN, HAS FORBIDDEN THE PRIVILEGE OF THE COURT.
SIGH. COME, RICHARD.

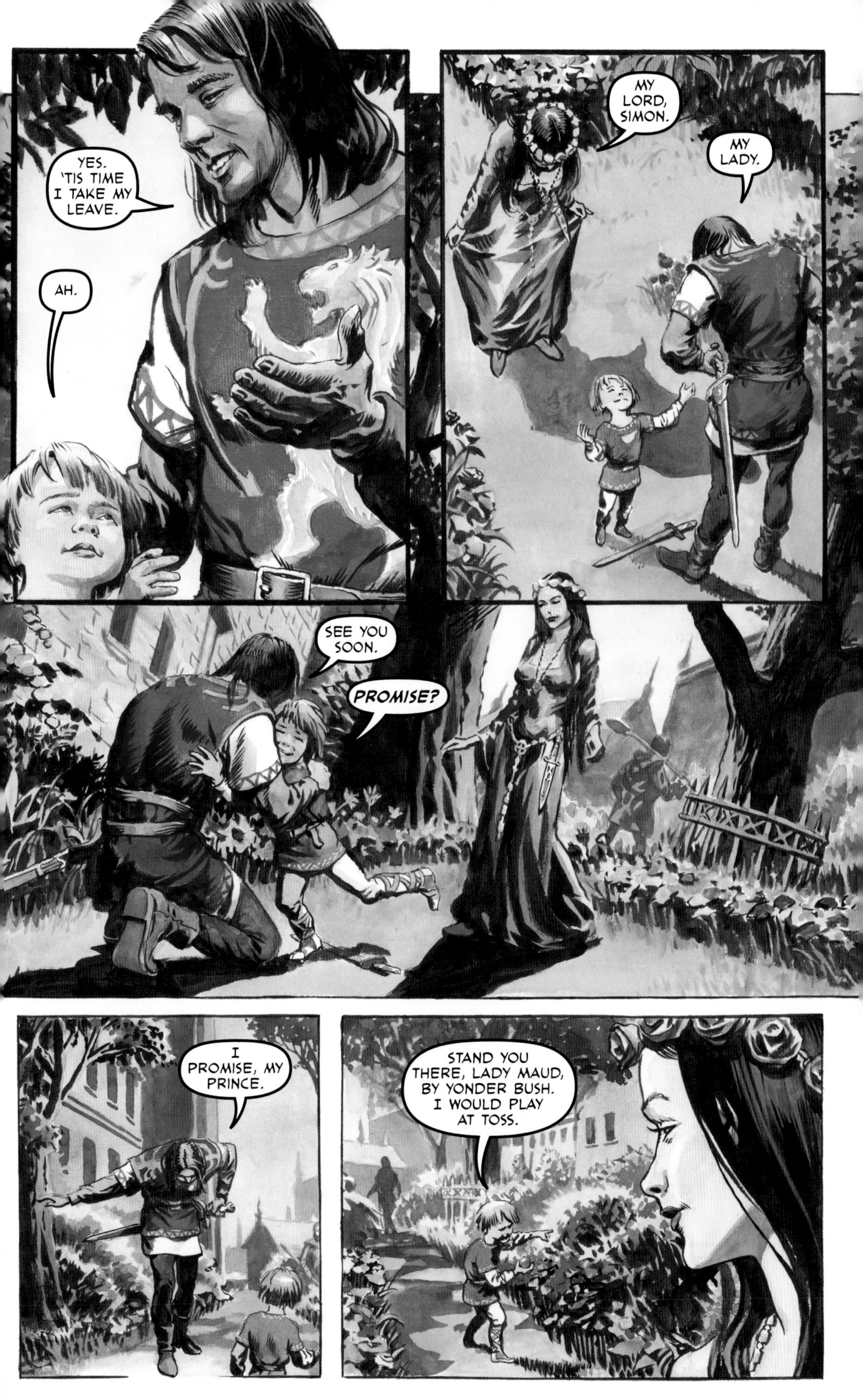
YES. 'TIS TIME I TAKE MY LEAVE.
AH.
MY LORD, SIMON.
MY LADY.
SEE YOU SOON.
PROMISE?
I PROMISE, MY PRINCE.
STAND YOU THERE, LADY MAUD, BY YONDER BUSH. I WOULD PLAY AT TOSS.

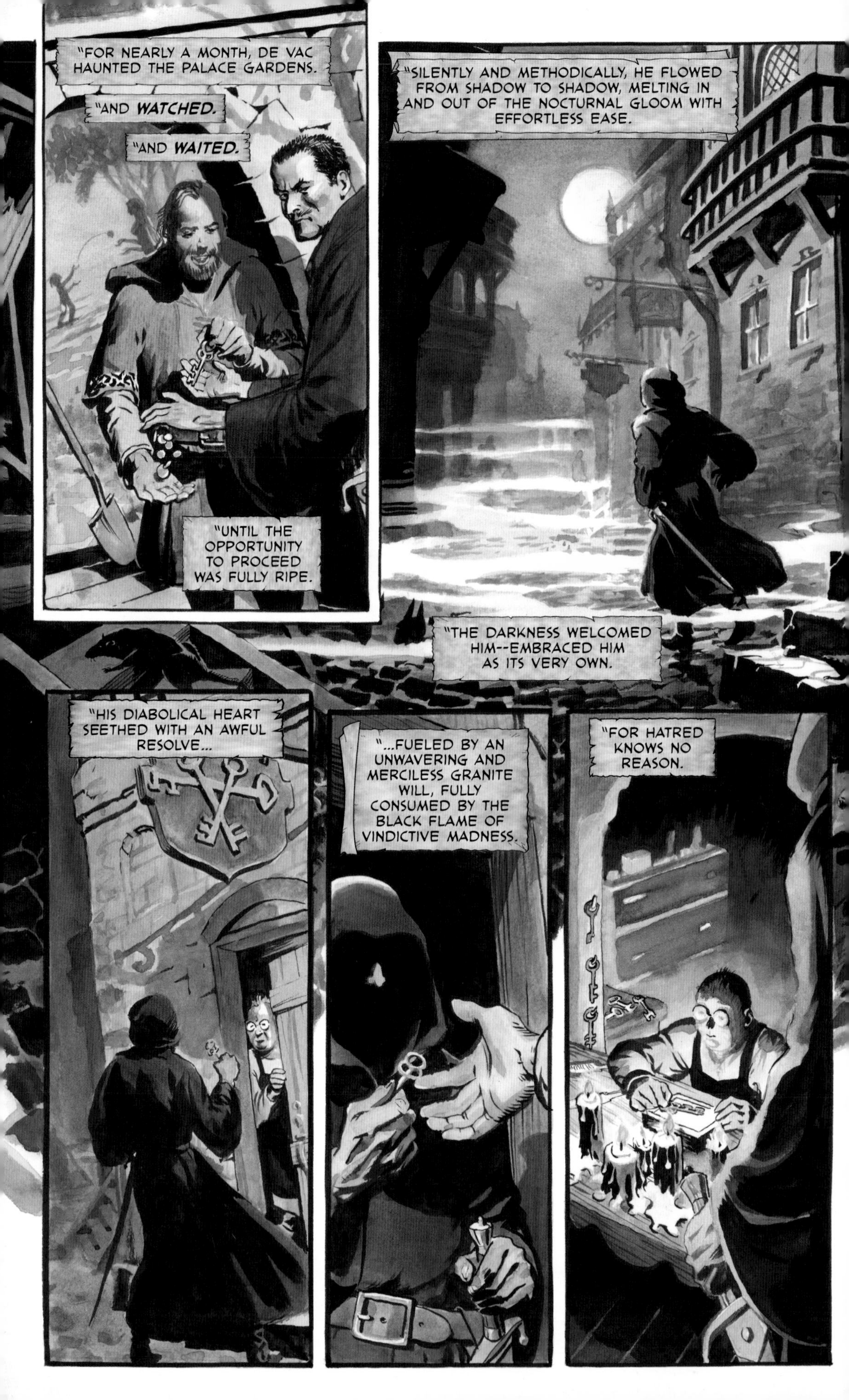

"FOR NEARLY A MONTH, DE VAC HAUNTED THE PALACE GARDENS.
"AND WATCHED.
"AND WAITED.
"UNTIL THE OPPORTUNITY TO PROCEED WAS FULLY RIPE.
"SILENTLY AND METHODICALLY, HE FLOWED FROM SHADOW TO SHADOW, MELTING IN AND OUT OF THE NOCTURNAL GLOOM WITH EFFORTLESS EASE.
"THE DARKNESS WELCOMED HIM--EMBRACED HIM AS ITS VERY OWN.
"HIS DIABOLICAL HEART SEETHED WITH AN AWFUL RESOLVE...
"...FUELED BY AN UNWAVERING AND MERCILESS GRANITE WILL, FULLY CONSUMED BY THE BLACK FLAME OF VINDICTIVE MADNESS.
"FOR HATRED KNOWS NO REASON.

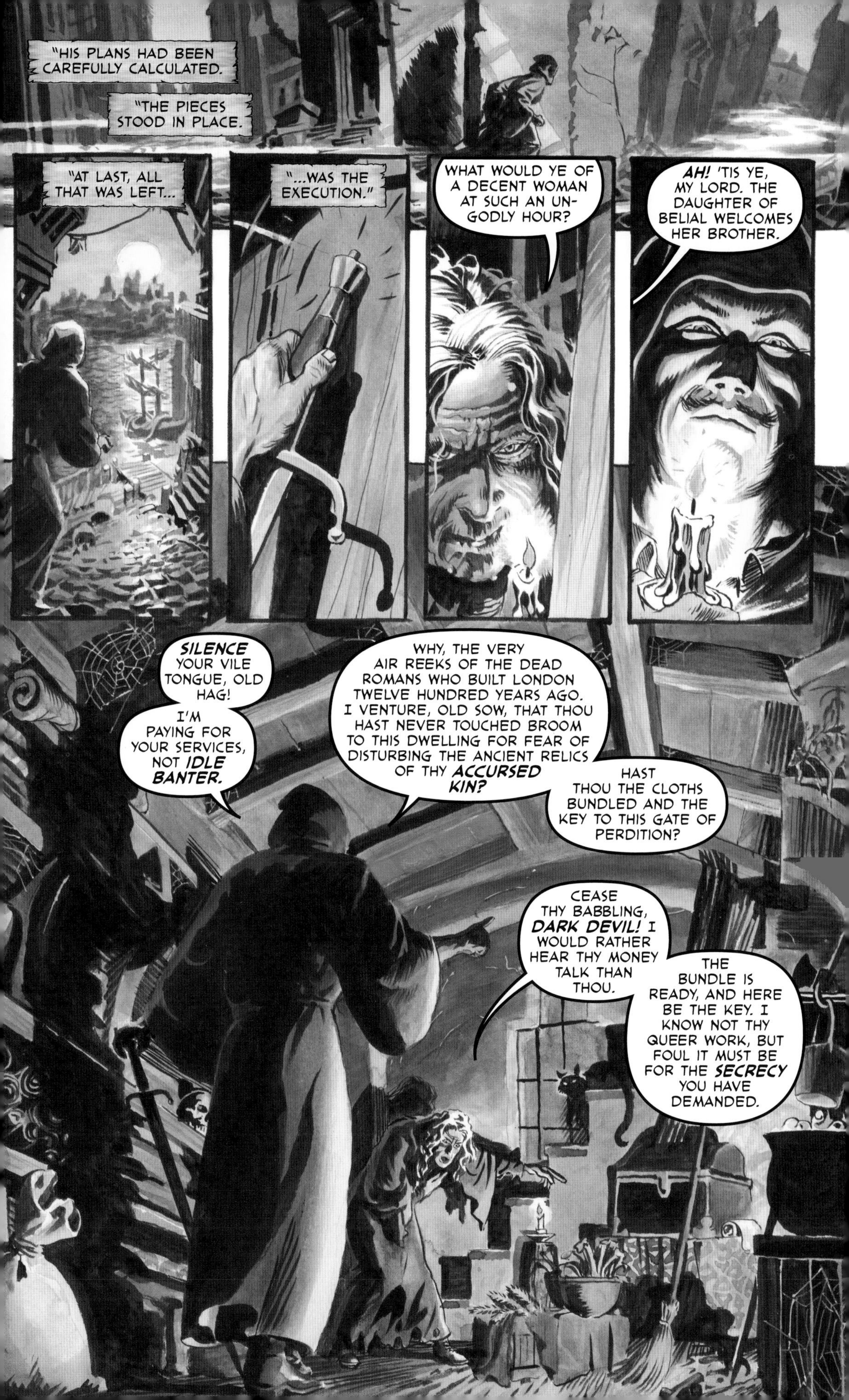
"HIS PLANS HAD BEEN CAREFULLY CALCULATED.
"THE PIECES STOOD IN PLACE.
"AT LAST, ALL THAT WAS LEFT...
"...WAS THE EXECUTION."
WHAT WOULD YE OF A DECENT WOMAN AT SUCH AN UNGODLY HOUR?
AH! 'TIS YE, MY LORD. THE DAUGHTER OF BELIAL WELCOMES HER BROTHER.
SILENCE YOUR VILE TONGUE, OLD HAG!
I'M PAYING FOR YOUR SERVICES, NOT IDLE BANTER.
WHY, THE VERY AIR REEKS OF THE DEAD ROMANS WHO BUILT LONDON TWELVE HUNDRED YEARS AGO. I VENTURE, OLD SOW, THAT THOU HAST NEVER TOUCHED BROOM TO THIS DWELLING FOR FEAR OF DISTURBING THE ANCIENT RELICS OF THY ACCURSED KIN?
HAST THOU THE CLOTHS BUNDLED AND THE KEY TO THIS GATE OF PERDITION?
CEASE THY BABBLING, DARK DEVIL! I WOULD RATHER HEAR THY MONEY TALK THAN THOU.
THE BUNDLE IS READY, AND HERE BE THE KEY. I KNOW NOT THY QUEER WORK, BUT FOUL IT MUST BE FOR THE SECRECY YOU HAVE DEMANDED.

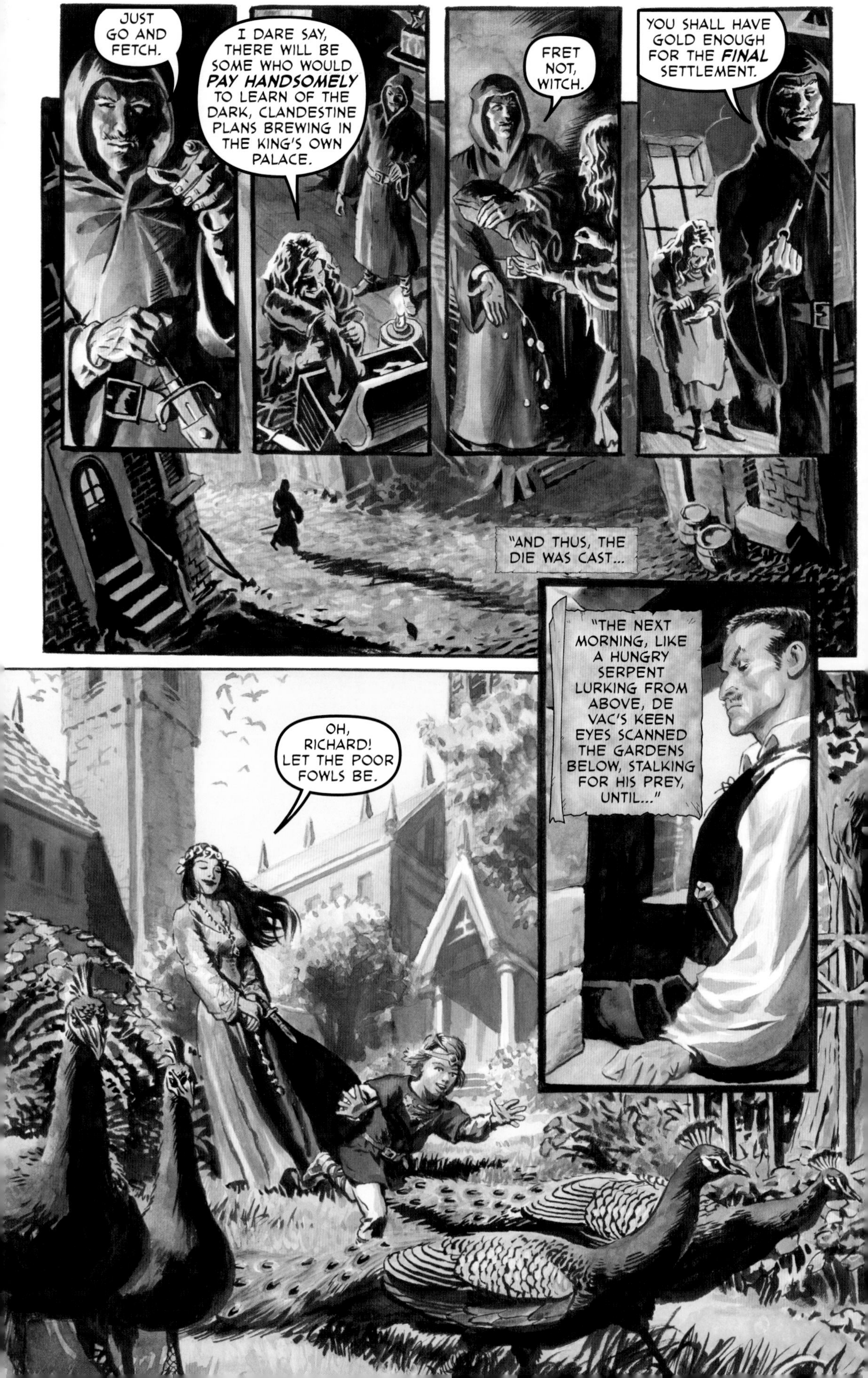
JUST GO AND FETCH.
I DARE SAY, THERE WILL BE SOME WHO WOULD PAY HANDSOMELY TO LEARN OF THE DARK, CLANDESTINE PLANS BREWING IN THE KING'S OWN PALACE.
FRET NOT, WITCH.
YOU SHALL HAVE GOLD ENOUGH FOR THE FINAL SETTLEMENT.
"AND THUS, THE DIE WAS CAST...
"THE NEXT MORNING, LIKE A HUNGRY SERPENT LURKING FROM ABOVE, DE VAC'S KEEN EYES SCANNED THE GARDENS BELOW, STALKING FOR HIS PREY, UNTIL..."
OH, RICHARD! LET THE POOR FOWLS BE.

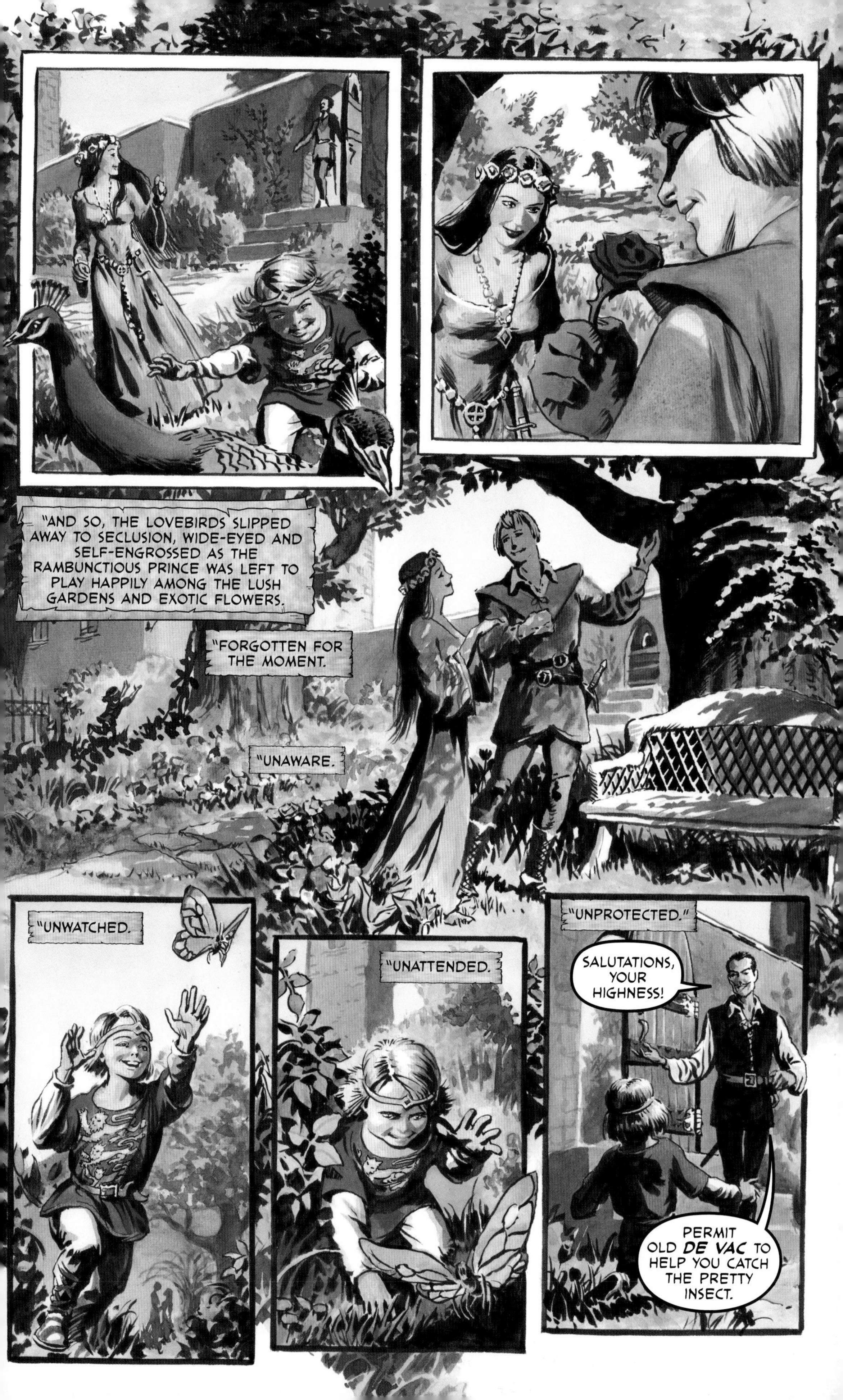
"AND SO, THE LOVEBIRDS SLIPPED AWAY TO SECLUSION, WIDE-EYED AND SELF-ENGROSSED AS THE RAMBUNCTIOUS PRINCE WAS LEFT TO PLAY HAPPILY AMONG THE LUSH GARDENS AND EXOTIC FLOWERS.
"FORGOTTEN FOR THE MOMENT.
"UNAWARE.
"UNWATCHED.
"UNATTENDED.
"UNPROTECTED."
SALUTATIONS, YOUR HIGHNESS!
PERMIT OLD DE VAC TO HELP YOU CATCH THE PRETTY INSECT.

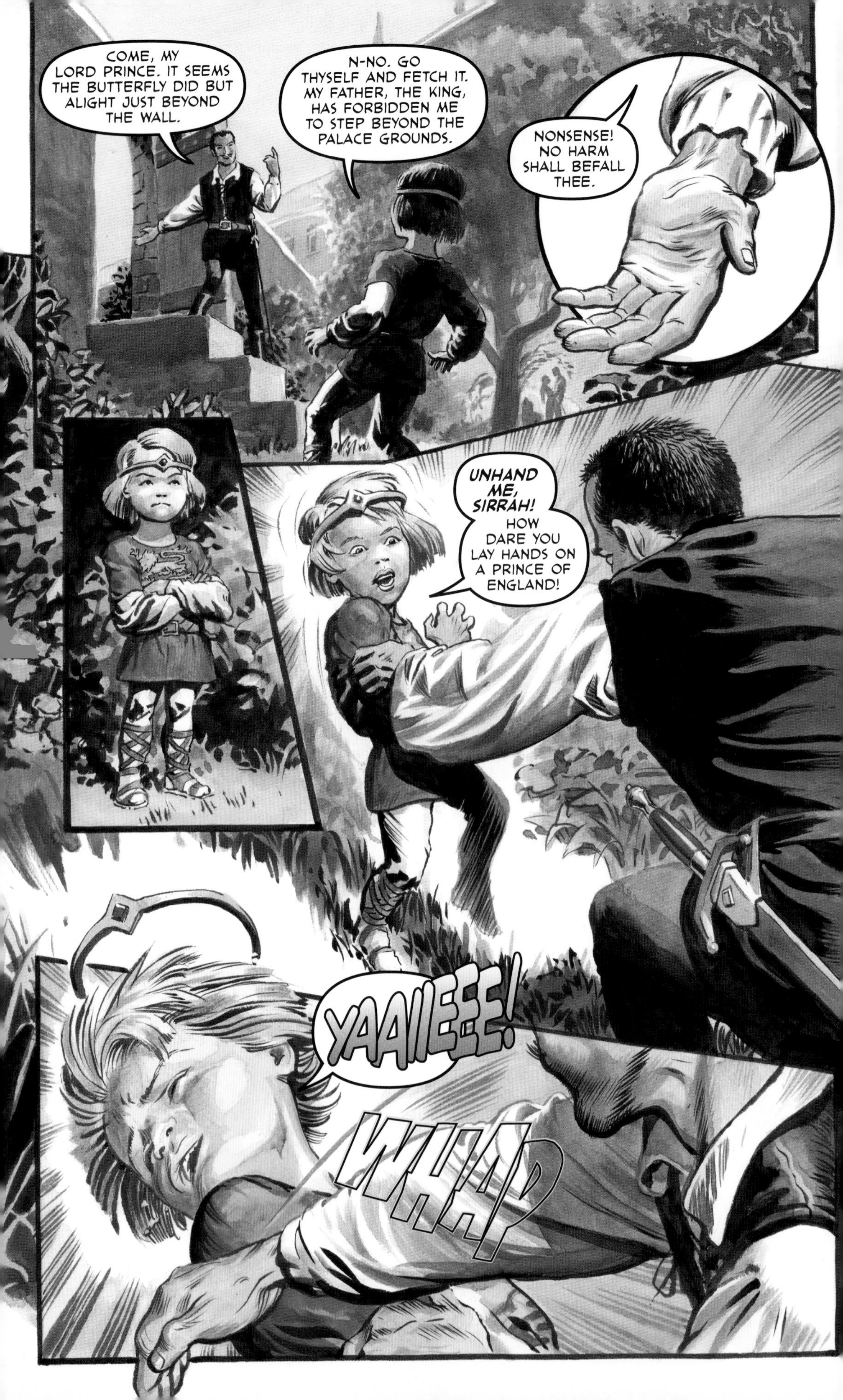
COME, MY LORD PRINCE. IT SEEMS THE BUTTERFLY DID BUT ALIGHT JUST BEYOND THE WALL.
N-NO. GO THYSELF AND FETCH IT. MY FATHER, THE KING, HAS FORBIDDEN ME TO STEP BEYOND THE PALACE GROUNDS.
NONSENSE! NO HARM SHALL BEFALL THEE.
UNHAND ME, SIRRAH! HOW DARE YOU LAY HANDS ON A PRINCE OF ENGLAND!
YAAIIEEE!
WHAP

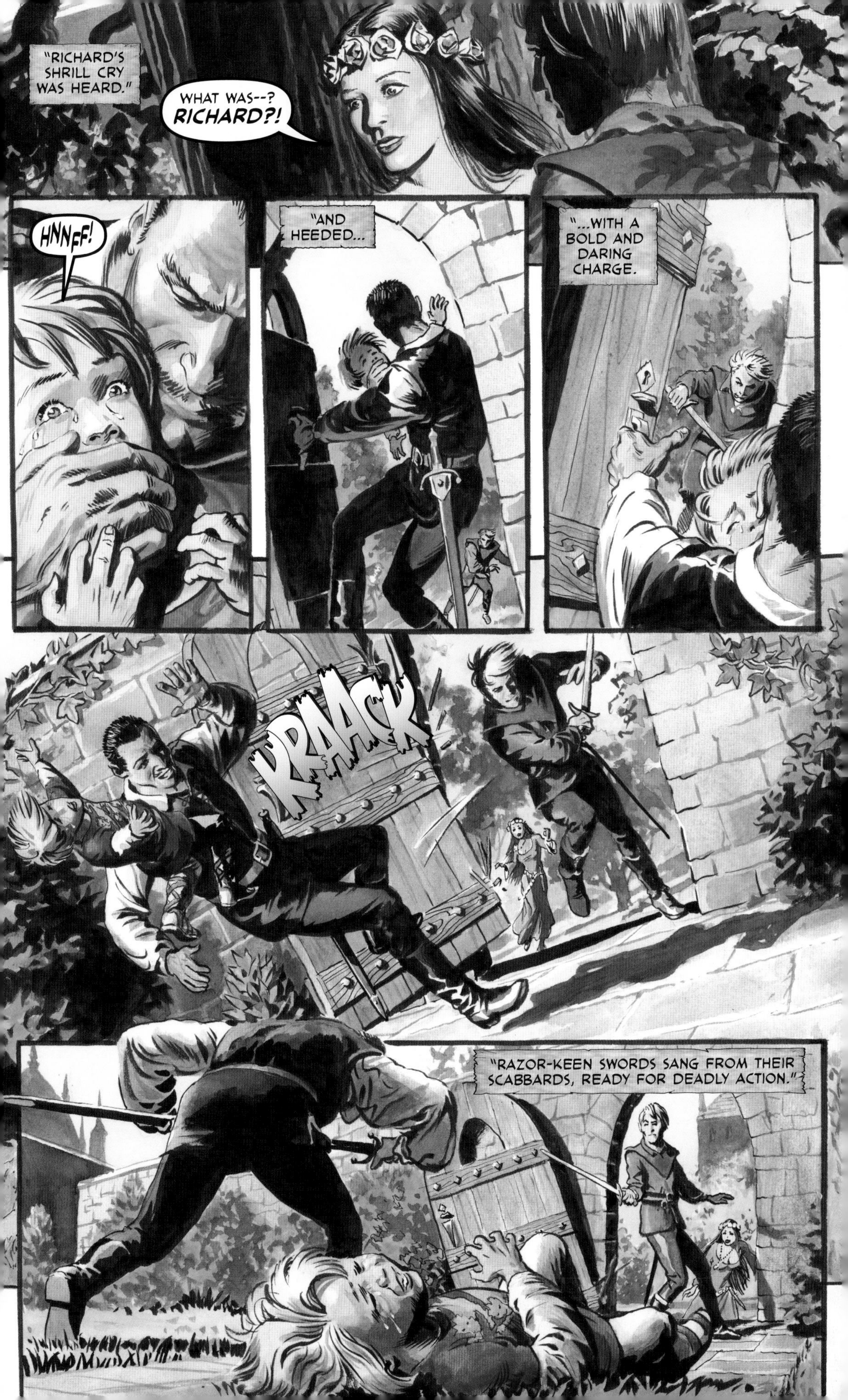
"RICHARD'S SHRILL CRY WAS HEARD."
WHAT WAS--? RICHARD?!
HNNFF!
"AND HEEDED...
"...WITH A BOLD AND DARING CHARGE.
KRAACK
"RAZOR-KEEN SWORDS SANG FROM THEIR SCABBARDS, READY FOR DEADLY ACTION."

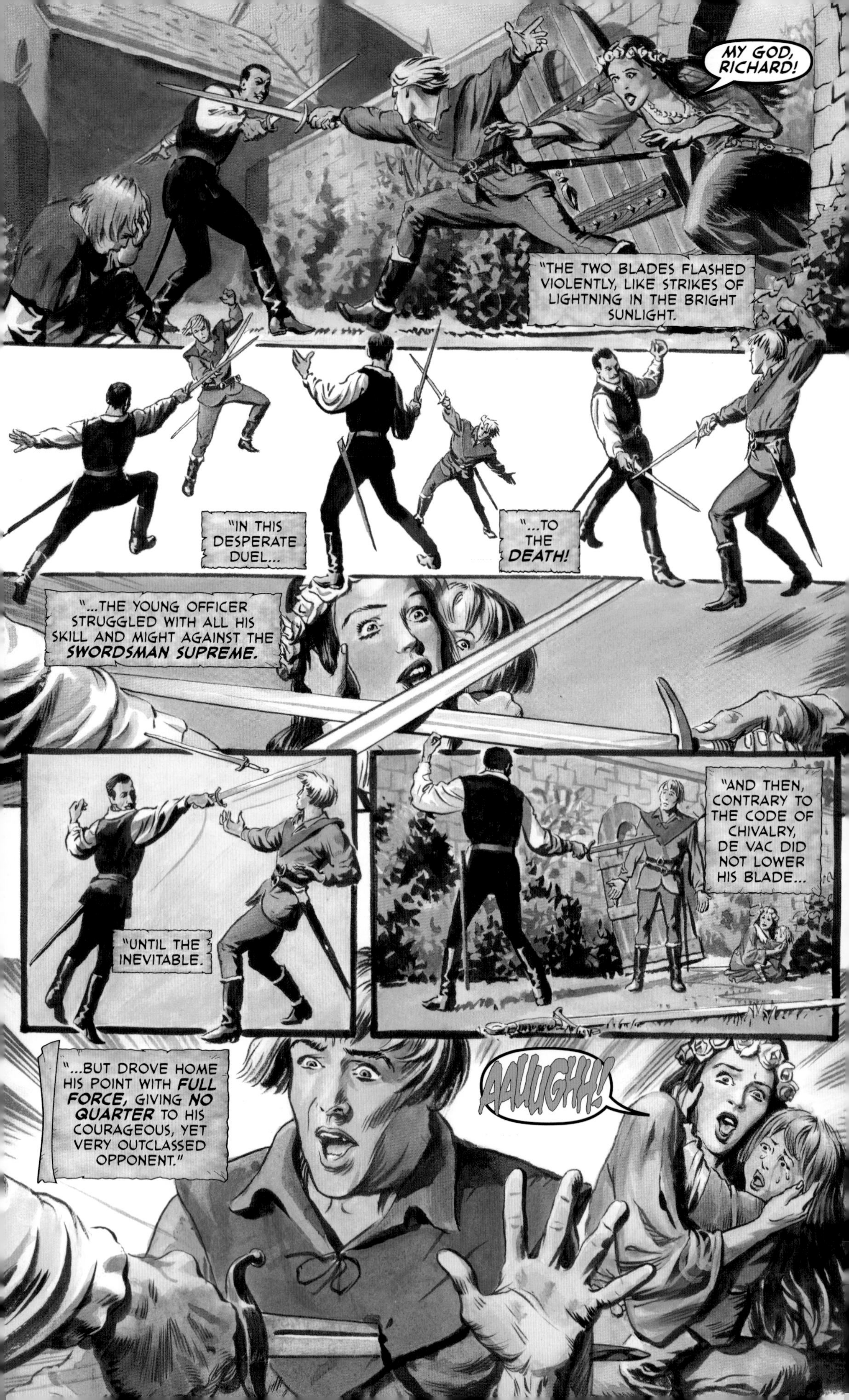
MY GOD, RICHARD!
"THE TWO BLADES FLASHED VIOLENTLY, LIKE STRIKES OF LIGHTNING IN THE BRIGHT SUNLIGHT.
"IN THIS DESPERATE DUEL...
"...TO THE DEATH!
"...THE YOUNG OFFICER STRUGGLED WITH ALL HIS SKILL AND MIGHT AGAINST THE SWORDSMAN SUPREME.
"UNTIL THE INEVITABLE.
"AND THEN, CONTRARY TO THE CODE OF CHIVALRY, DE VAC DID NOT LOWER HIS BLADE...
"...BUT DROVE HOME HIS POINT WITH FULL FORCE, GIVING NO QUARTER TO HIS COURAGEOUS, YET VERY OUTCLASSED OPPONENT."
AAUUGHH!

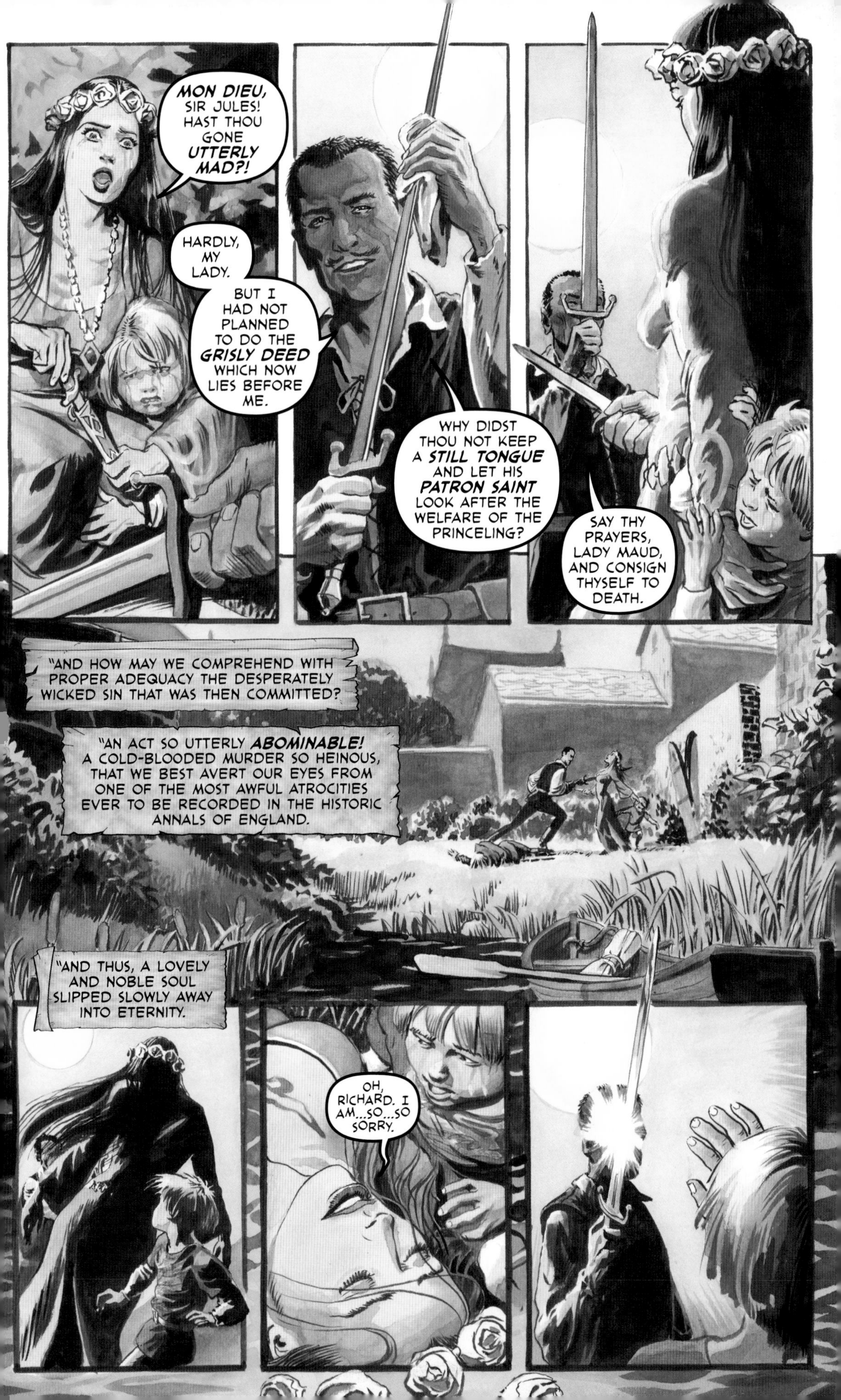
MON DIEU, SIR JULES! HAST THOU GONE UTTERLY MAD?!
HARDLY, MY LADY.
BUT I HAD NOT PLANNED TO DO THE GRISLY DEED WHICH NOW LIES BEFORE ME.
WHY DIDST THOU NOT KEEP A STILL TONGUE AND LET HIS PATRON SAINT LOOK AFTER THE WELFARE OF THE PRINCELING?
SAY THY PRAYERS, LADY MAUD, AND CONSIGN THYSELF TO DEATH.
"AND HOW MAY WE COMPREHEND WITH PROPER ADEQUACY THE DESPERATELY WICKED SIN THAT WAS THEN COMMITTED?
"AN ACT SO UTTERLY ABOMINABLE! A COLD-BLOODED MURDER SO HEINOUS, THAT WE BEST AVERT OUR EYES FROM ONE OF THE MOST AWFUL ATROCITIES EVER TO BE RECORDED IN THE HISTORIC ANNALS OF ENGLAND.
"AND THUS, A LOVELY AND NOBLE SOUL SLIPPED SLOWLY AWAY INTO ETERNITY.
OH, RICHARD. I AM...SO...SO SORRY.

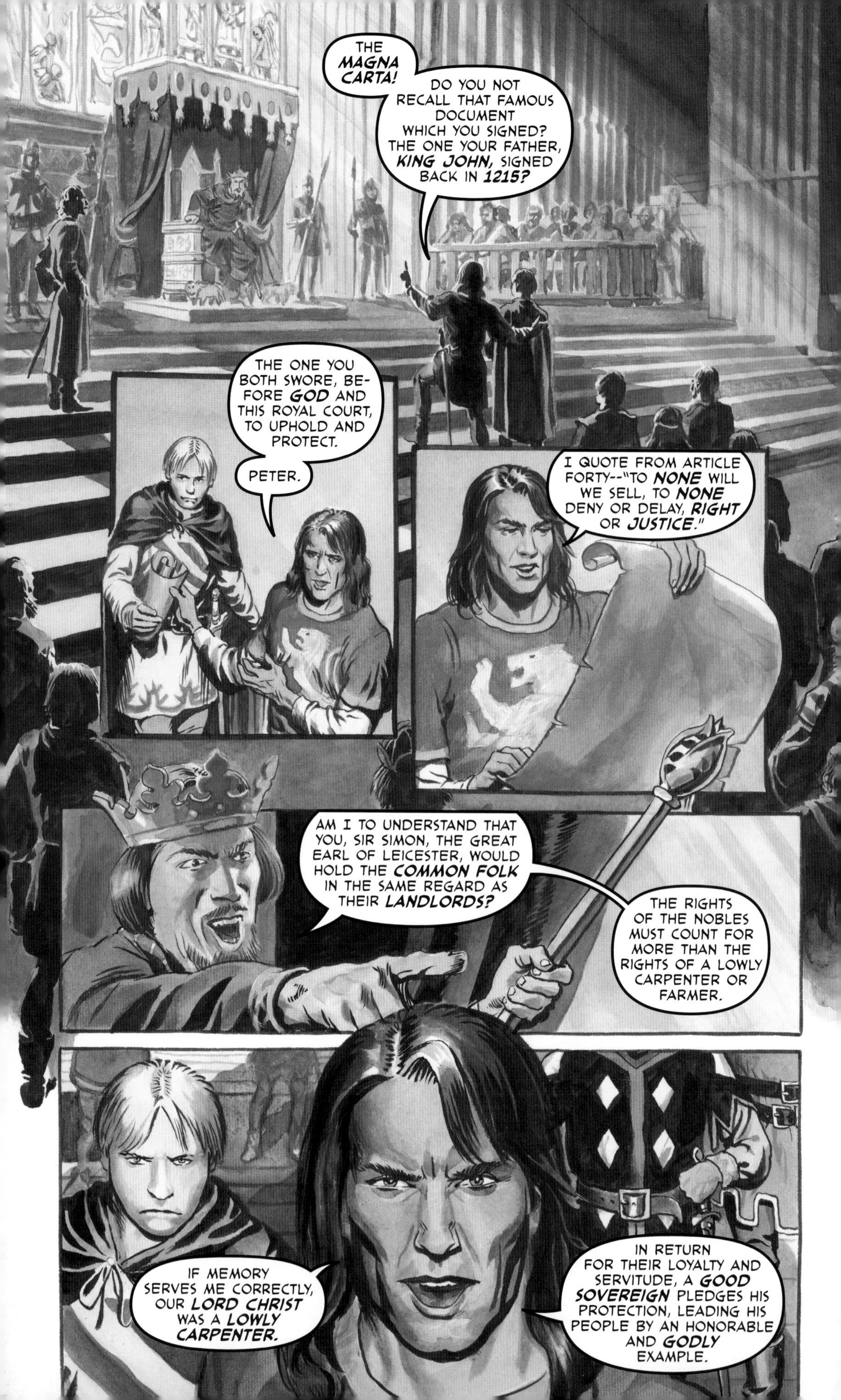
THE MAGNA CARTA!
DO YOU NOT RECALL THAT FAMOUS DOCUMENT WHICH YOU SIGNED? THE ONE YOUR FATHER, KING JOHN, SIGNED BACK IN 1215?
THE ONE YOU BOTH SWORE, BE- FORE GOD AND THIS ROYAL COURT, TO UPHOLD AND PROTECT.
PETER.
I QUOTE FROM ARTICLE FORTY--"TO NONE WILL WE SELL, TO NONE DENY OR DELAY, RIGHT OR JUSTICE."
AM I TO UNDERSTAND THAT YOU, SIR SIMON, THE GREAT EARL OF LEICESTER, WOULD HOLD THE COMMON FOLK IN THE SAME REGARD AS THEIR LANDLORDS?
THE RIGHTS OF THE NOBLES MUST COUNT FOR MORE THAN THE RIGHTS OF A LOWLY CARPENTER OR FARMER.
IF MEMORY SERVES ME CORRECTLY, OUR LORD CHRIST WAS A LOWLY CARPENTER.
IN RETURN FOR THEIR LOYALTY AND SERVITUDE, A GOOD SOVEREIGN PLEDGES HIS PROTECTION, LEADING HIS PEOPLE BY AN HONORABLE AND GODLY EXAMPLE.

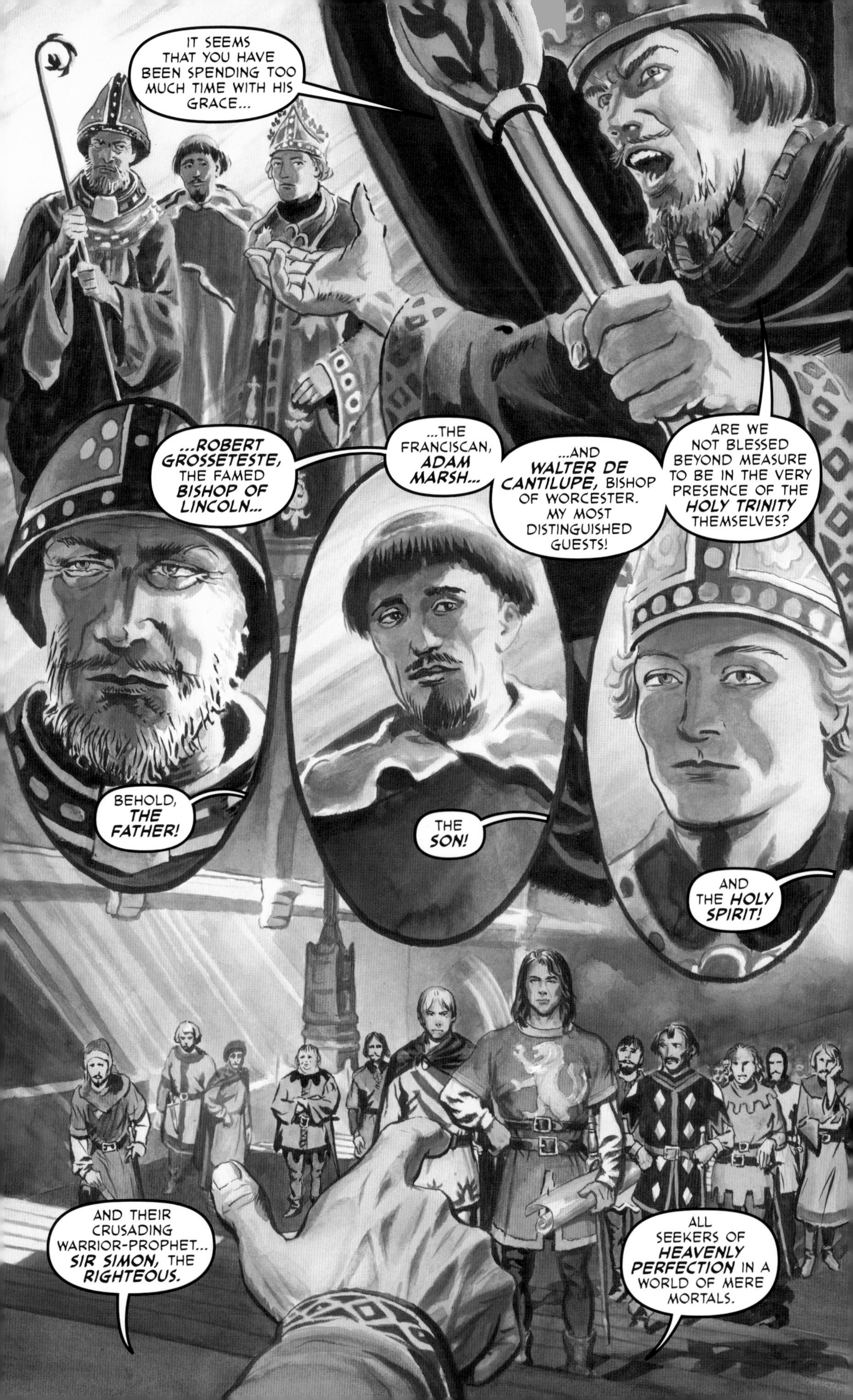
IT SEEMS THAT YOU HAVE BEEN SPENDING TOO MUCH TIME WITH HIS GRACE...
ARE WE NOT BLESSED BEYOND MEASURE TO BE IN THE VERY PRESENCE OF THE HOLY TRINITY THEMSELVES?
...ROBERT GROSSETESTE, THE FAMED BISHOP OF LINCOLN...
...THE FRANCISCAN, ADAM MARSH...
...AND WALTER DE CANTILUPE, BISHOP OF WORCESTER. MY MOST DISTINGUISHED GUESTS!
BEHOLD, THE FATHER!
THE SON!
AND THE HOLY SPIRIT!
AND THEIR CRUSADING WARRIOR-PROPHET... SIR SIMON, THE RIGHTEOUS.
ALL SEEKERS OF HEAVENLY PERFECTION IN A WORLD OF MERE MORTALS.

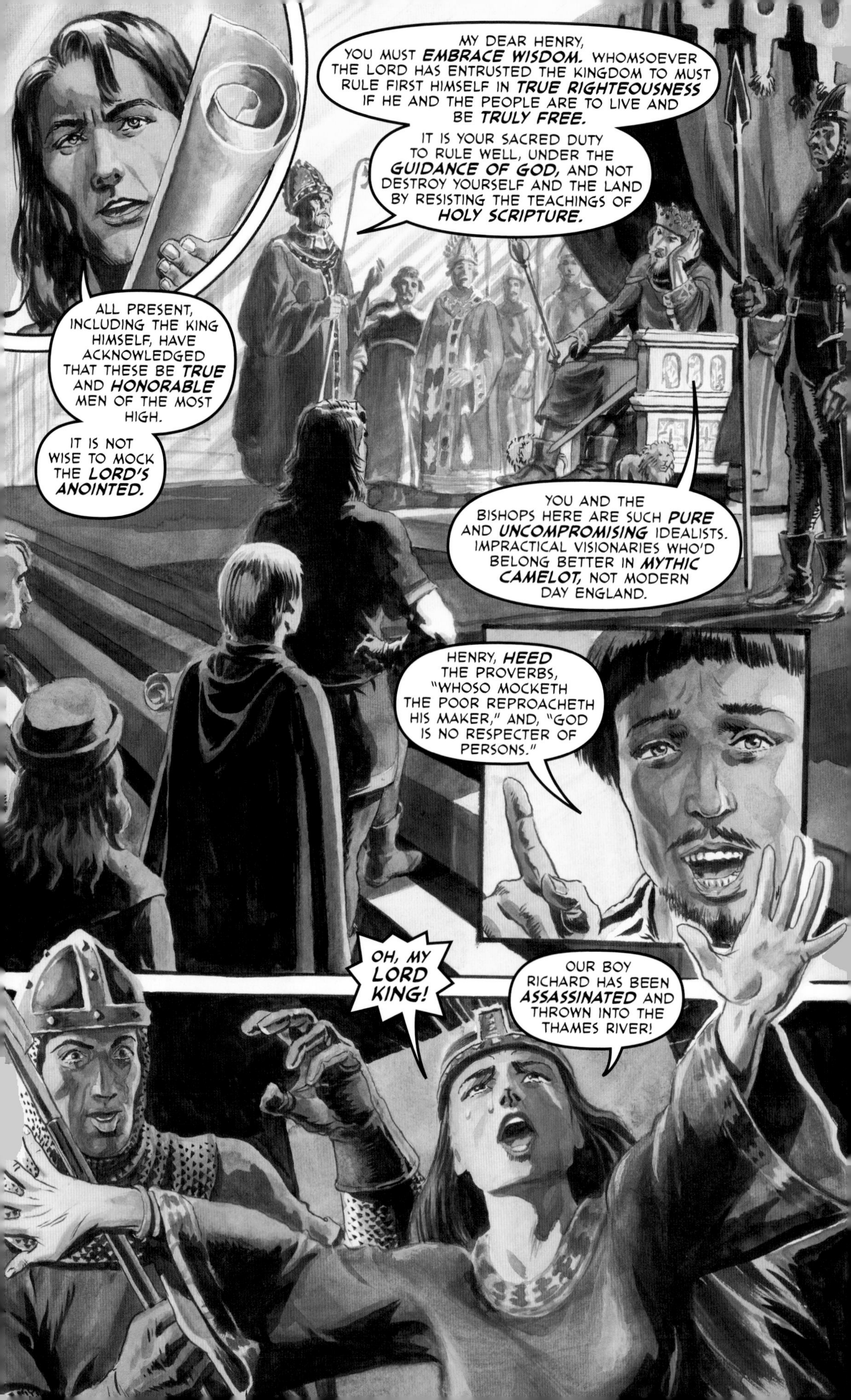
MY DEAR HENRY, YOU MUST EMBRACE WISDOM. WHOMSOEVER THE LORD HAS ENTRUSTED THE KINGDOM TO MUST RULE FIRST HIMSELF IN TRUE RIGHTEOUSNESS IF HE AND THE PEOPLE ARE TO LIVE AND BE TRULY FREE.
IT IS YOUR SACRED DUTY TO RULE WELL, UNDER THE GUIDANCE OF GOD, AND NOT DESTROY YOURSELF AND THE LAND BY RESISTING THE TEACHINGS OF HOLY SCRIPTURE.
ALL PRESENT, INCLUDING THE KING HIMSELF, HAVE ACKNOWLEDGED THAT THESE BE TRUE AND HONORABLE MEN OF THE MOST HIGH.
IT IS NOT WISE TO MOCK THE LORD'S ANOINTED.
YOU AND THE BISHOPS HERE ARE SUCH PURE AND UNCOMPROMISING IDEALISTS. IMPRACTICAL VISIONARIES WHO'D BELONG BETTER IN MYTHIC CAMELOT, NOT MODERN DAY ENGLAND.
HENRY, HEED THE PROVERBS, "WHOSO MOCKETH THE POOR REPROACHETH HIS MAKER," AND, "GOD IS NO RESPECTER OF PERSONS."
OH, MY LORD KING!
OUR BOY RICHARD HAS BEEN ASSASSINATED AND THROWN INTO THE THAMES RIVER!

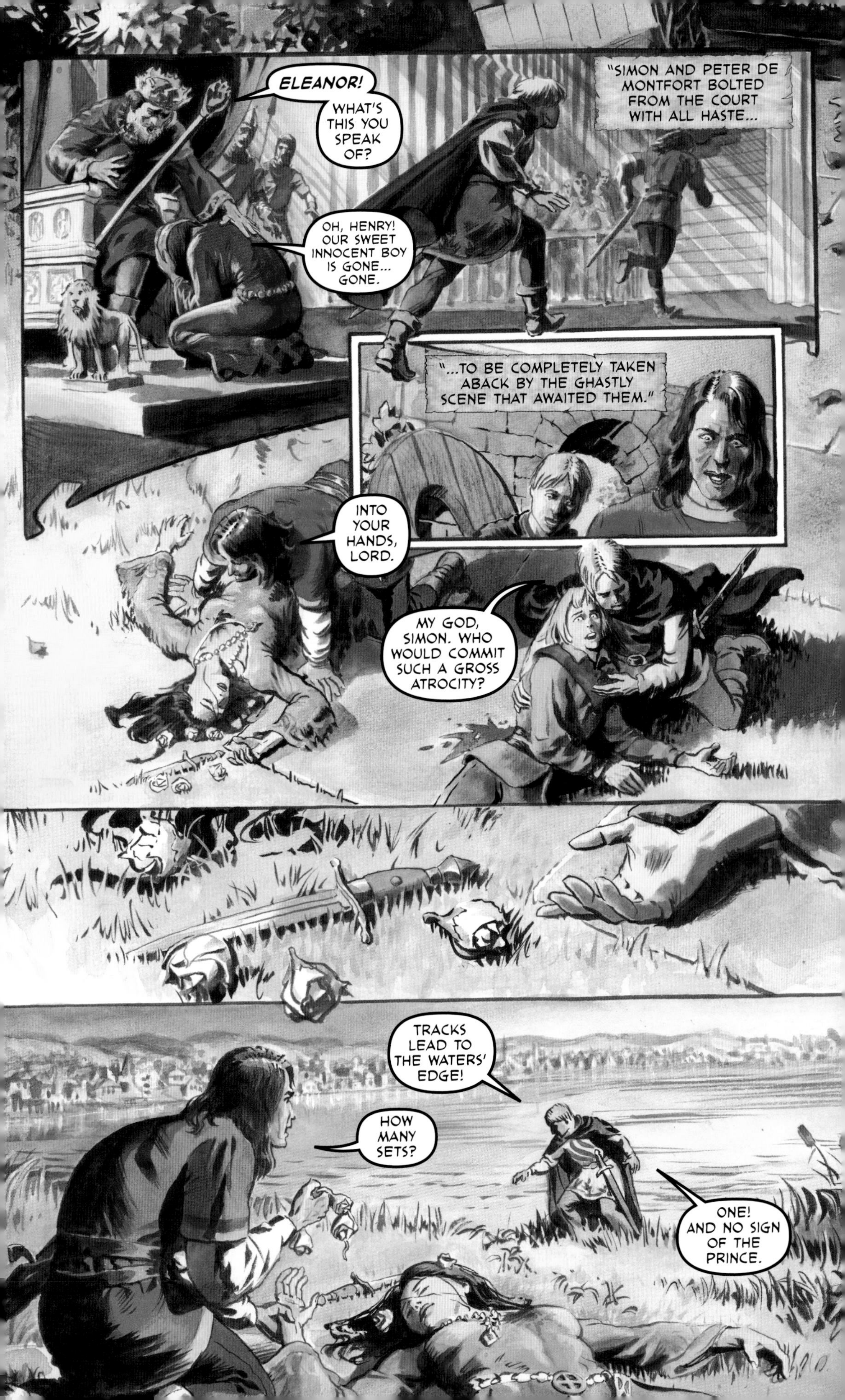
ELEANOR!
WHAT'S THIS YOU SPEAK OF?
"SIMON AND PETER DE MONTFORT BOLTED FROM THE COURT WITH ALL HASTE...
OH, HENRY! OUR SWEET INNOCENT BOY IS GONE... GONE.
"...TO BE COMPLETELY TAKEN ABACK BY THE GHASTLY SCENE THAT AWAITED THEM."
INTO YOUR HANDS, LORD.
MY GOD, SIMON. WHO WOULD COMMIT SUCH A GROSS ATROCITY?
TRACKS LEAD TO THE WATERS' EDGE!
HOW MANY SETS?
ONE! AND NO SIGN OF THE PRINCE.

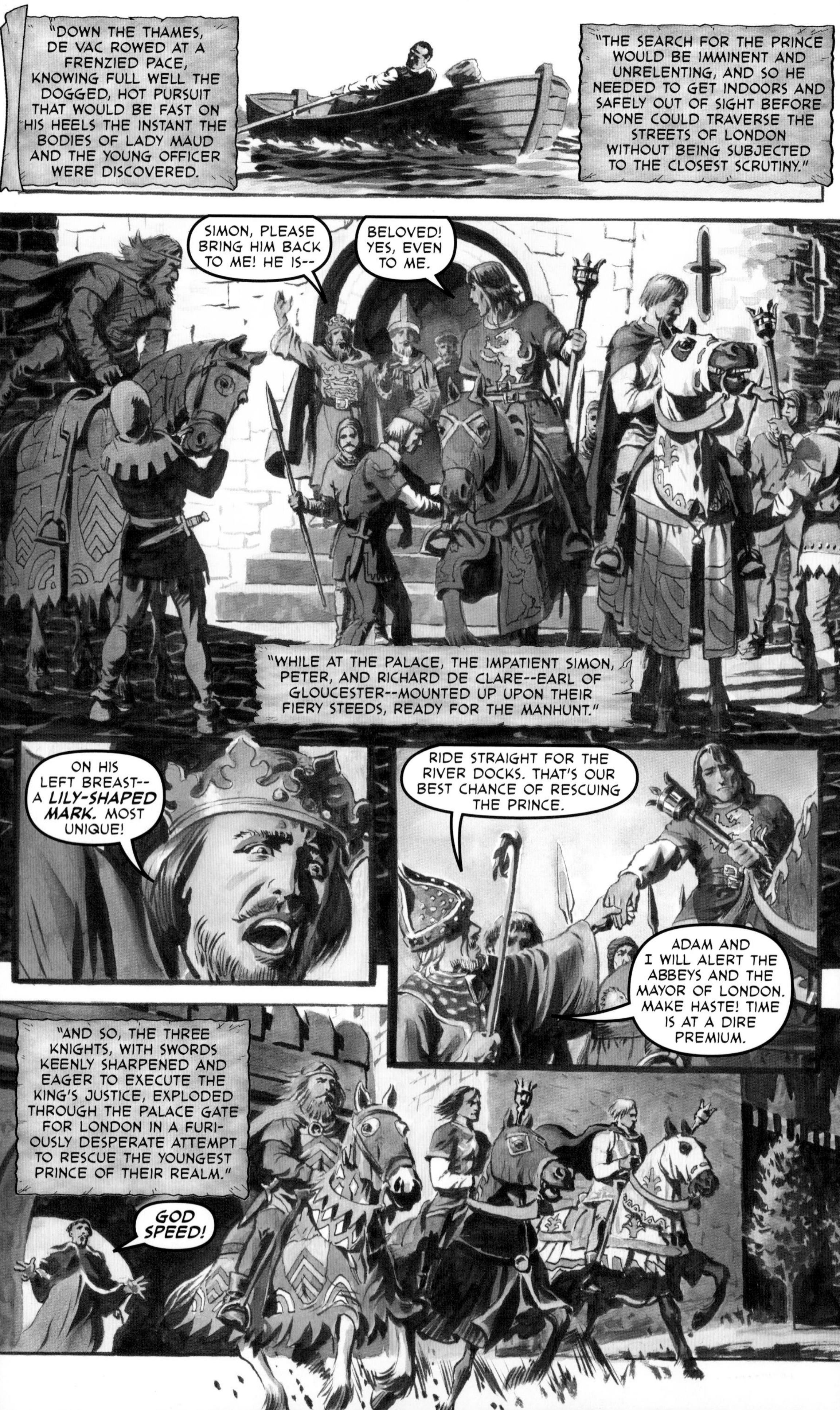
"DOWN THE THAMES, DE VAC ROWED AT A FRENZIED PACE, KNOWING FULL WELL THE DOGGED, HOT PURSUIT THAT WOULD BE FAST ON HIS HEELS THE INSTANT THE BODIES OF LADY MAUD AND THE YOUNG OFFICER WERE DISCOVERED.
"THE SEARCH FOR THE PRINCE WOULD BE IMMINENT AND UNRELENTING, AND SO HE NEEDED TO GET INDOORS AND SAFELY OUT OF SIGHT BEFORE NONE COULD TRAVERSE THE STREETS OF LONDON WITHOUT BEING SUBJECTED TO THE CLOSEST SCRUTINY."
SIMON, PLEASE BRING HIM BACK TO ME! HE IS--
BELOVED! YES, EVEN TO ME.
"WHILE AT THE PALACE, THE IMPATIENT SIMON, PETER, AND RICHARD DE CLARE--EARL OF GLOUCESTER--MOUNTED UP UPON THEIR FIERY STEEDS, READY FOR THE MANHUNT."
ON HIS LEFT BREAST--A *LILY-SHAPED MARK.* MOST UNIQUE!
RIDE STRAIGHT FOR THE RIVER DOCKS. THAT'S OUR BEST CHANCE OF RESCUING THE PRINCE.
ADAM AND I WILL ALERT THE ABBEYS AND THE MAYOR OF LONDON. MAKE HASTE! TIME IS AT A DIRE PREMIUM.
"AND SO, THE THREE KNIGHTS, WITH SWORDS KEENLY SHARPENED AND EAGER TO EXECUTE THE KING'S JUSTICE, EXPLODED THROUGH THE PALACE GATE FOR LONDON IN A FURIOUSLY DESPERATE ATTEMPT TO RESCUE THE YOUNGEST PRINCE OF THEIR REALM."
GOD SPEED!

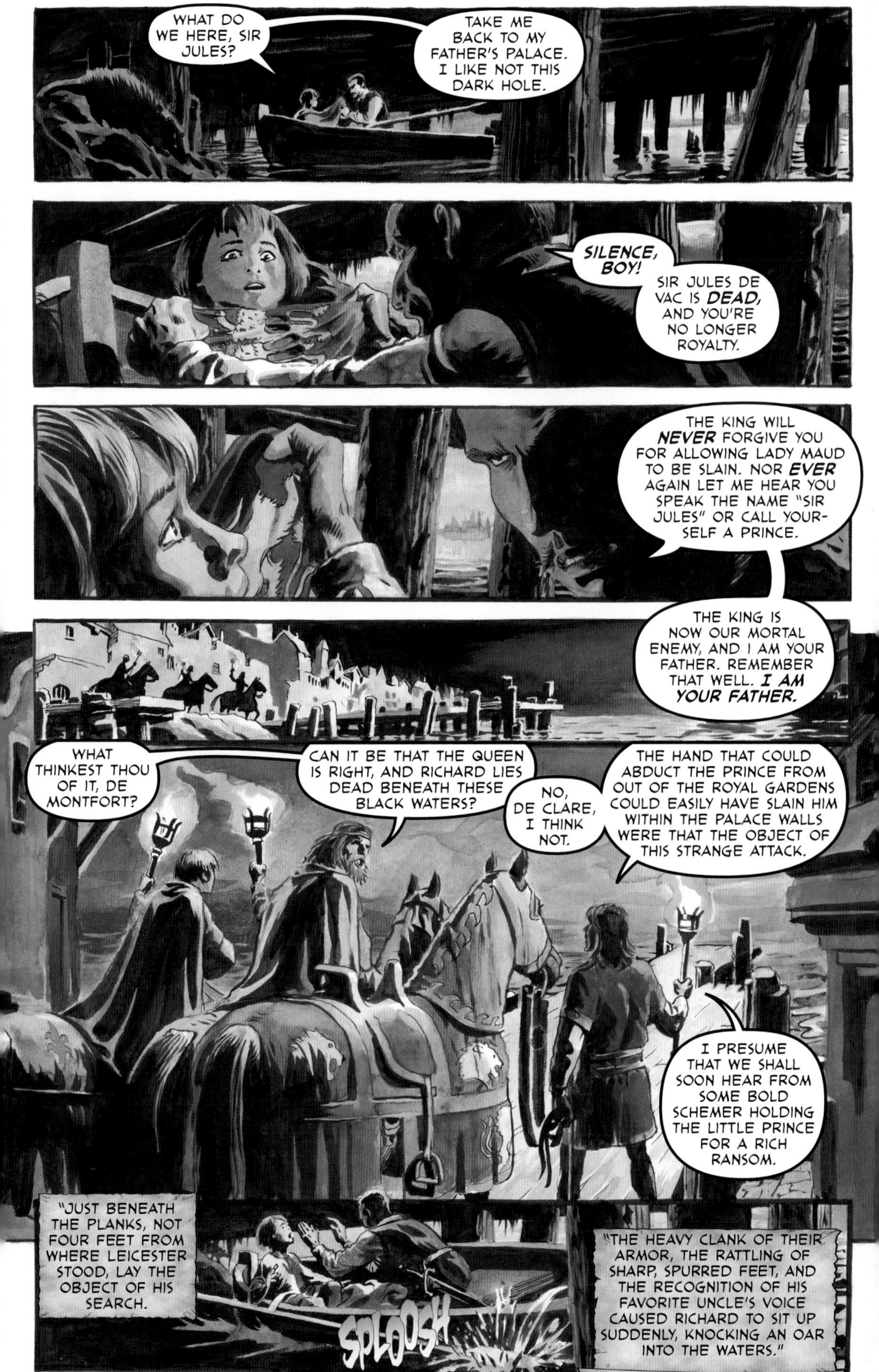
WHAT DO WE HERE, SIR JULES?
TAKE ME BACK TO MY FATHER'S PALACE. I LIKE NOT THIS DARK HOLE.
SILENCE, BOY!
SIR JULES DE VAC IS DEAD, AND YOU'RE NO LONGER ROYALTY.
THE KING WILL NEVER FORGIVE YOU FOR ALLOWING LADY MAUD TO BE SLAIN. NOR EVER AGAIN LET ME HEAR YOU SPEAK THE NAME "SIR JULES" OR CALL YOURSELF A PRINCE.
THE KING IS NOW OUR MORTAL ENEMY, AND I AM YOUR FATHER. REMEMBER THAT WELL. I AM YOUR FATHER.
WHAT THINKEST THOU OF IT, DE MONTFORT?
CAN IT BE THAT THE QUEEN IS RIGHT, AND RICHARD LIES DEAD BENEATH THESE BLACK WATERS?
NO, DE CLARE, I THINK NOT.
THE HAND THAT COULD ABDUCT THE PRINCE FROM OUT OF THE ROYAL GARDENS COULD EASILY HAVE SLAIN HIM WITHIN THE PALACE WALLS WERE THAT THE OBJECT OF THIS STRANGE ATTACK.
I PRESUME THAT WE SHALL SOON HEAR FROM SOME BOLD SCHEMER HOLDING THE LITTLE PRINCE FOR A RICH RANSOM.
"JUST BENEATH THE PLANKS, NOT FOUR FEET FROM WHERE LEICESTER STOOD, LAY THE OBJECT OF HIS SEARCH.
SPLOOSH
"THE HEAVY CLANK OF THEIR ARMOR, THE RATTLING OF SHARP, SPURRED FEET, AND THE RECOGNITION OF HIS FAVORITE UNCLE'S VOICE CAUSED RICHARD TO SIT UP SUDDENLY, KNOCKING AN OAR INTO THE WATERS."

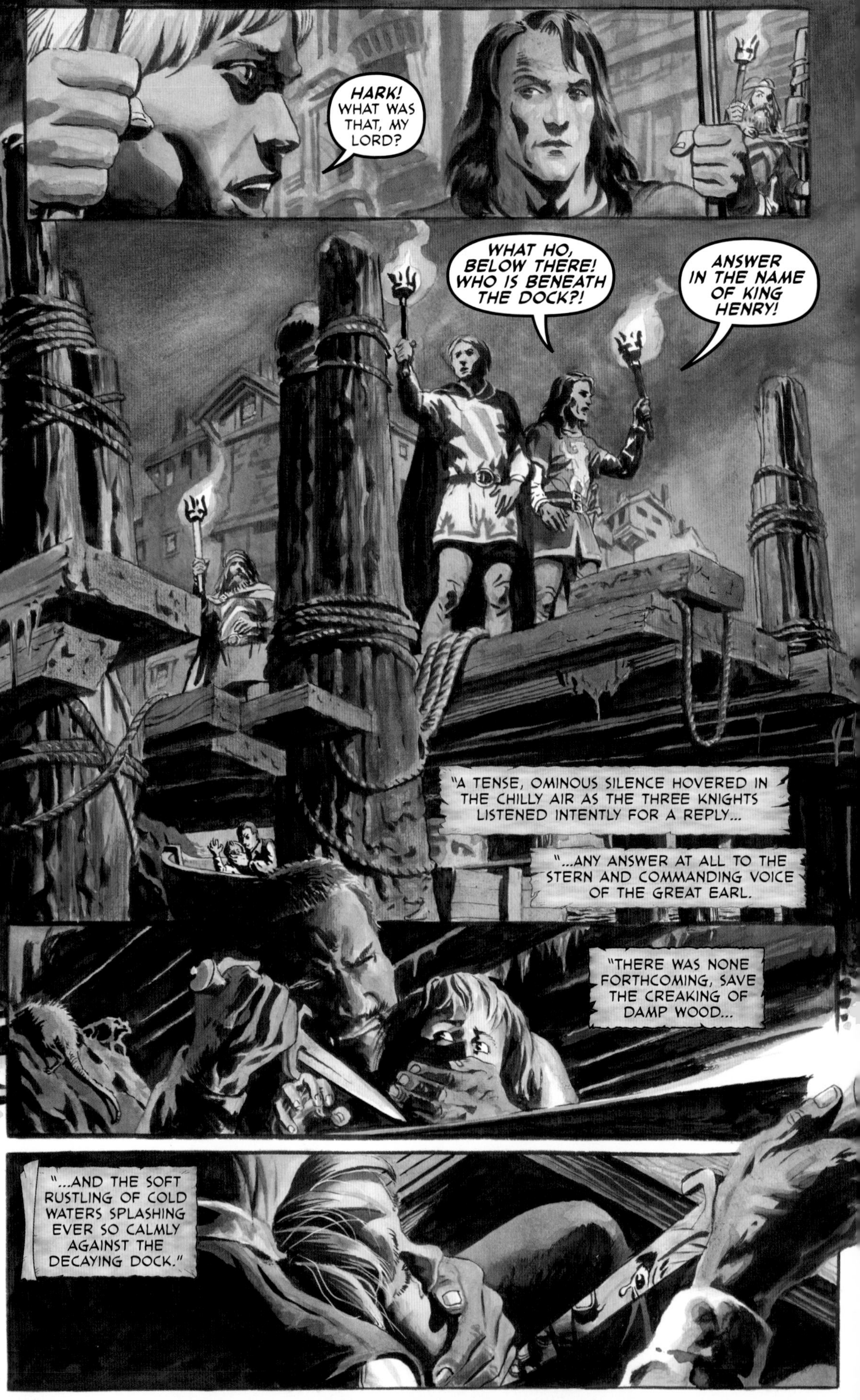
HARK! WHAT WAS THAT, MY LORD?
WHAT HO, BELOW THERE! WHO IS BENEATH THE DOCK?!
ANSWER IN THE NAME OF KING HENRY!
"A TENSE, OMINOUS SILENCE HOVERED IN THE CHILLY AIR AS THE THREE KNIGHTS LISTENED INTENTLY FOR A REPLY...
"...ANY ANSWER AT ALL TO THE STERN AND COMMANDING VOICE OF THE GREAT EARL.
"THERE WAS NONE FORTHCOMING, SAVE THE CREAKING OF DAMP WOOD...
"...AND THE SOFT RUSTLING OF COLD WATERS SPLASHING EVER SO CALMLY AGAINST THE DECAYING DOCK."

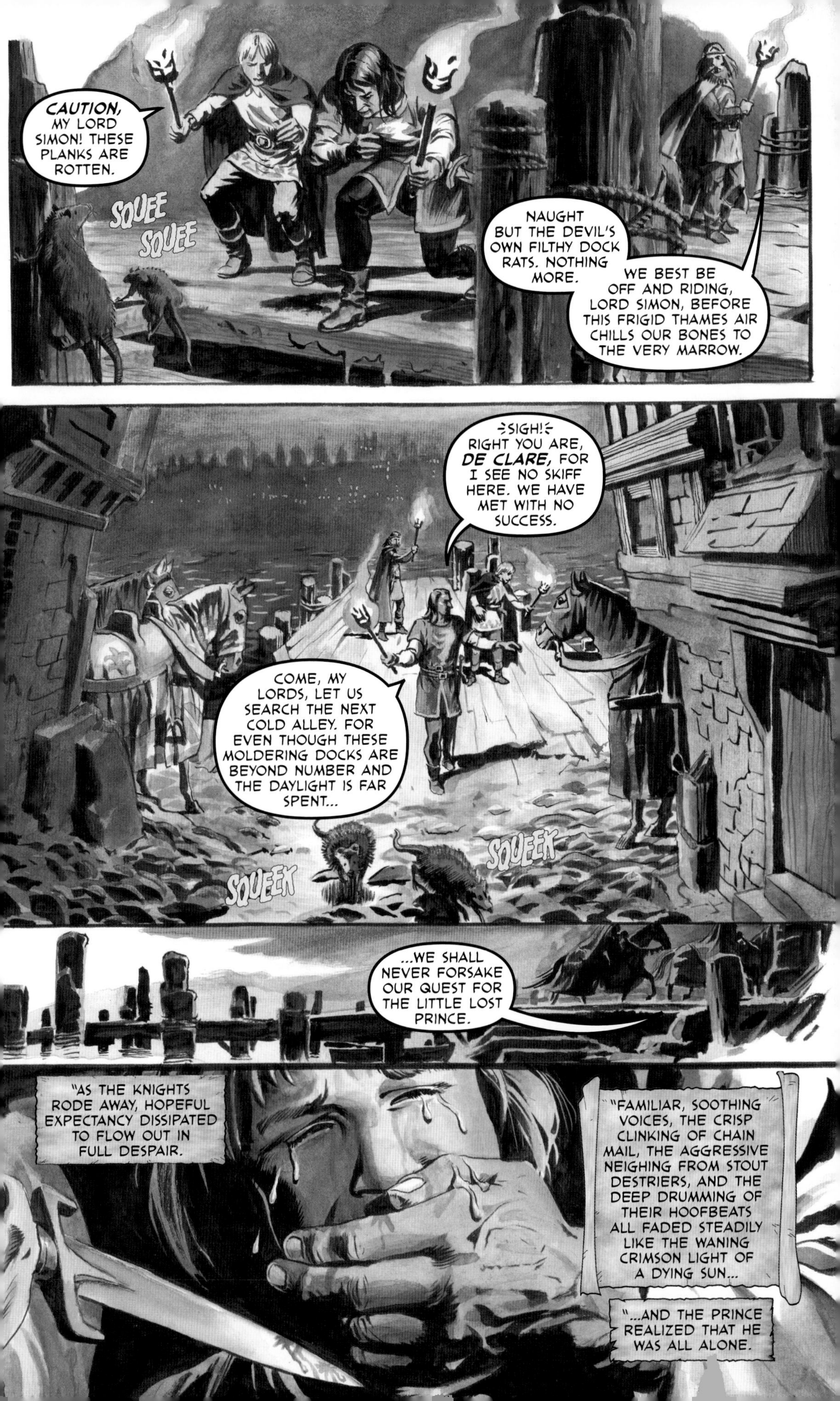
CAUTION, MY LORD SIMON! THESE PLANKS ARE ROTTEN.
SQUEE SQUEE
NAUGHT BUT THE DEVIL'S OWN FILTHY DOCK RATS. NOTHING MORE.
WE BEST BE OFF AND RIDING, LORD SIMON, BEFORE THIS FRIGID THAMES AIR CHILLS OUR BONES TO THE VERY MARROW.
SIGH! RIGHT YOU ARE, DE CLARE, FOR I SEE NO SKIFF HERE. WE HAVE MET WITH NO SUCCESS.
COME, MY LORDS, LET US SEARCH THE NEXT COLD ALLEY. FOR EVEN THOUGH THESE MOLDERING DOCKS ARE BEYOND NUMBER AND THE DAYLIGHT IS FAR SPENT...
SQUEEK
SQUEEK
...WE SHALL NEVER FORSAKE OUR QUEST FOR THE LITTLE LOST PRINCE.
"AS THE KNIGHTS RODE AWAY, HOPEFUL EXPECTANCY DISSIPATED TO FLOW OUT IN FULL DESPAIR.
"FAMILIAR, SOOTHING VOICES, THE CRISP CLINKING OF CHAIN MAIL, THE AGGRESSIVE NEIGHING FROM STOUT DESTRIERS, AND THE DEEP DRUMMING OF THEIR HOOFBEATS ALL FADED STEADILY LIKE THE WANING CRIMSON LIGHT OF A DYING SUN...
"...AND THE PRINCE REALIZED THAT HE WAS ALL ALONE.

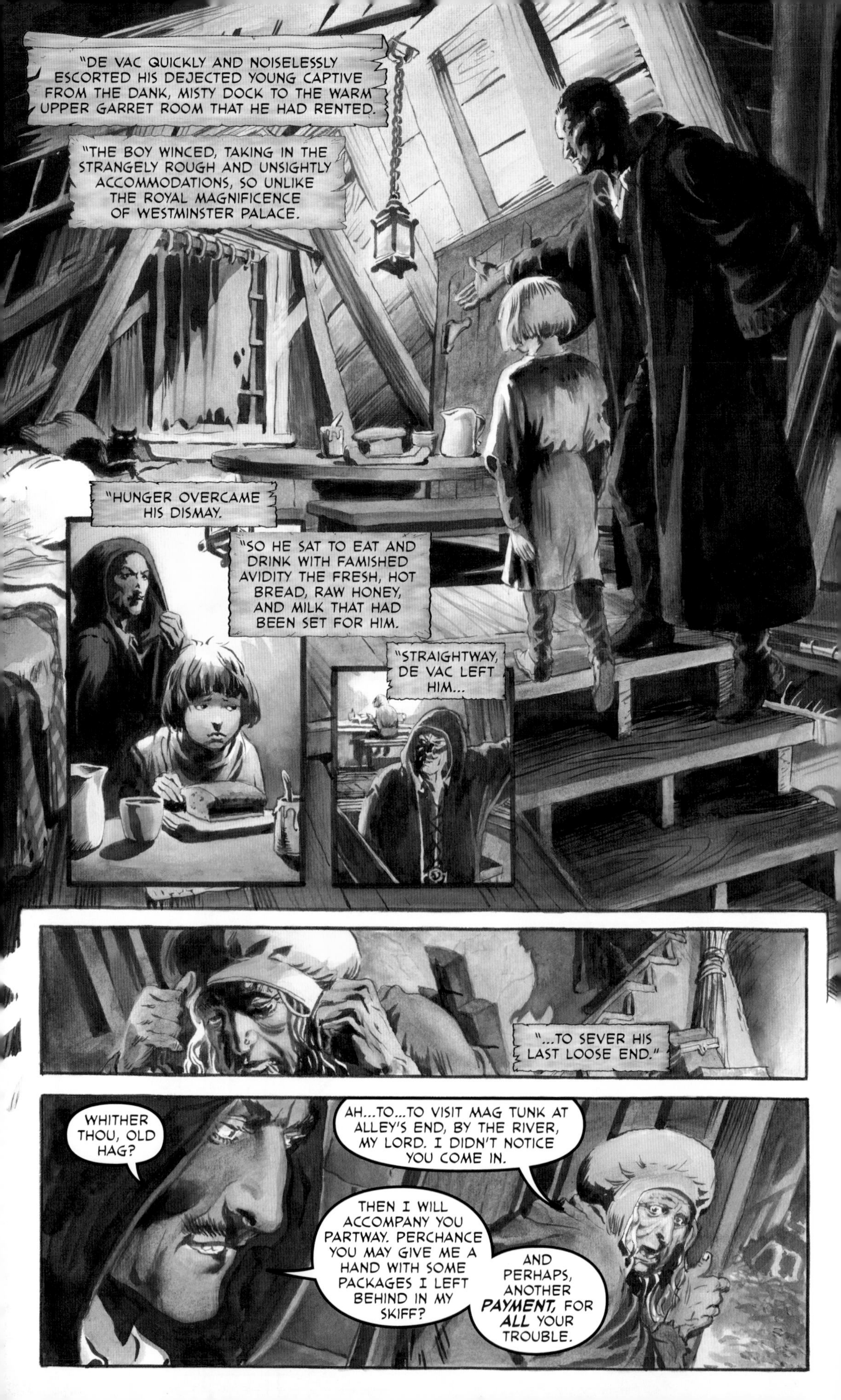
"DE VAC QUICKLY AND NOISELESSLY ESCORTED HIS DEJECTED YOUNG CAPTIVE FROM THE DANK, MISTY DOCK TO THE WARM UPPER GARRET ROOM THAT HE HAD RENTED.
"THE BOY WINCED, TAKING IN THE STRANGELY ROUGH AND UNSIGHTLY ACCOMMODATIONS, SO UNLIKE THE ROYAL MAGNIFICENCE OF WESTMINSTER PALACE.
"HUNGER OVERCAME HIS DISMAY.
"SO HE SAT TO EAT AND DRINK WITH FAMISHED AVIDITY THE FRESH, HOT BREAD, RAW HONEY, AND MILK THAT HAD BEEN SET FOR HIM.
"STRAIGHTWAY, DE VAC LEFT HIM...
"...TO SEVER HIS LAST LOOSE END."
WHITHER THOU, OLD HAG?
AH...TO...TO VISIT MAG TUNK AT ALLEY'S END, BY THE RIVER, MY LORD. I DIDN'T NOTICE YOU COME IN.
THEN I WILL ACCOMPANY YOU PARTWAY. PERCHANCE YOU MAY GIVE ME A HAND WITH SOME PACKAGES I LEFT BEHIND IN MY SKIFF?
AND PERHAPS, ANOTHER *PAYMENT,* FOR *ALL* YOUR TROUBLE.

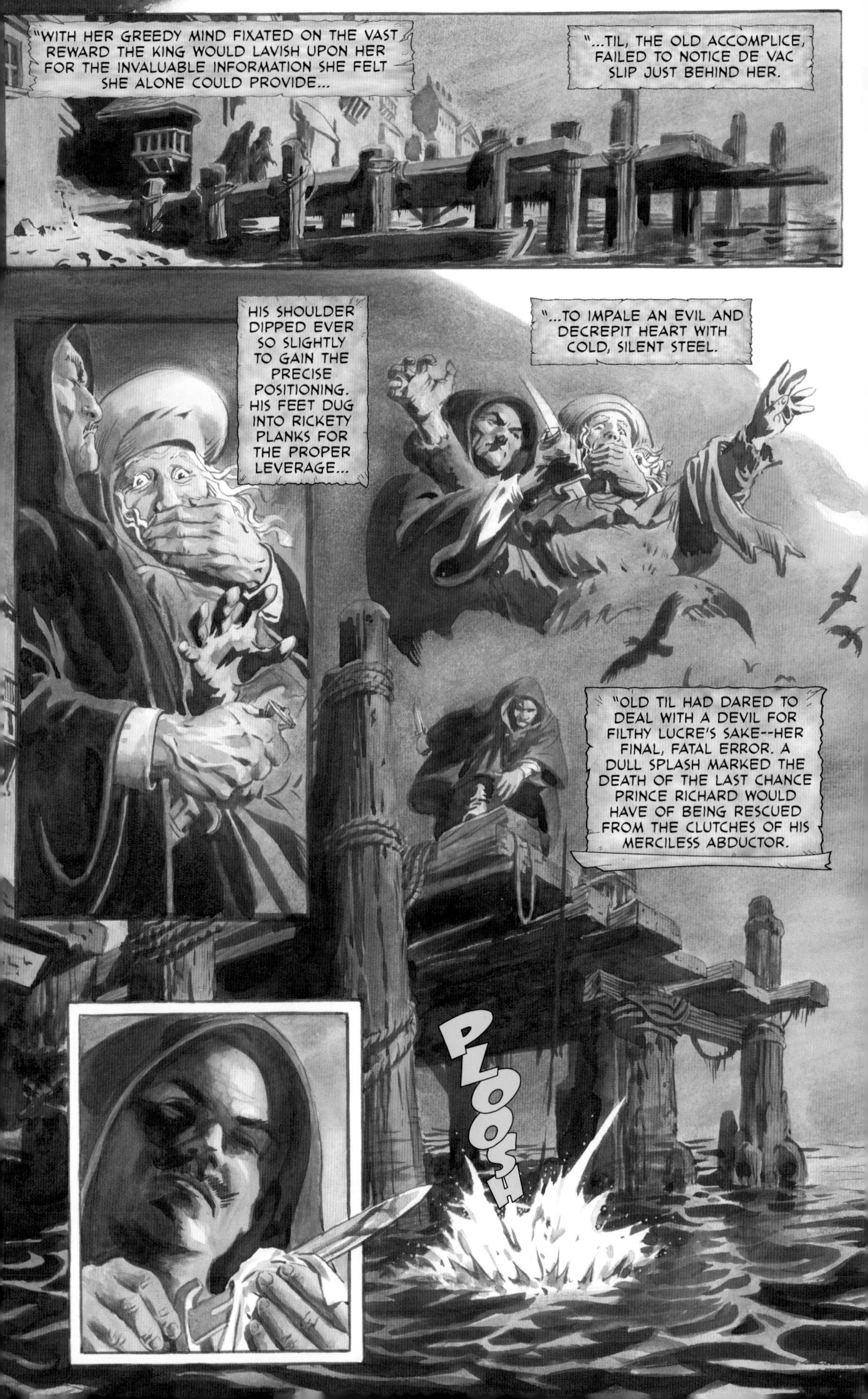
"WITH HER GREEDY MIND FIXATED ON THE VAST REWARD THE KING WOULD LAVISH UPON HER FOR THE INVALUABLE INFORMATION SHE FELT SHE ALONE COULD PROVIDE...
"...TIL, THE OLD ACCOMPLICE, FAILED TO NOTICE DE VAC SLIP JUST BEHIND HER.
HIS SHOULDER DIPPED EVER SO SLIGHTLY TO GAIN THE PRECISE POSITIONING. HIS FEET DUG INTO RICKETY PLANKS FOR THE PROPER LEVERAGE...
"...TO IMPALE AN EVIL AND DECREPIT HEART WITH COLD, SILENT STEEL.
"OLD TIL HAD DARED TO DEAL WITH A DEVIL FOR FILTHY LUCRE'S SAKE--HER FINAL, FATAL ERROR. A DULL SPLASH MARKED THE DEATH OF THE LAST CHANCE PRINCE RICHARD WOULD HAVE OF BEING RESCUED FROM THE CLUTCHES OF HIS MERCILESS ABDUCTOR.
PLOOSH

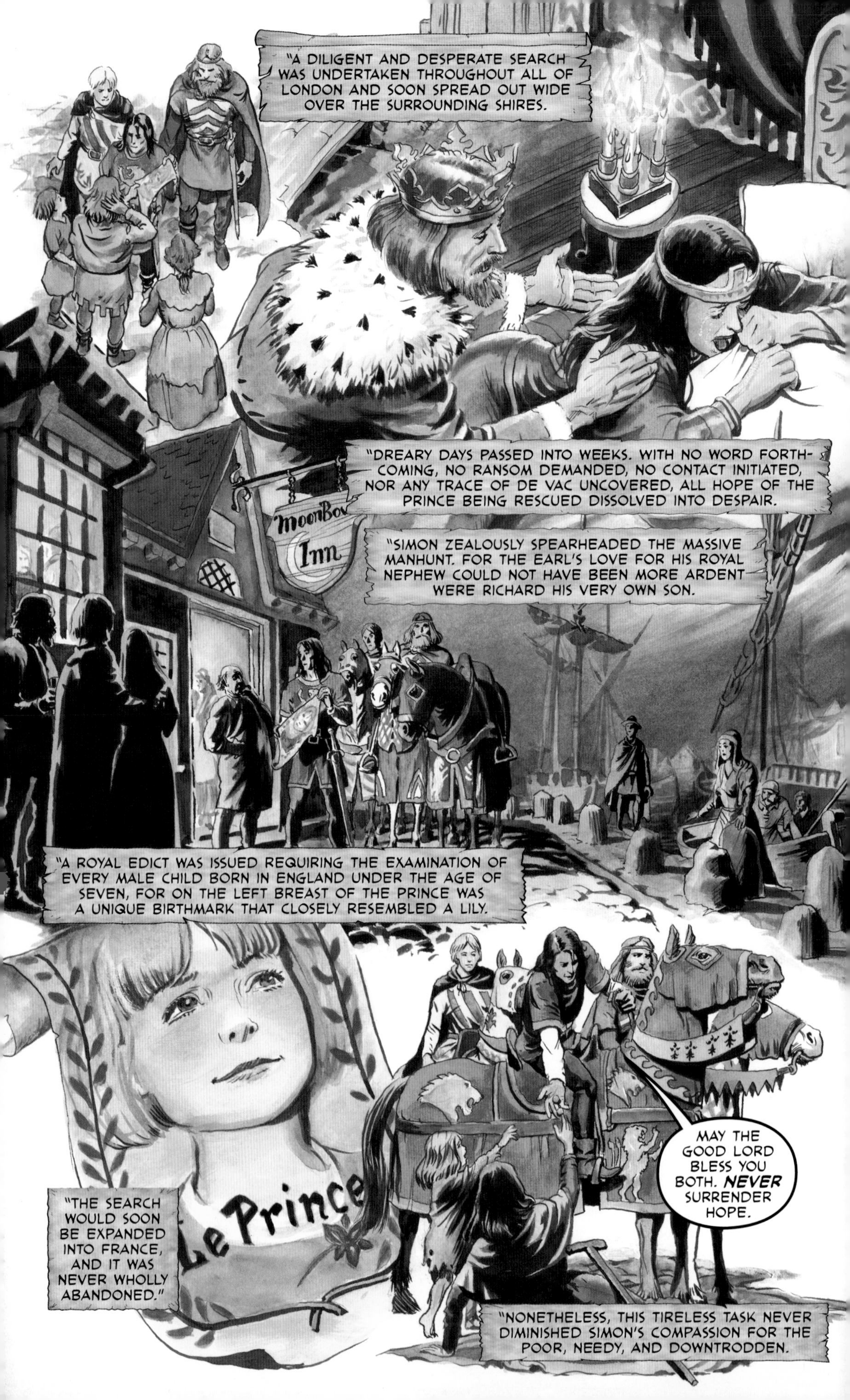
"A DILIGENT AND DESPERATE SEARCH WAS UNDERTAKEN THROUGHOUT ALL OF LONDON AND SOON SPREAD OUT WIDE OVER THE SURROUNDING SHIRES.
"DREARY DAYS PASSED INTO WEEKS. WITH NO WORD FORTHCOMING, NO RANSOM DEMANDED, NO CONTACT INITIATED, NOR ANY TRACE OF DE VAC UNCOVERED, ALL HOPE OF THE PRINCE BEING RESCUED DISSOLVED INTO DESPAIR.
moonBow Inn
"SIMON ZEALOUSLY SPEARHEADED THE MASSIVE MANHUNT. FOR THE EARL'S LOVE FOR HIS ROYAL NEPHEW COULD NOT HAVE BEEN MORE ARDENT WERE RICHARD HIS VERY OWN SON.
"A ROYAL EDICT WAS ISSUED REQUIRING THE EXAMINATION OF EVERY MALE CHILD BORN IN ENGLAND UNDER THE AGE OF SEVEN, FOR ON THE LEFT BREAST OF THE PRINCE WAS A UNIQUE BIRTHMARK THAT CLOSELY RESEMBLED A LILY.
Le Prince
"THE SEARCH WOULD SOON BE EXPANDED INTO FRANCE, AND IT WAS NEVER WHOLLY ABANDONED."
MAY THE GOOD LORD BLESS YOU BOTH. NEVER SURRENDER HOPE.
"NONETHELESS, THIS TIRELESS TASK NEVER DIMINISHED SIMON'S COMPASSION FOR THE POOR, NEEDY, AND DOWNTRODDEN.

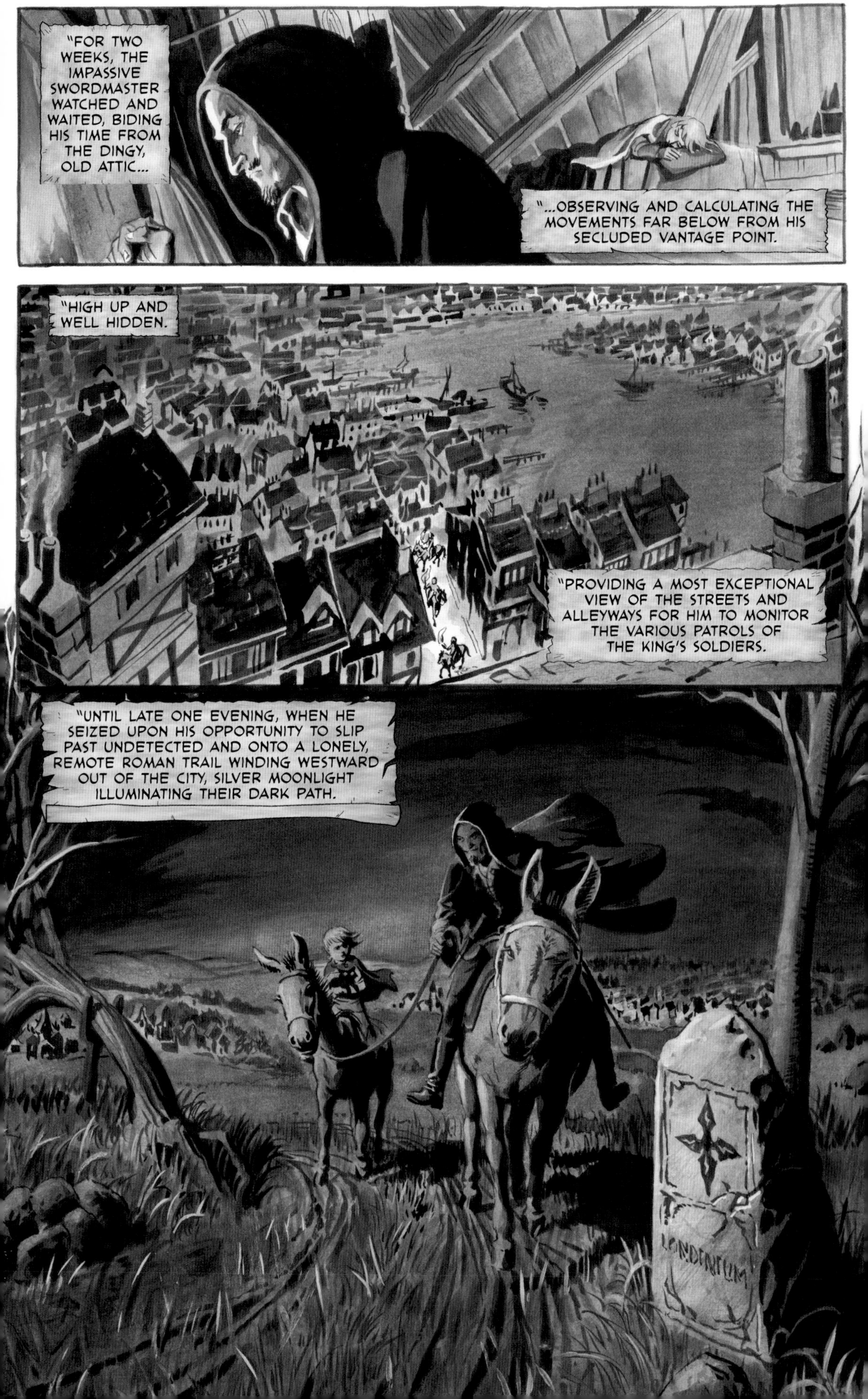
"FOR TWO WEEKS, THE IMPASSIVE SWORDMASTER WATCHED AND WAITED, BIDING HIS TIME FROM THE DINGY, OLD ATTIC...
"...OBSERVING AND CALCULATING THE MOVEMENTS FAR BELOW FROM HIS SECLUDED VANTAGE POINT.
"HIGH UP AND WELL HIDDEN.
"PROVIDING A MOST EXCEPTIONAL VIEW OF THE STREETS AND ALLEYWAYS FOR HIM TO MONITOR THE VARIOUS PATROLS OF THE KING'S SOLDIERS.
"UNTIL LATE ONE EVENING, WHEN HE SEIZED UPON HIS OPPORTUNITY TO SLIP PAST UNDETECTED AND ONTO A LONELY, REMOTE ROMAN TRAIL WINDING WESTWARD OUT OF THE CITY, SILVER MOONLIGHT ILLUMINATING THEIR DARK PATH.
LONDINIUM

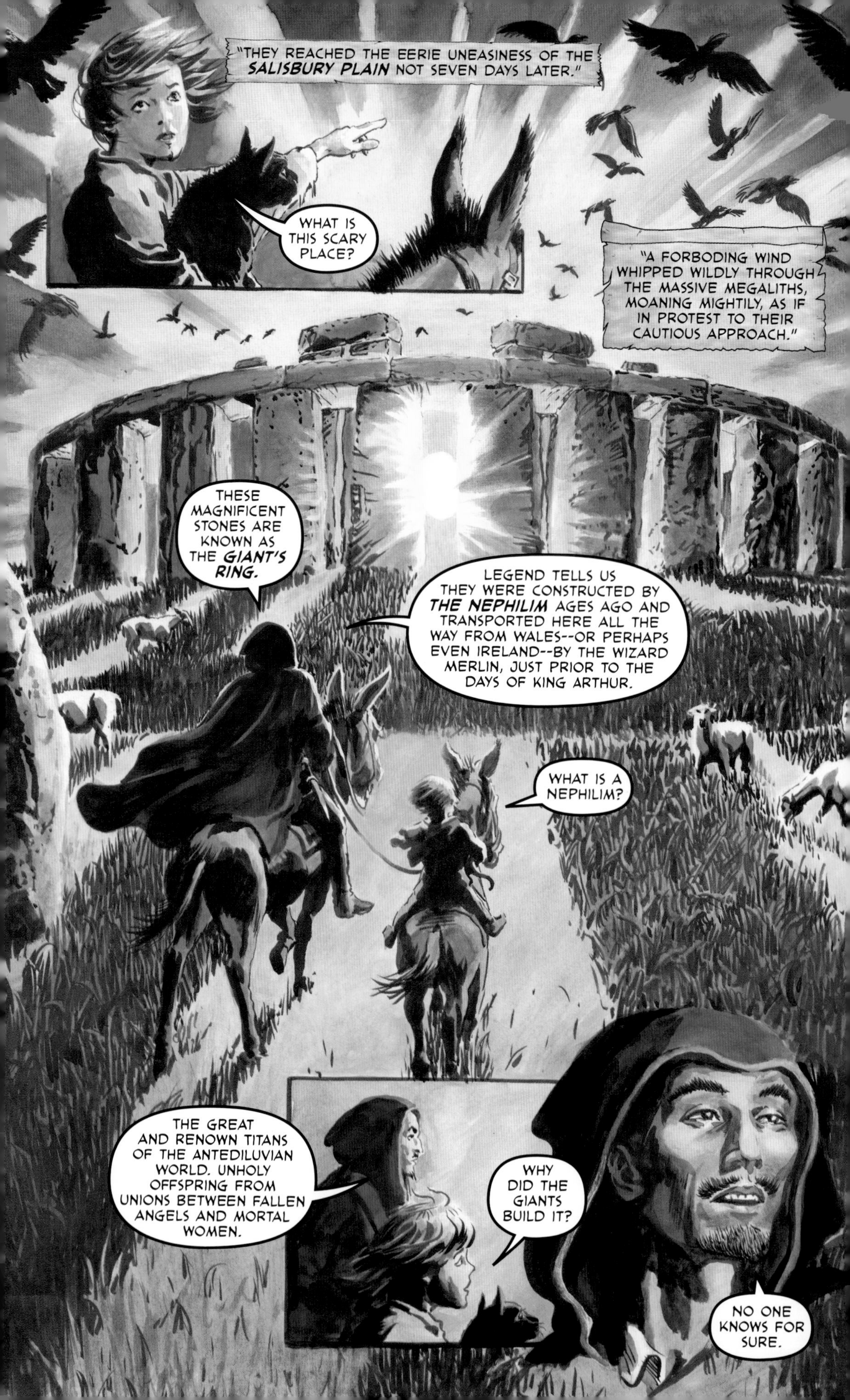
"THEY REACHED THE EERIE UNEASINESS OF THE *SALISBURY PLAIN* NOT SEVEN DAYS LATER."
WHAT IS THIS SCARY PLACE?
"A FORBODING WIND WHIPPED WILDLY THROUGH THE MASSIVE MEGALITHS, MOANING MIGHTILY, AS IF IN PROTEST TO THEIR CAUTIOUS APPROACH."
THESE MAGNIFICENT STONES ARE KNOWN AS THE *GIANT'S RING.*
LEGEND TELLS US THEY WERE CONSTRUCTED BY *THE NEPHILIM* AGES AGO AND TRANSPORTED HERE ALL THE WAY FROM WALES--OR PERHAPS EVEN IRELAND--BY THE WIZARD MERLIN, JUST PRIOR TO THE DAYS OF KING ARTHUR.
WHAT IS A NEPHILIM?
THE GREAT AND RENOWN TITANS OF THE ANTEDILUVIAN WORLD. UNHOLY OFFSPRING FROM UNIONS BETWEEN FALLEN ANGELS AND MORTAL WOMEN.
WHY DID THE GIANTS BUILD IT?
NO ONE KNOWS FOR SURE.

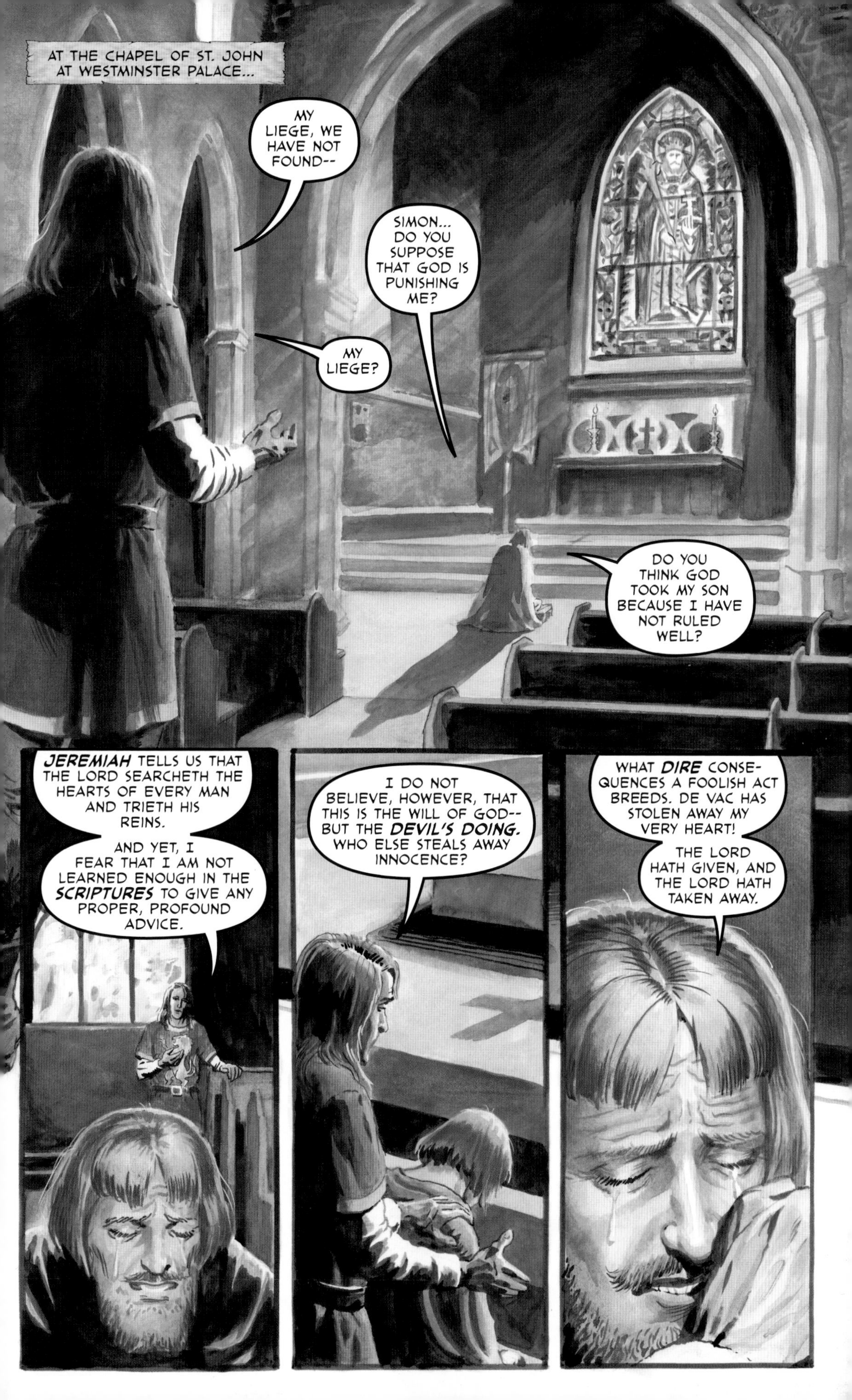
AT THE CHAPEL OF ST. JOHN AT WESTMINSTER PALACE...
MY LIEGE, WE HAVE NOT FOUND--
MY LIEGE?
SIMON... DO YOU SUPPOSE THAT GOD IS PUNISHING ME?
DO YOU THINK GOD TOOK MY SON BECAUSE I HAVE NOT RULED WELL?
JEREMIAH TELLS US THAT THE LORD SEARCHETH THE HEARTS OF EVERY MAN AND TRIETH HIS REINS.
AND YET, I FEAR THAT I AM NOT LEARNED ENOUGH IN THE SCRIPTURES TO GIVE ANY PROPER, PROFOUND ADVICE.
I DO NOT BELIEVE, HOWEVER, THAT THIS IS THE WILL OF GOD-- BUT THE DEVIL'S DOING. WHO ELSE STEALS AWAY INNOCENCE?
WHAT DIRE CONSE-QUENCES A FOOLISH ACT BREEDS. DE VAC HAS STOLEN AWAY MY VERY HEART!
THE LORD HATH GIVEN, AND THE LORD HATH TAKEN AWAY.

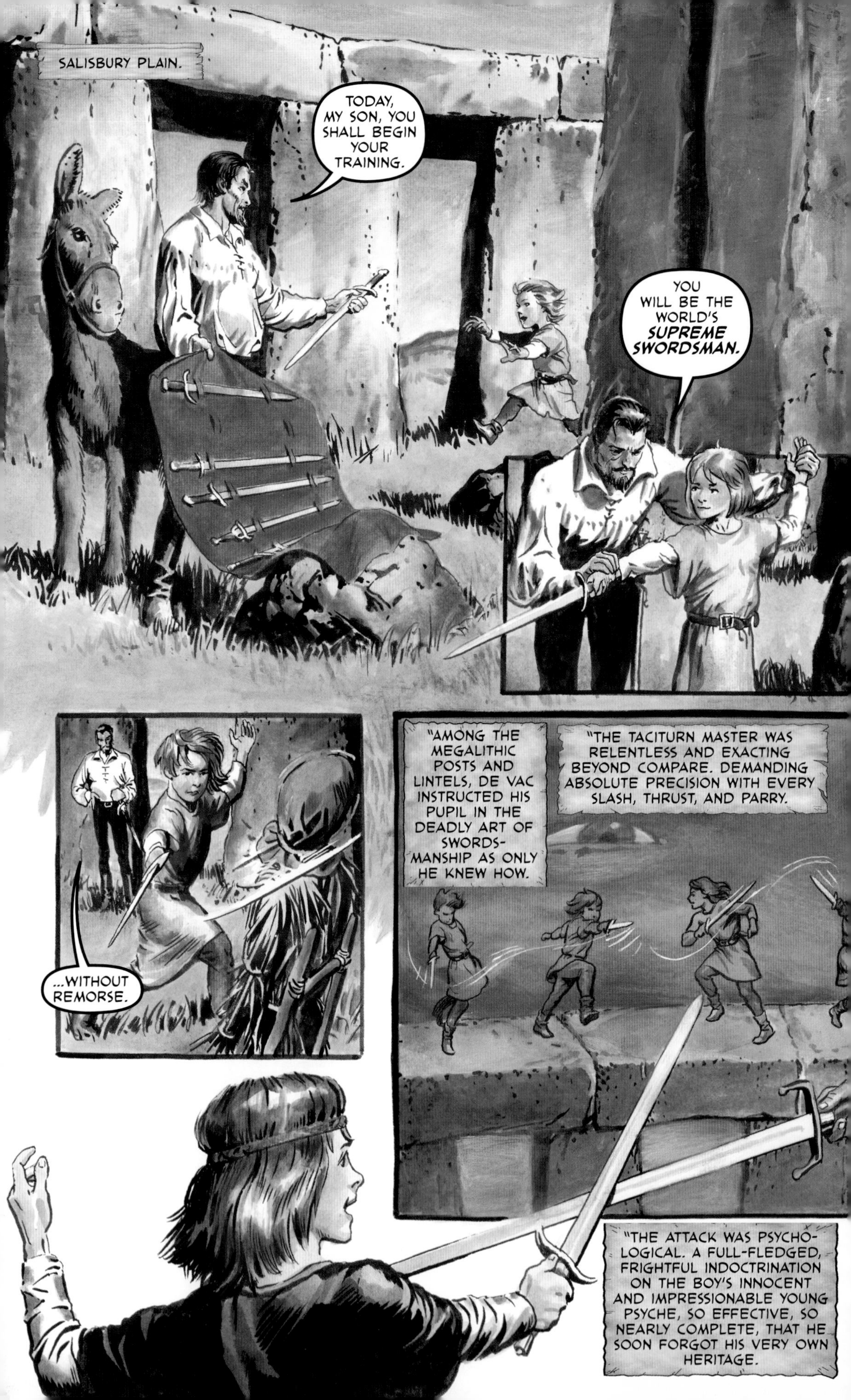
SALISBURY PLAIN.
TODAY, MY SON, YOU SHALL BEGIN YOUR TRAINING.
YOU WILL BE THE WORLD'S *SUPREME SWORDSMAN.*
...WITHOUT REMORSE.
"AMONG THE MEGALITHIC POSTS AND LINTELS, DE VAC INSTRUCTED HIS PUPIL IN THE DEADLY ART OF SWORDS-MANSHIP AS ONLY HE KNEW HOW.
"THE TACITURN MASTER WAS RELENTLESS AND EXACTING BEYOND COMPARE. DEMANDING ABSOLUTE PRECISION WITH EVERY SLASH, THRUST, AND PARRY.
"THE ATTACK WAS PSYCHO-LOGICAL. A FULL-FLEDGED, FRIGHTFUL INDOCTRINATION ON THE BOY'S INNOCENT AND IMPRESSIONABLE YOUNG PSYCHE, SO EFFECTIVE, SO NEARLY COMPLETE, THAT HE SOON FORGOT HIS VERY OWN HERITAGE.

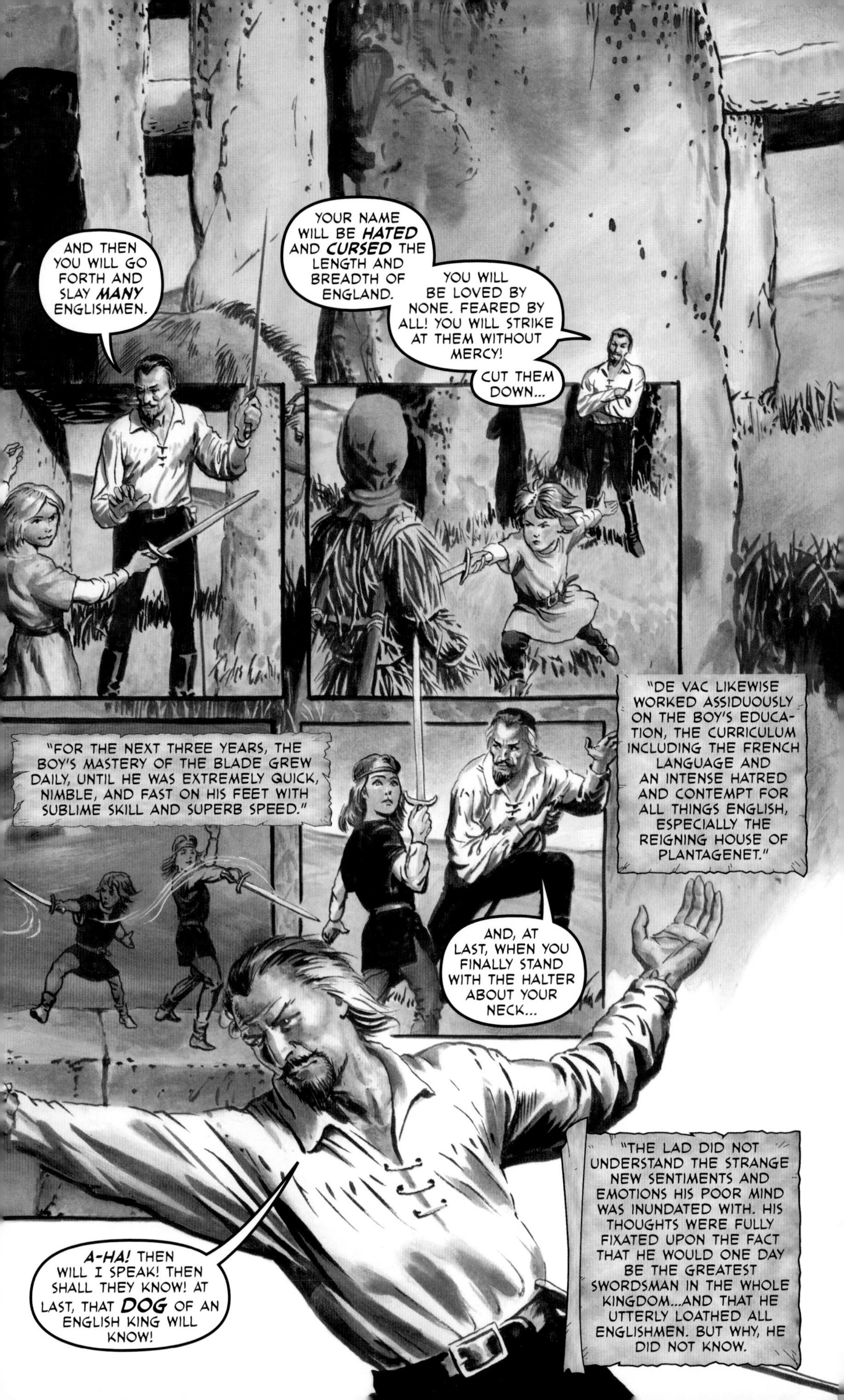
AND THEN YOU WILL GO FORTH AND SLAY *MANY* ENGLISHMEN.
YOUR NAME WILL BE *HATED* AND *CURSED* THE LENGTH AND BREADTH OF ENGLAND.
YOU WILL BE LOVED BY NONE. FEARED BY ALL! YOU WILL STRIKE AT THEM WITHOUT MERCY!
CUT THEM DOWN...
"FOR THE NEXT THREE YEARS, THE BOY'S MASTERY OF THE BLADE GREW DAILY, UNTIL HE WAS EXTREMELY QUICK, NIMBLE, AND FAST ON HIS FEET WITH SUBLIME SKILL AND SUPERB SPEED."
"DE VAC LIKEWISE WORKED ASSIDUOUSLY ON THE BOY'S EDUCATION, THE CURRICULUM INCLUDING THE FRENCH LANGUAGE AND AN INTENSE HATRED AND CONTEMPT FOR ALL THINGS ENGLISH, ESPECIALLY THE REIGNING HOUSE OF PLANTAGENET."
AND, AT LAST, WHEN YOU FINALLY STAND WITH THE HALTER ABOUT YOUR NECK...
A-HA! THEN WILL I SPEAK! THEN SHALL THEY KNOW! AT LAST, THAT *DOG* OF AN ENGLISH KING WILL KNOW!
"THE LAD DID NOT UNDERSTAND THE STRANGE NEW SENTIMENTS AND EMOTIONS HIS POOR MIND WAS INUNDATED WITH. HIS THOUGHTS WERE FULLY FIXATED UPON THE FACT THAT HE WOULD ONE DAY BE THE GREATEST SWORDSMAN IN THE WHOLE KINGDOM...AND THAT HE UTTERLY LOATHED ALL ENGLISHMEN. BUT WHY, HE DID NOT KNOW.

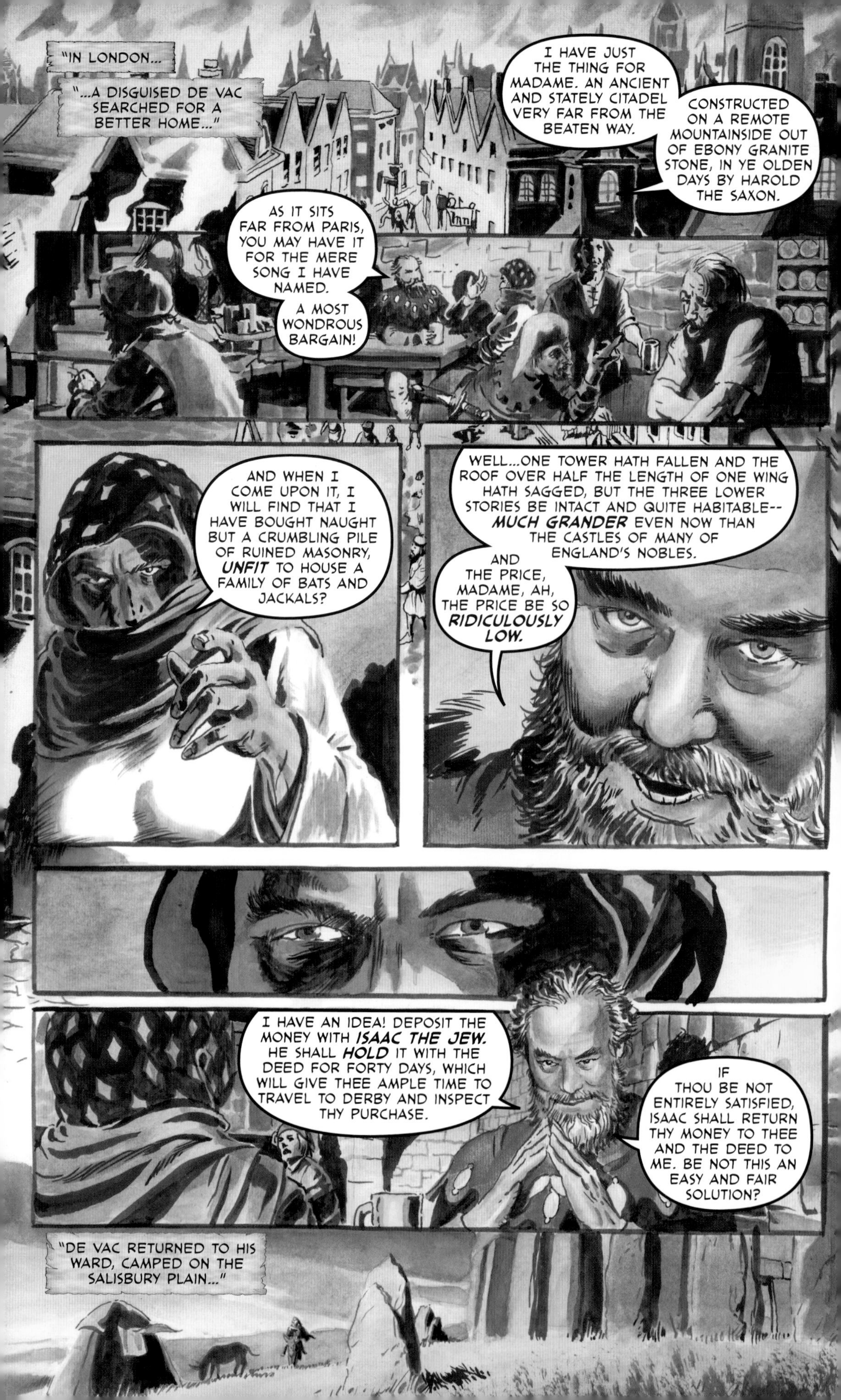
"IN LONDON...
"...A DISGUISED DE VAC SEARCHED FOR A BETTER HOME..."
I HAVE JUST THE THING FOR MADAME. AN ANCIENT AND STATELY CITADEL VERY FAR FROM THE BEATEN WAY.
CONSTRUCTED ON A REMOTE MOUNTAINSIDE OUT OF EBONY GRANITE STONE, IN YE OLDEN DAYS BY HAROLD THE SAXON.
AS IT SITS FAR FROM PARIS, YOU MAY HAVE IT FOR THE MERE SONG I HAVE NAMED.
A MOST WONDROUS BARGAIN!
AND WHEN I COME UPON IT, I WILL FIND THAT I HAVE BOUGHT NAUGHT BUT A CRUMBLING PILE OF RUINED MASONRY, UNFIT TO HOUSE A FAMILY OF BATS AND JACKALS?
WELL...ONE TOWER HATH FALLEN AND THE ROOF OVER HALF THE LENGTH OF ONE WING HATH SAGGED, BUT THE THREE LOWER STORIES BE INTACT AND QUITE HABITABLE-- MUCH GRANDER EVEN NOW THAN THE CASTLES OF MANY OF ENGLAND'S NOBLES.
AND THE PRICE, MADAME, AH, THE PRICE BE SO RIDICULOUSLY LOW.
I HAVE AN IDEA! DEPOSIT THE MONEY WITH ISAAC THE JEW. HE SHALL HOLD IT WITH THE DEED FOR FORTY DAYS, WHICH WILL GIVE THEE AMPLE TIME TO TRAVEL TO DERBY AND INSPECT THY PURCHASE.
IF THOU BE NOT ENTIRELY SATISFIED, ISAAC SHALL RETURN THY MONEY TO THEE AND THE DEED TO ME. BE NOT THIS AN EASY AND FAIR SOLUTION?
"DE VAC RETURNED TO HIS WARD, CAMPED ON THE SALISBURY PLAIN..."

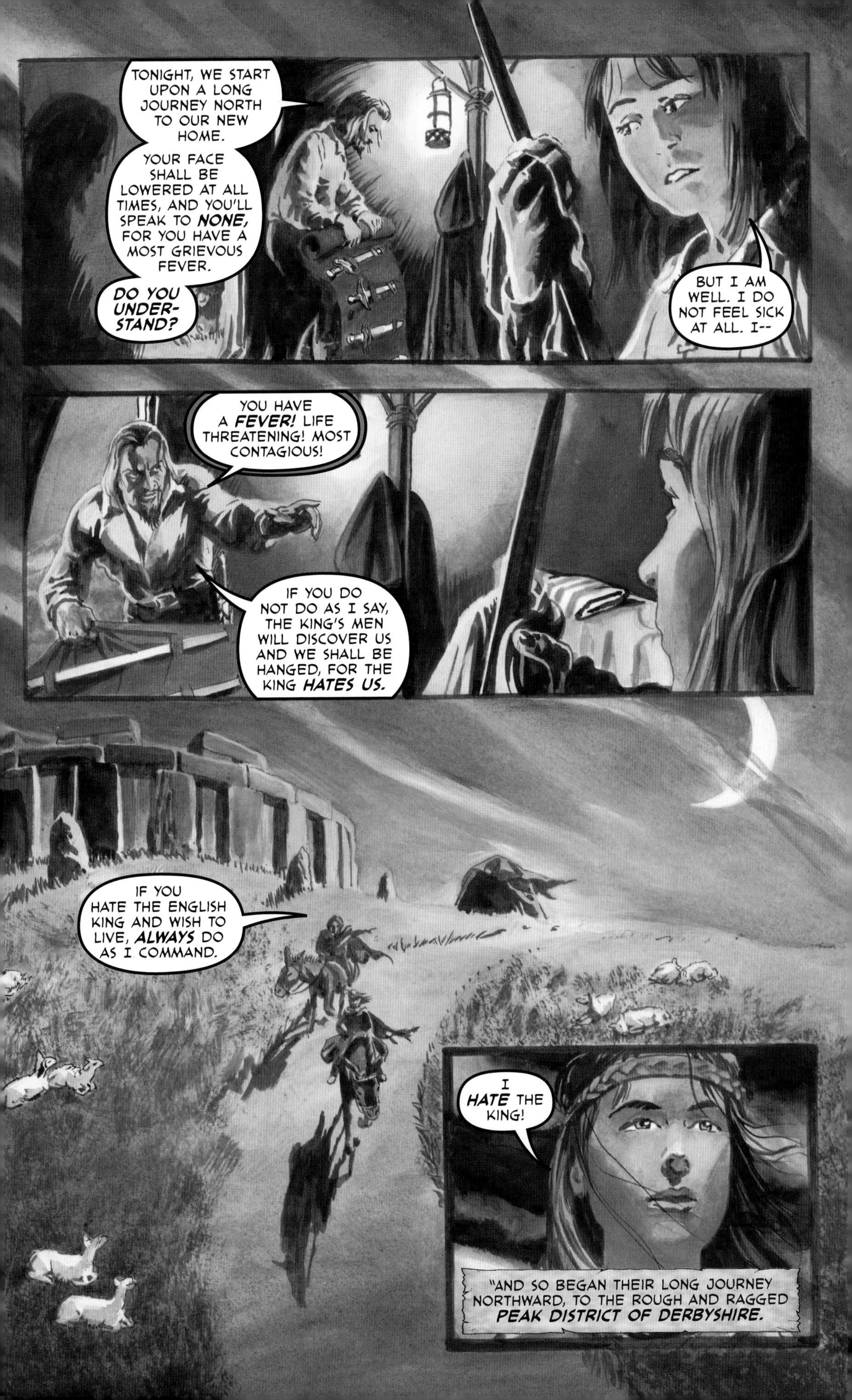
TONIGHT, WE START UPON A LONG JOURNEY NORTH TO OUR NEW HOME.
YOUR FACE SHALL BE LOWERED AT ALL TIMES, AND YOU'LL SPEAK TO NONE, FOR YOU HAVE A MOST GRIEVOUS FEVER.
DO YOU UNDER-STAND?
BUT I AM WELL. I DO NOT FEEL SICK AT ALL. I--
YOU HAVE A FEVER! LIFE THREATENING! MOST CONTAGIOUS!
IF YOU DO NOT DO AS I SAY, THE KING'S MEN WILL DISCOVER US AND WE SHALL BE HANGED, FOR THE KING HATES US.
IF YOU HATE THE ENGLISH KING AND WISH TO LIVE, ALWAYS DO AS I COMMAND.
I HATE THE KING!
"AND SO BEGAN THEIR LONG JOURNEY NORTHWARD, TO THE ROUGH AND RAGGED PEAK DISTRICT OF DERBYSHIRE.

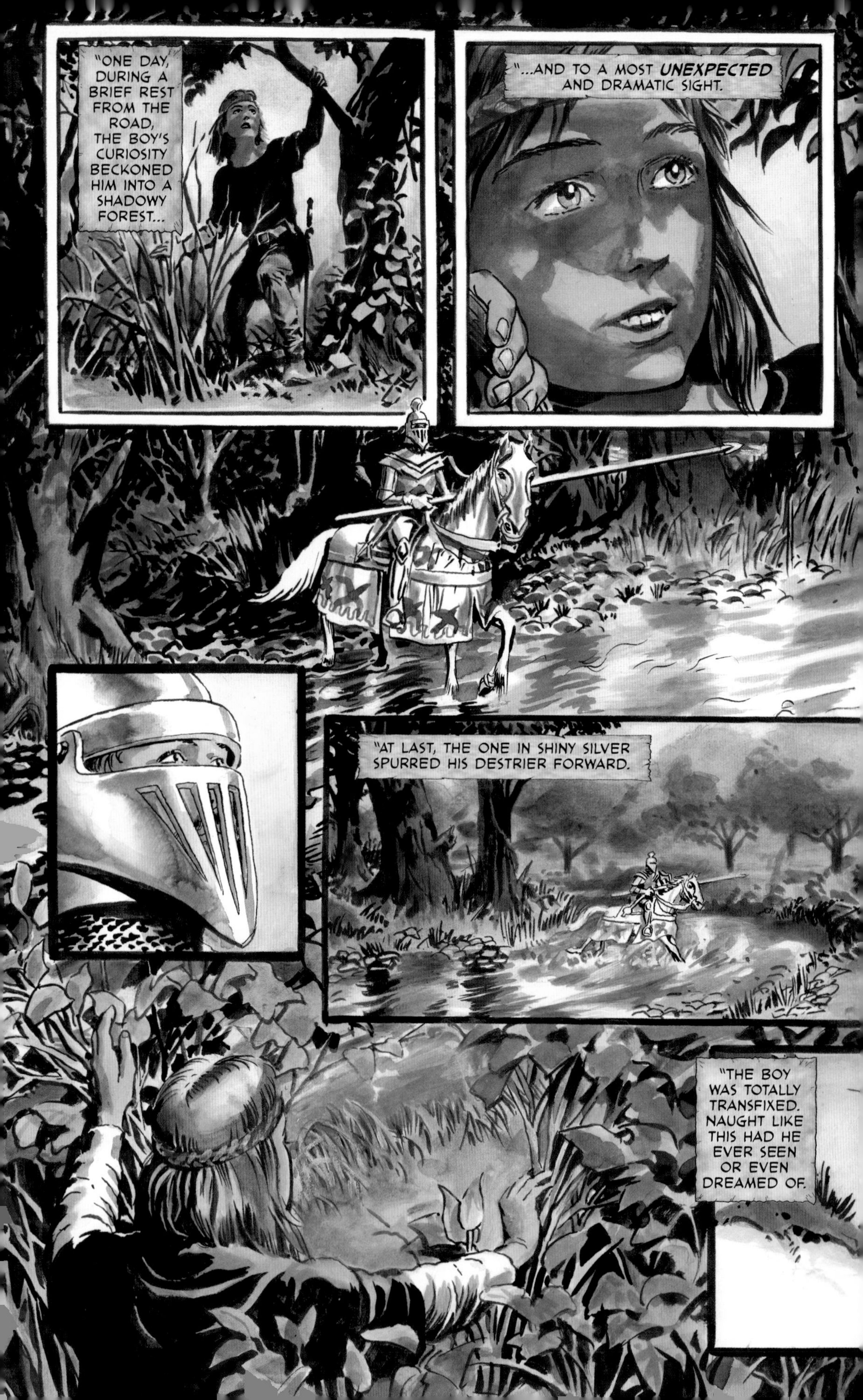
"ONE DAY, DURING A BRIEF REST FROM THE ROAD, THE BOY'S CURIOSITY BECKONED HIM INTO A SHADOWY FOREST...
"...AND TO A MOST UNEXPECTED AND DRAMATIC SIGHT.
"AT LAST, THE ONE IN SHINY SILVER SPURRED HIS DESTRIER FORWARD.
"THE BOY WAS TOTALLY TRANSFIXED. NAUGHT LIKE THIS HAD HE EVER SEEN OR EVEN DREAMED OF.

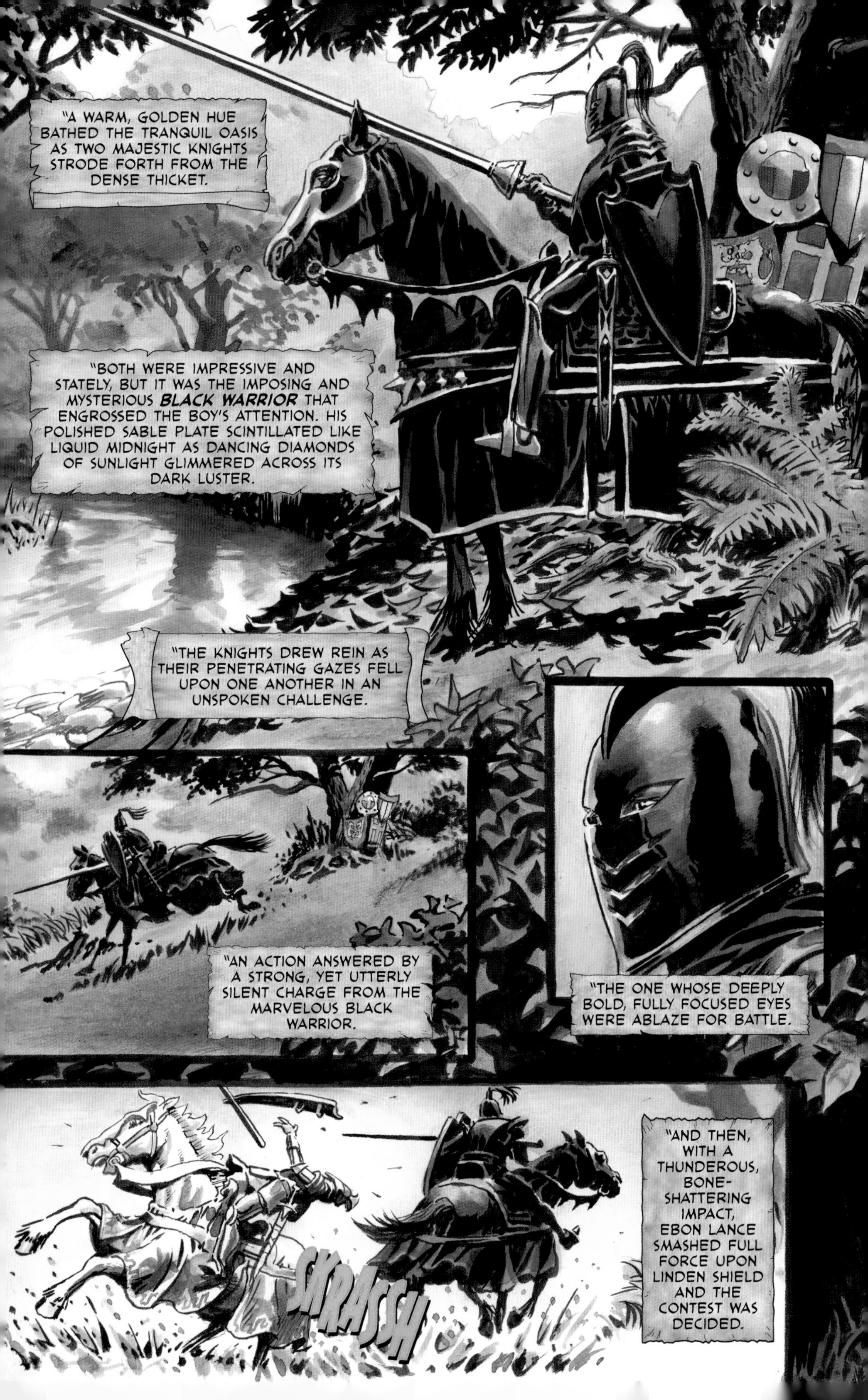
"A WARM, GOLDEN HUE BATHED THE TRANQUIL OASIS AS TWO MAJESTIC KNIGHTS STRODE FORTH FROM THE DENSE THICKET.
"BOTH WERE IMPRESSIVE AND STATELY, BUT IT WAS THE IMPOSING AND MYSTERIOUS BLACK WARRIOR THAT ENGROSSED THE BOY'S ATTENTION. HIS POLISHED SABLE PLATE SCINTILLATED LIKE LIQUID MIDNIGHT AS DANCING DIAMONDS OF SUNLIGHT GLIMMERED ACROSS ITS DARK LUSTER.
"THE KNIGHTS DREW REIN AS THEIR PENETRATING GAZES FELL UPON ONE ANOTHER IN AN UNSPOKEN CHALLENGE.
"AN ACTION ANSWERED BY A STRONG, YET UTTERLY SILENT CHARGE FROM THE MARVELOUS BLACK WARRIOR.
"THE ONE WHOSE DEEPLY BOLD, FULLY FOCUSED EYES WERE ABLAZE FOR BATTLE.
"AND THEN, WITH A THUNDEROUS, BONE-SHATTERING IMPACT, EBON LANCE SMASHED FULL FORCE UPON LINDEN SHIELD AND THE CONTEST WAS DECIDED.
SKRASSH

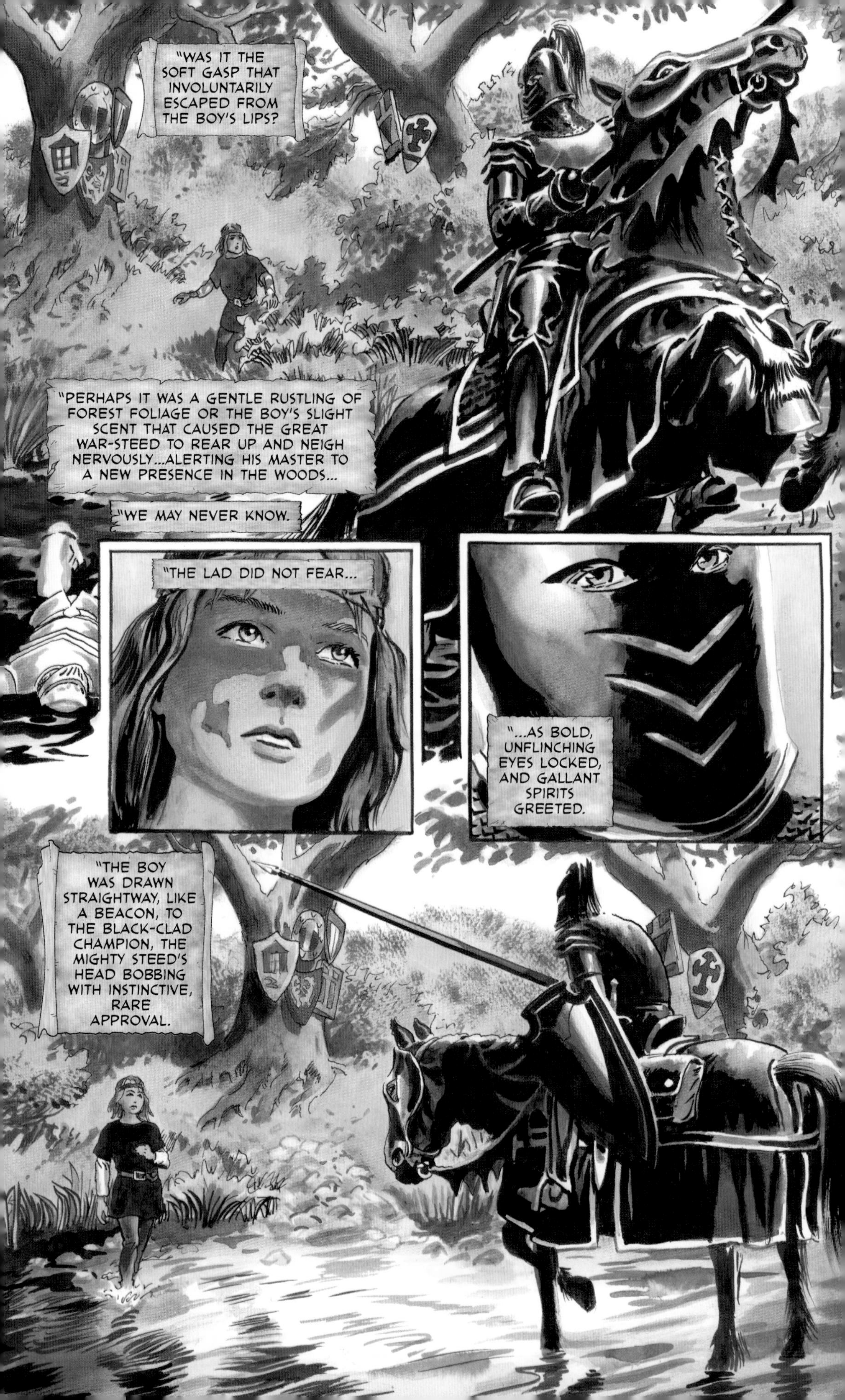
"WAS IT THE SOFT GASP THAT INVOLUNTARILY ESCAPED FROM THE BOY'S LIPS?
"PERHAPS IT WAS A GENTLE RUSTLING OF FOREST FOLIAGE OR THE BOY'S SLIGHT SCENT THAT CAUSED THE GREAT WAR-STEED TO REAR UP AND NEIGH NERVOUSLY...ALERTING HIS MASTER TO A NEW PRESENCE IN THE WOODS...
"WE MAY NEVER KNOW.
"THE LAD DID NOT FEAR...
"...AS BOLD, UNFLINCHING EYES LOCKED, AND GALLANT SPIRITS GREETED.
"THE BOY WAS DRAWN STRAIGHTWAY, LIKE A BEACON, TO THE BLACK-CLAD CHAMPION, THE MIGHTY STEED'S HEAD BOBBING WITH INSTINCTIVE, RARE APPROVAL.

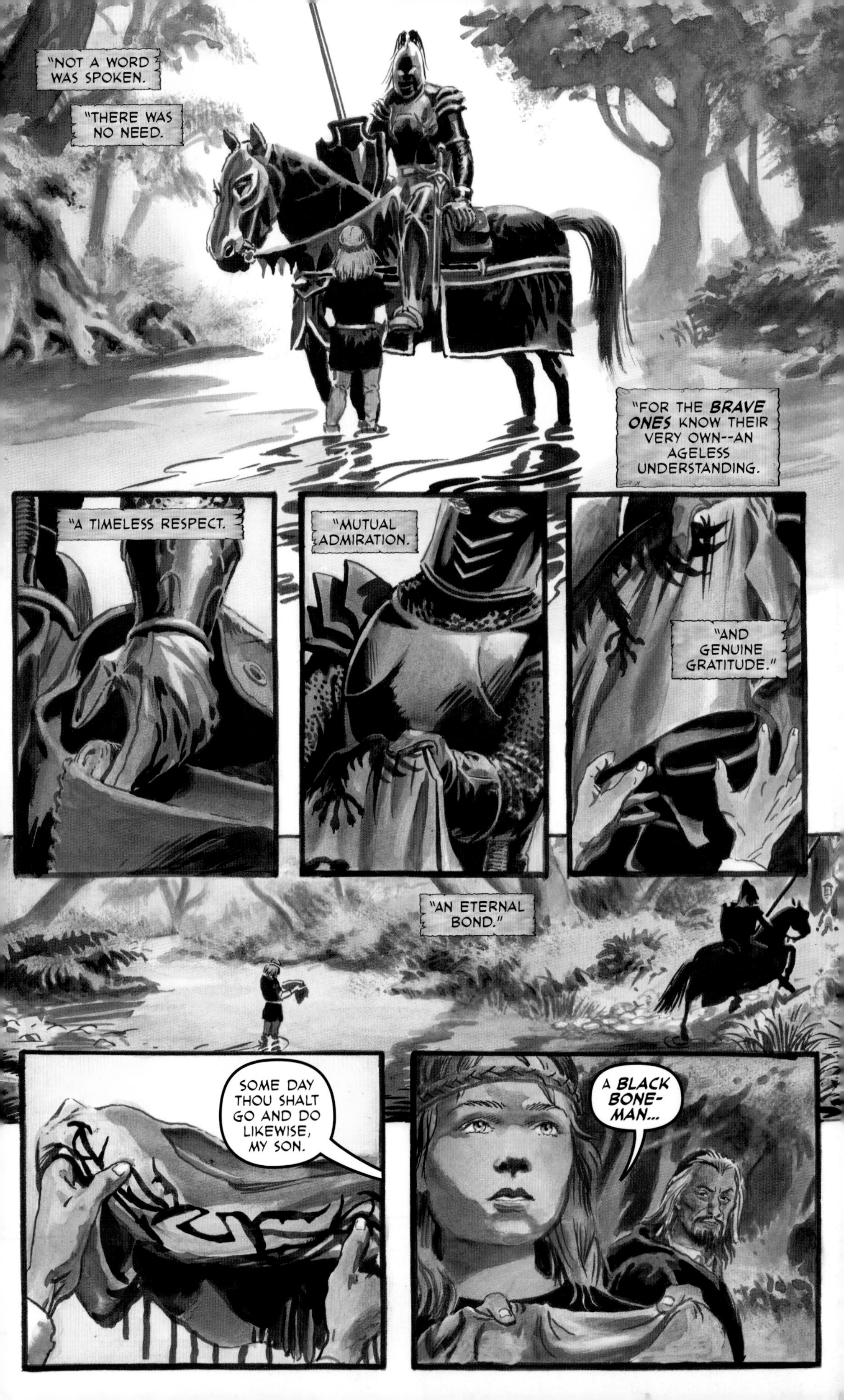
"NOT A WORD WAS SPOKEN.
"THERE WAS NO NEED.
"FOR THE BRAVE ONES KNOW THEIR VERY OWN--AN AGELESS UNDERSTANDING.
"A TIMELESS RESPECT.
"MUTUAL ADMIRATION.
"AND GENUINE GRATITUDE."
"AN ETERNAL BOND."
SOME DAY THOU SHALT GO AND DO LIKEWISE, MY SON.
A BLACK BONE-MAN...

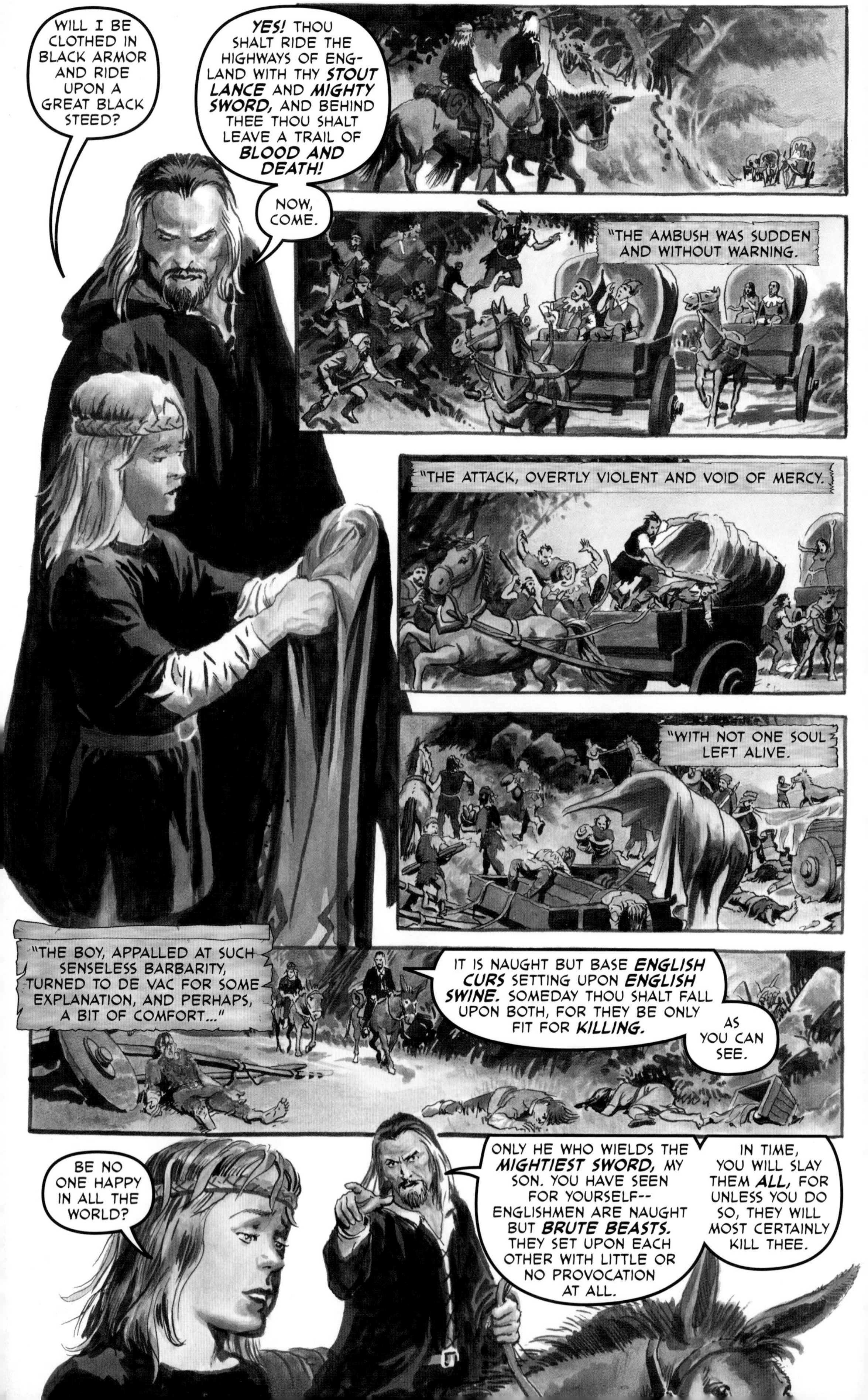
WILL I BE CLOTHED IN BLACK ARMOR AND RIDE UPON A GREAT BLACK STEED?
YES! THOU SHALT RIDE THE HIGHWAYS OF ENG-LAND WITH THY STOUT LANCE AND MIGHTY SWORD, AND BEHIND THEE THOU SHALT LEAVE A TRAIL OF BLOOD AND DEATH!
NOW, COME.
"THE AMBUSH WAS SUDDEN AND WITHOUT WARNING.
"THE ATTACK, OVERTLY VIOLENT AND VOID OF MERCY.
"WITH NOT ONE SOUL LEFT ALIVE.
"THE BOY, APPALLED AT SUCH SENSELESS BARBARITY, TURNED TO DE VAC FOR SOME EXPLANATION, AND PERHAPS, A BIT OF COMFORT..."
IT IS NAUGHT BUT BASE ENGLISH CURS SETTING UPON ENGLISH SWINE. SOMEDAY THOU SHALT FALL UPON BOTH, FOR THEY BE ONLY FIT FOR KILLING.
AS YOU CAN SEE.
BE NO ONE HAPPY IN ALL THE WORLD?
ONLY HE WHO WIELDS THE MIGHTIEST SWORD, MY SON. YOU HAVE SEEN FOR YOURSELF-- ENGLISHMEN ARE NAUGHT BUT BRUTE BEASTS. THEY SET UPON EACH OTHER WITH LITTLE OR NO PROVOCATION AT ALL.
IN TIME, YOU WILL SLAY THEM ALL, FOR UNLESS YOU DO SO, THEY WILL MOST CERTAINLY KILL THEE.

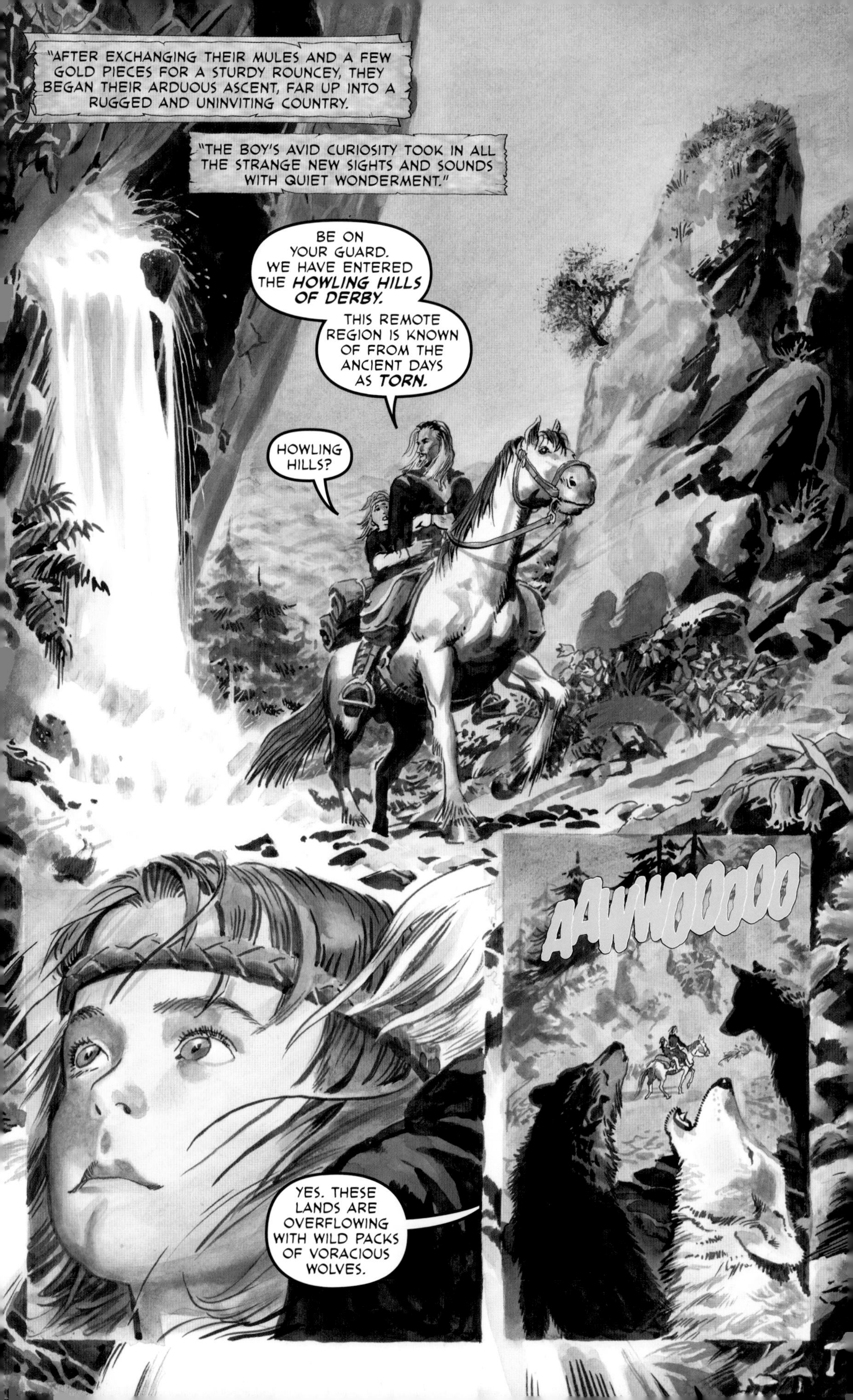
"AFTER EXCHANGING THEIR MULES AND A FEW GOLD PIECES FOR A STURDY ROUNCEY, THEY BEGAN THEIR ARDUOUS ASCENT, FAR UP INTO A RUGGED AND UNINVITING COUNTRY.
"THE BOY'S AVID CURIOSITY TOOK IN ALL THE STRANGE NEW SIGHTS AND SOUNDS WITH QUIET WONDERMENT."
BE ON YOUR GUARD. WE HAVE ENTERED THE *HOWLING HILLS OF DERBY.*
THIS REMOTE REGION IS KNOWN OF FROM THE ANCIENT DAYS AS *TORN.*
HOWLING HILLS?
YES. THESE LANDS ARE OVERFLOWING WITH WILD PACKS OF VORACIOUS WOLVES.
AAWHOOOOO

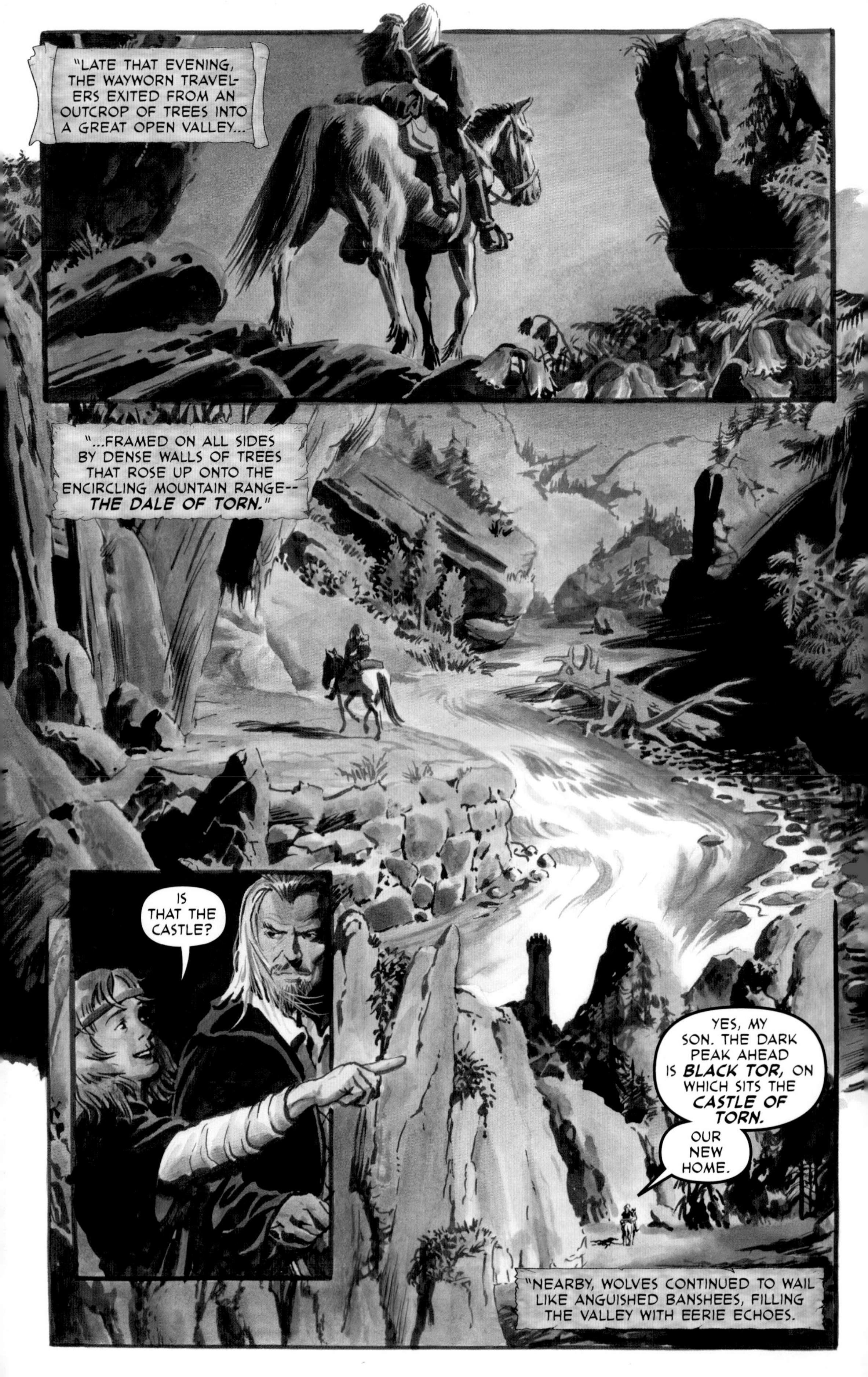
"LATE THAT EVENING, THE WAYWORN TRAVELERS EXITED FROM AN OUTCROP OF TREES INTO A GREAT OPEN VALLEY...
"...FRAMED ON ALL SIDES BY DENSE WALLS OF TREES THAT ROSE UP ONTO THE ENCIRCLING MOUNTAIN RANGE-- THE DALE OF TORN."
IS THAT THE CASTLE?
YES, MY SON. THE DARK PEAK AHEAD IS BLACK TOR, ON WHICH SITS THE CASTLE OF TORN.
OUR NEW HOME.
"NEARBY, WOLVES CONTINUED TO WAIL LIKE ANGUISHED BANSHEES, FILLING THE VALLEY WITH EERIE ECHOES.

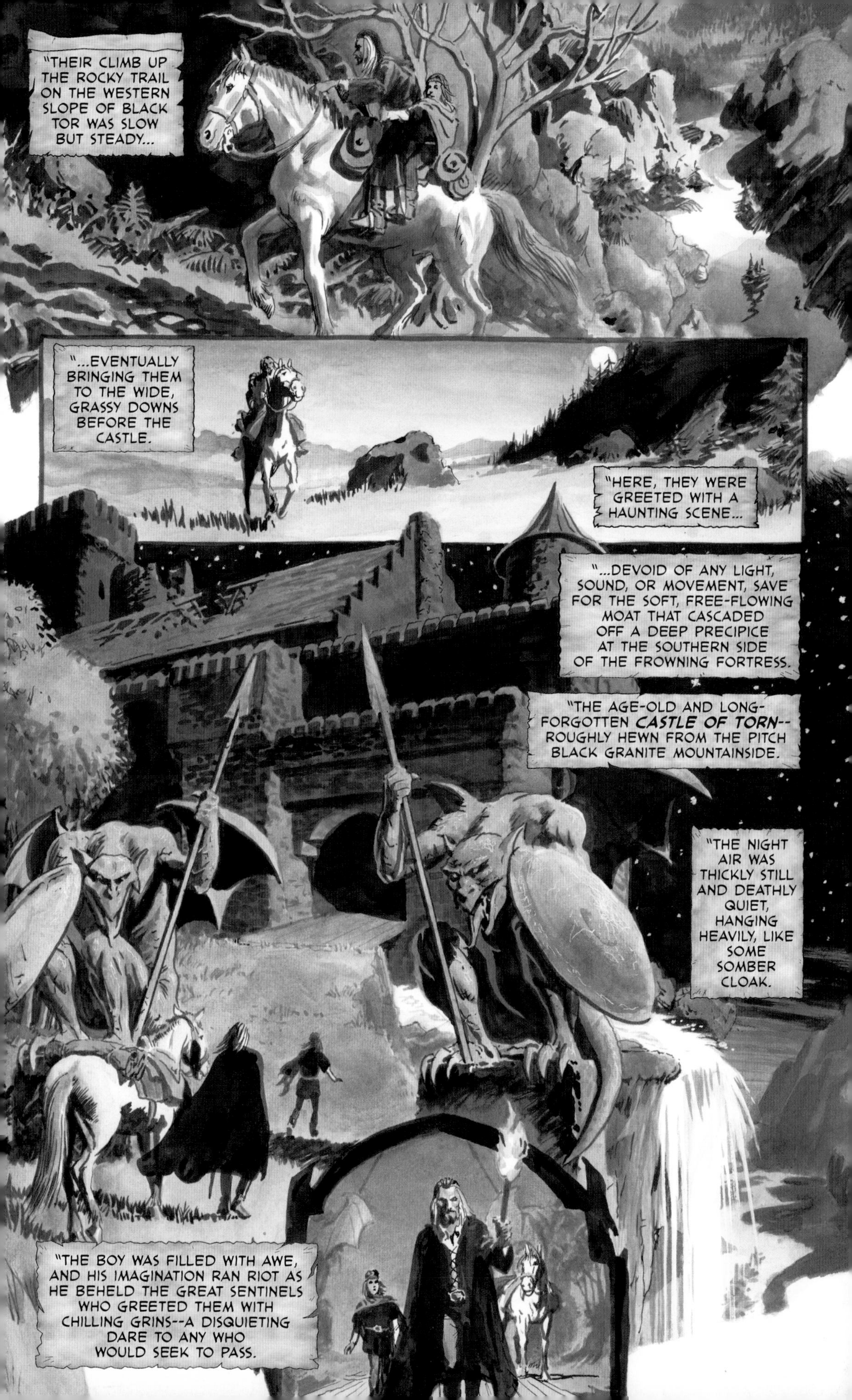
"THEIR CLIMB UP THE ROCKY TRAIL ON THE WESTERN SLOPE OF BLACK TOR WAS SLOW BUT STEADY...
"...EVENTUALLY BRINGING THEM TO THE WIDE, GRASSY DOWNS BEFORE THE CASTLE.
"HERE, THEY WERE GREETED WITH A HAUNTING SCENE...
"...DEVOID OF ANY LIGHT, SOUND, OR MOVEMENT, SAVE FOR THE SOFT, FREE-FLOWING MOAT THAT CASCADED OFF A DEEP PRECIPICE AT THE SOUTHERN SIDE OF THE FROWNING FORTRESS.
"THE AGE-OLD AND LONG-FORGOTTEN *CASTLE OF TORN*--ROUGHLY HEWN FROM THE PITCH BLACK GRANITE MOUNTAINSIDE.
"THE NIGHT AIR WAS THICKLY STILL AND DEATHLY QUIET, HANGING HEAVILY, LIKE SOME SOMBER CLOAK.
"THE BOY WAS FILLED WITH AWE, AND HIS IMAGINATION RAN RIOT AS HE BEHELD THE GREAT SENTINELS WHO GREETED THEM WITH CHILLING GRINS--A DISQUIETING DARE TO ANY WHO WOULD SEEK TO PASS.

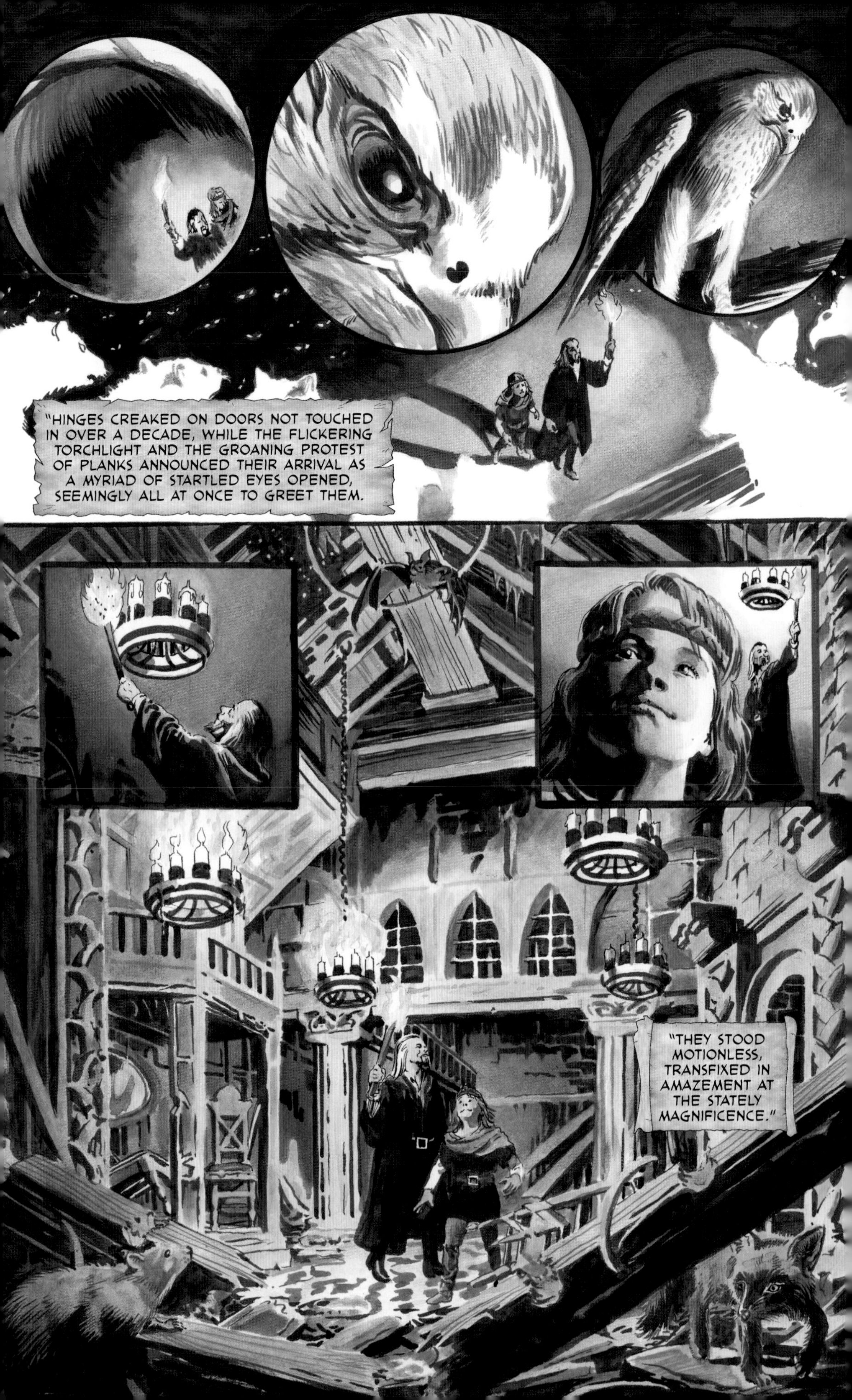
"HINGES CREAKED ON DOORS NOT TOUCHED IN OVER A DECADE, WHILE THE FLICKERING TORCHLIGHT AND THE GROANING PROTEST OF PLANKS ANNOUNCED THEIR ARRIVAL AS A MYRIAD OF STARTLED EYES OPENED, SEEMINGLY ALL AT ONCE TO GREET THEM.
"THEY STOOD MOTIONLESS, TRANSFIXED IN AMAZEMENT AT THE STATELY MAGNIFICENCE."

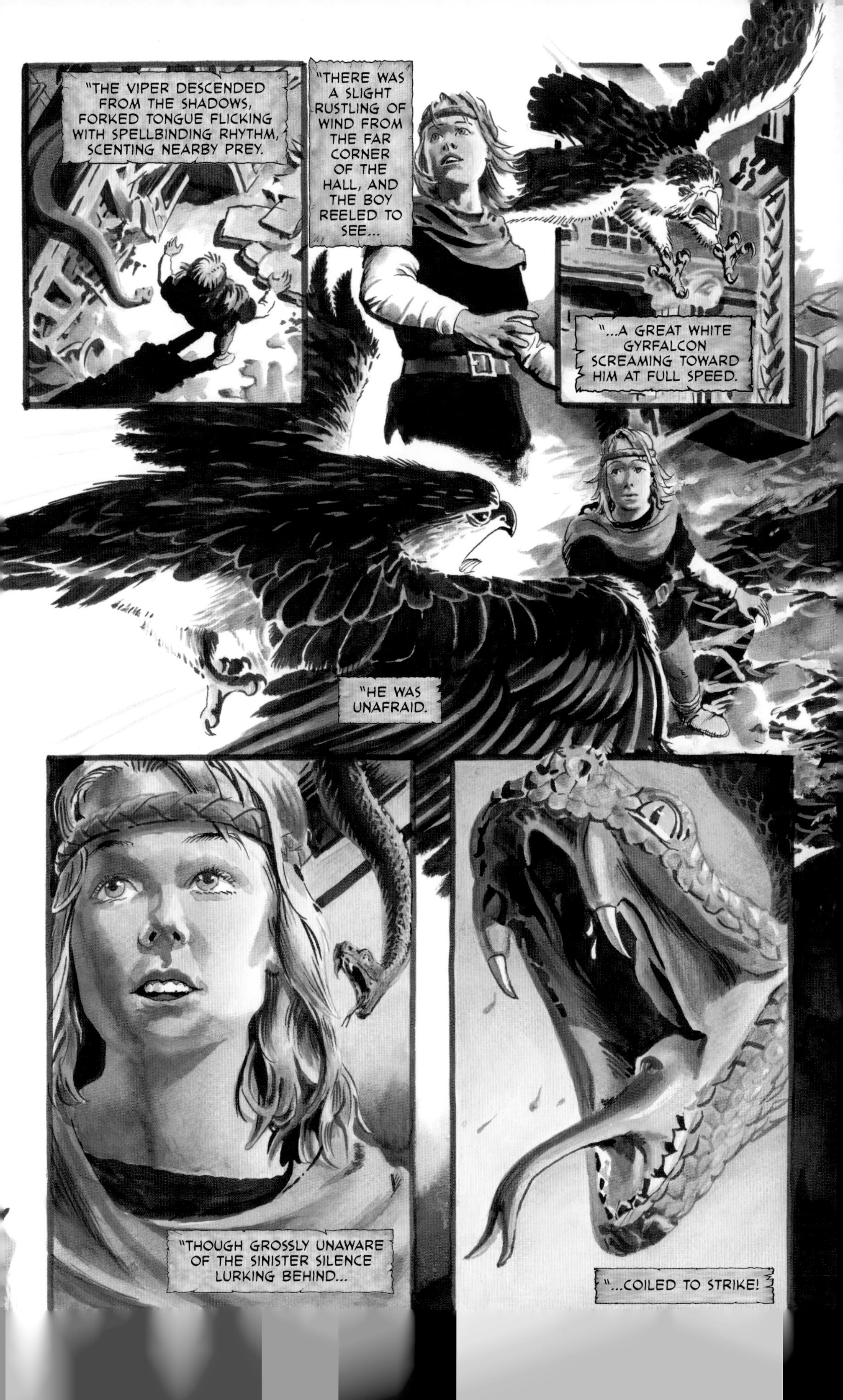
"THE VIPER DESCENDED FROM THE SHADOWS, FORKED TONGUE FLICKING WITH SPELLBINDING RHYTHM, SCENTING NEARBY PREY.
"THERE WAS A SLIGHT RUSTLING OF WIND FROM THE FAR CORNER OF THE HALL, AND THE BOY REELED TO SEE...
"...A GREAT WHITE GYRFALCON SCREAMING TOWARD HIM AT FULL SPEED.
"HE WAS UNAFRAID.
"THOUGH GROSSLY UNAWARE OF THE SINISTER SILENCE LURKING BEHIND...
"...COILED TO STRIKE!

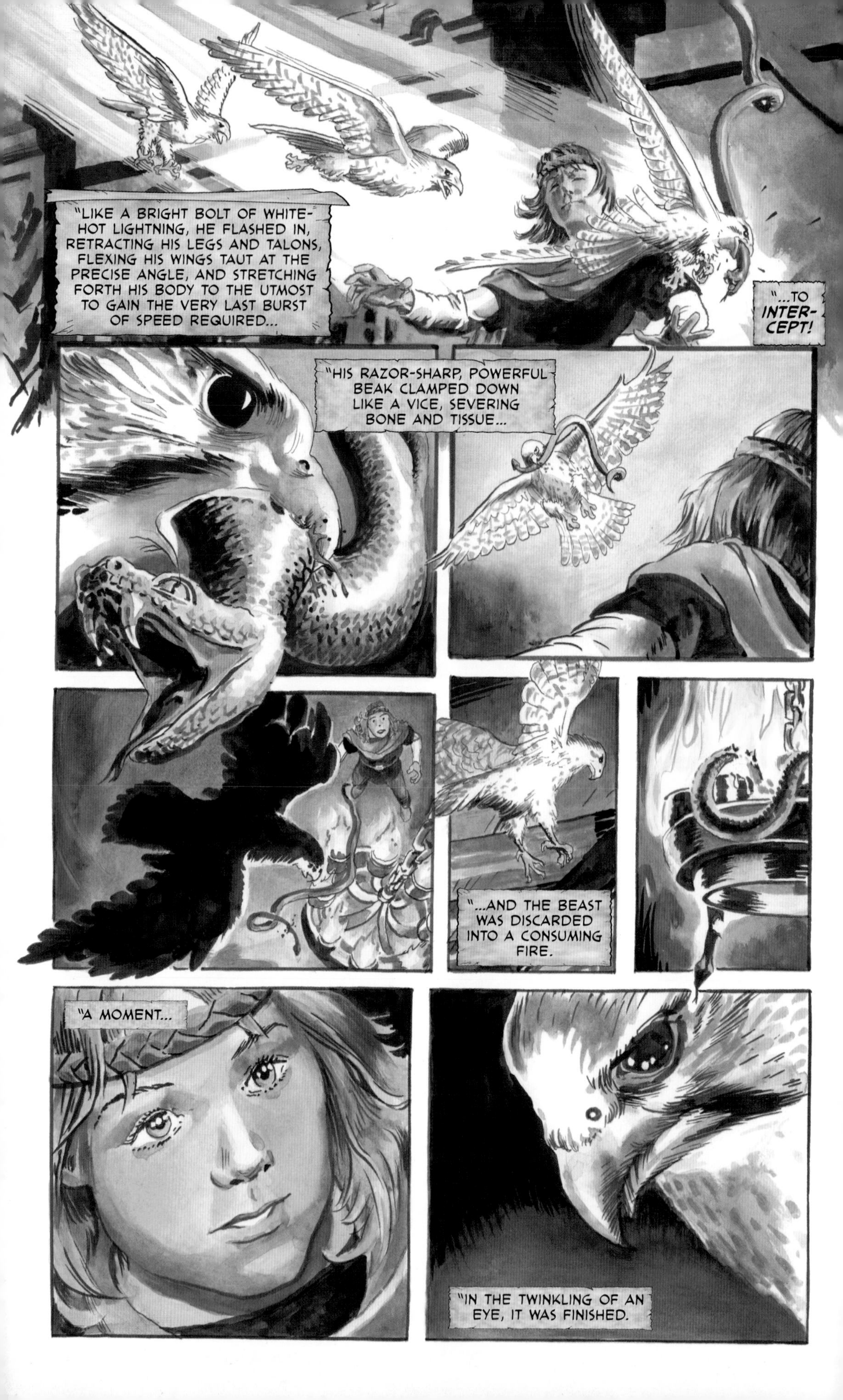
"LIKE A BRIGHT BOLT OF WHITE-HOT LIGHTNING, HE FLASHED IN, RETRACTING HIS LEGS AND TALONS, FLEXING HIS WINGS TAUT AT THE PRECISE ANGLE, AND STRETCHING FORTH HIS BODY TO THE UTMOST TO GAIN THE VERY LAST BURST OF SPEED REQUIRED...
"...TO INTERCEPT!
"HIS RAZOR-SHARP, POWERFUL BEAK CLAMPED DOWN LIKE A VICE, SEVERING BONE AND TISSUE...
"...AND THE BEAST WAS DISCARDED INTO A CONSUMING FIRE.
"A MOMENT...
"IN THE TWINKLING OF AN EYE, IT WAS FINISHED.

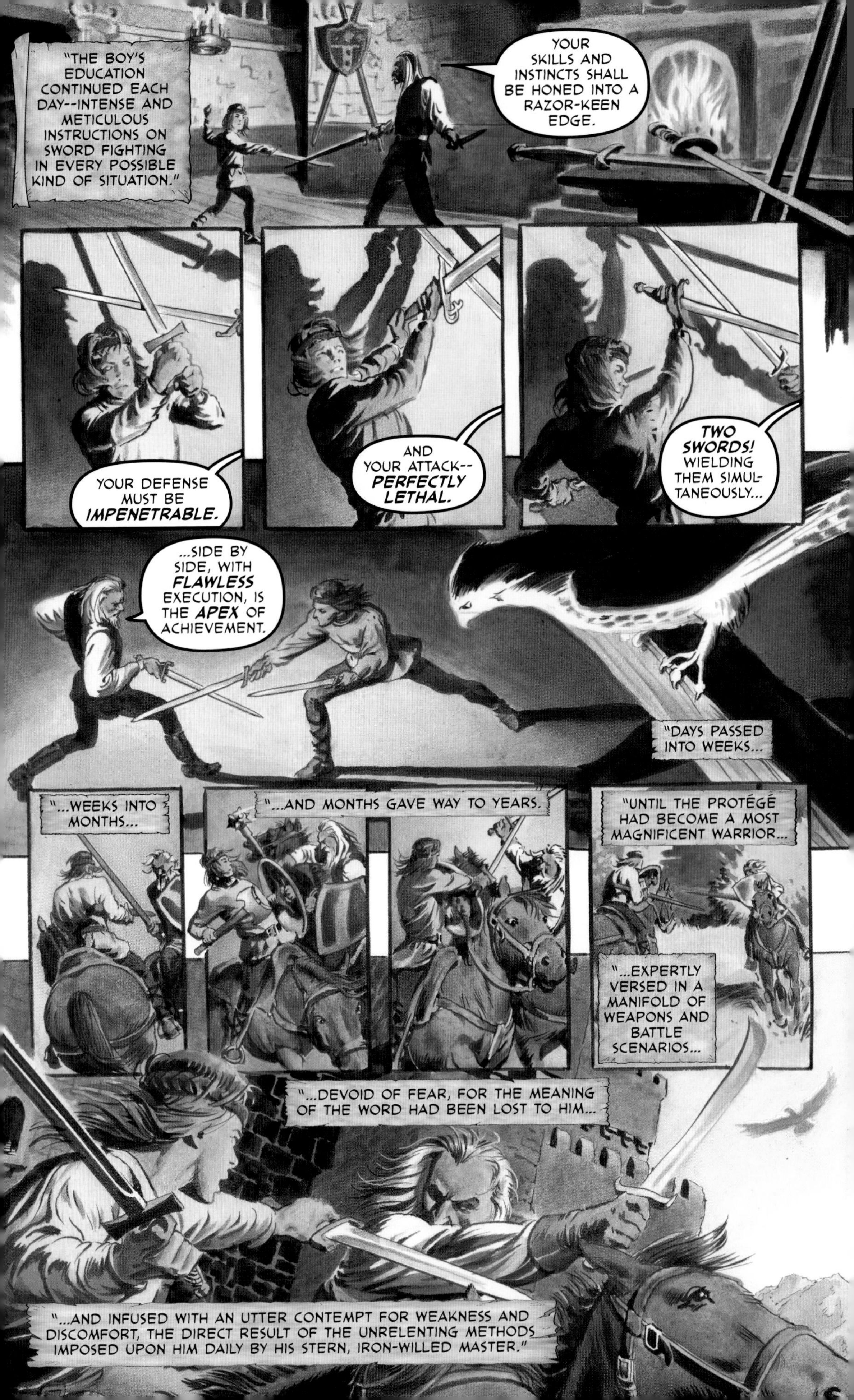
"THE BOY'S EDUCATION CONTINUED EACH DAY--INTENSE AND METICULOUS INSTRUCTIONS ON SWORD FIGHTING IN EVERY POSSIBLE KIND OF SITUATION."
YOUR SKILLS AND INSTINCTS SHALL BE HONED INTO A RAZOR-KEEN EDGE.
YOUR DEFENSE MUST BE IMPENETRABLE.
AND YOUR ATTACK-- PERFECTLY LETHAL.
TWO SWORDS! WIELDING THEM SIMUL-TANEOUSLY...
...SIDE BY SIDE, WITH FLAWLESS EXECUTION, IS THE APEX OF ACHIEVEMENT.
"DAYS PASSED INTO WEEKS...
"...WEEKS INTO MONTHS...
"...AND MONTHS GAVE WAY TO YEARS.
"UNTIL THE PROTÉGÉ HAD BECOME A MOST MAGNIFICENT WARRIOR...
"...EXPERTLY VERSED IN A MANIFOLD OF WEAPONS AND BATTLE SCENARIOS...
"...DEVOID OF FEAR, FOR THE MEANING OF THE WORD HAD BEEN LOST TO HIM...
"...AND INFUSED WITH AN UTTER CONTEMPT FOR WEAKNESS AND DISCOMFORT, THE DIRECT RESULT OF THE UNRELENTING METHODS IMPOSED UPON HIM DAILY BY HIS STERN, IRON-WILLED MASTER."

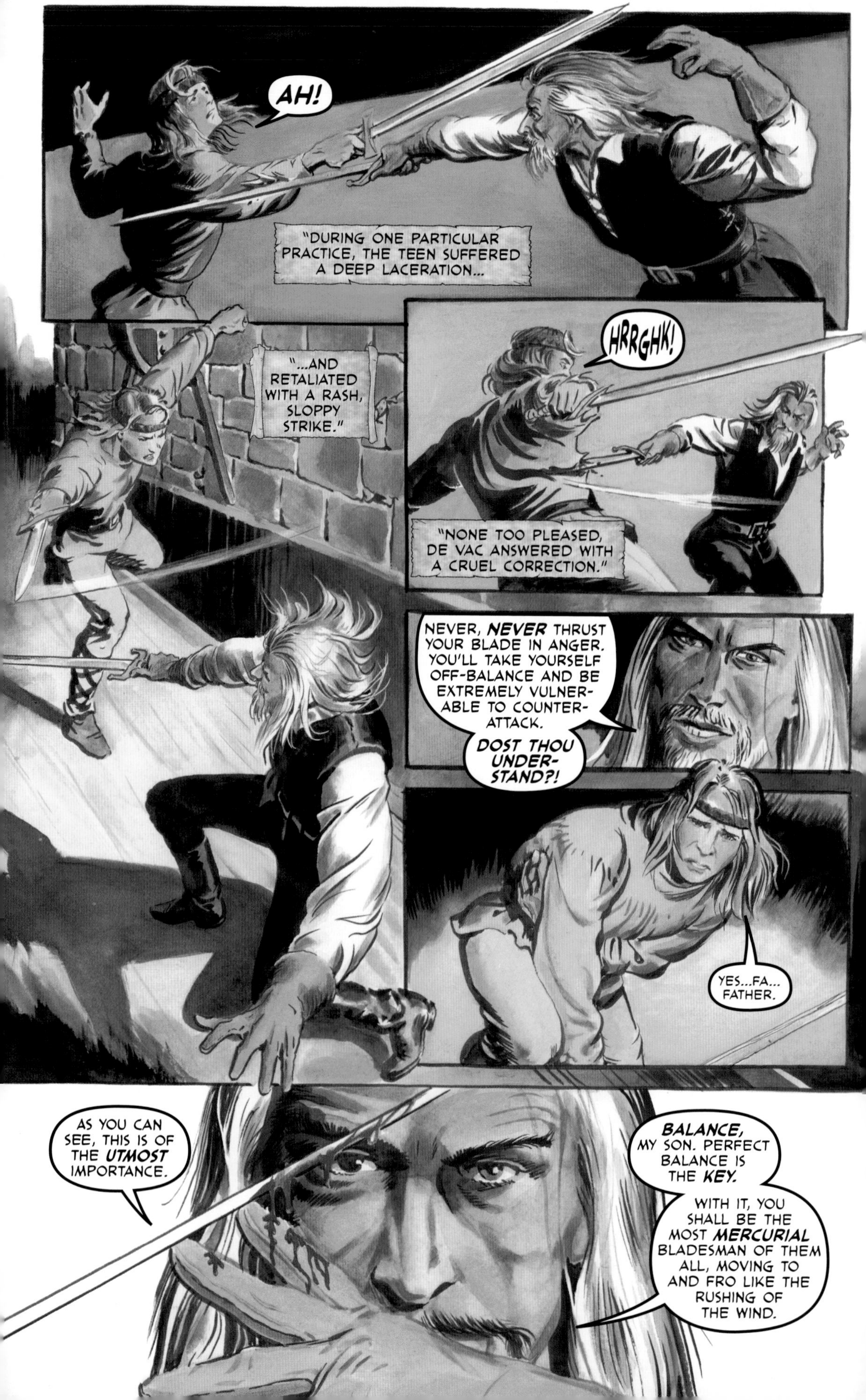

AH!
"DURING ONE PARTICULAR PRACTICE, THE TEEN SUFFERED A DEEP LACERATION...
"...AND RETALIATED WITH A RASH, SLOPPY STRIKE."
HRRGHK!
"NONE TOO PLEASED, DE VAC ANSWERED WITH A CRUEL CORRECTION."
NEVER, NEVER THRUST YOUR BLADE IN ANGER. YOU'LL TAKE YOURSELF OFF-BALANCE AND BE EXTREMELY VULNERABLE TO COUNTERATTACK.
DOST THOU UNDERSTAND?!
YES...FA... FATHER.
AS YOU CAN SEE, THIS IS OF THE UTMOST IMPORTANCE.
BALANCE, MY SON. PERFECT BALANCE IS THE KEY.
WITH IT, YOU SHALL BE THE MOST MERCURIAL BLADESMAN OF THEM ALL, MOVING TO AND FRO LIKE THE RUSHING OF THE WIND.

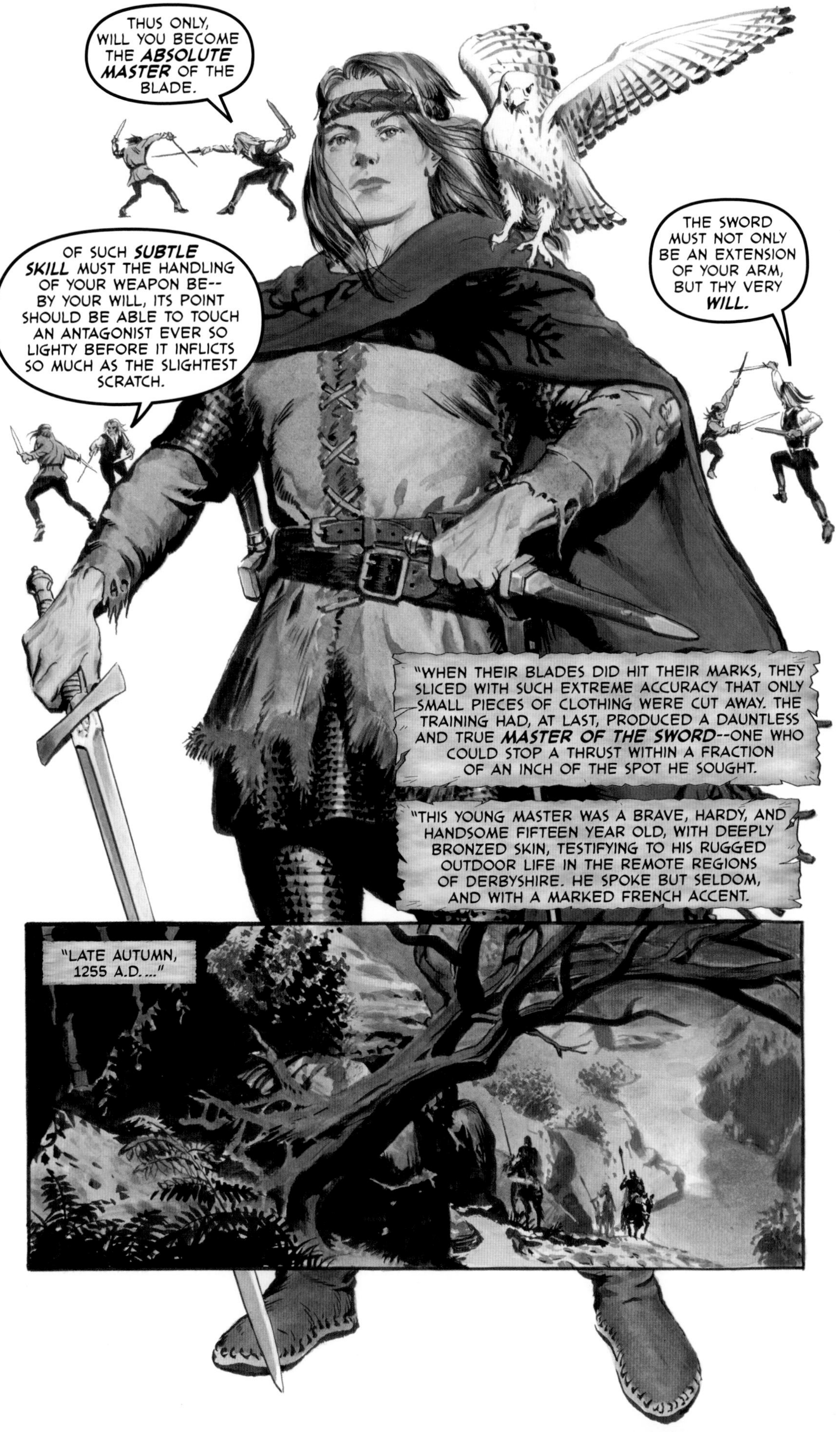
THUS ONLY, WILL YOU BECOME THE ABSOLUTE MASTER OF THE BLADE.
OF SUCH SUBTLE SKILL MUST THE HANDLING OF YOUR WEAPON BE-- BY YOUR WILL, ITS POINT SHOULD BE ABLE TO TOUCH AN ANTAGONIST EVER SO LIGHTY BEFORE IT INFLICTS SO MUCH AS THE SLIGHTEST SCRATCH.
THE SWORD MUST NOT ONLY BE AN EXTENSION OF YOUR ARM, BUT THY VERY WILL.
"WHEN THEIR BLADES DID HIT THEIR MARKS, THEY SLICED WITH SUCH EXTREME ACCURACY THAT ONLY SMALL PIECES OF CLOTHING WERE CUT AWAY. THE TRAINING HAD, AT LAST, PRODUCED A DAUNTLESS AND TRUE MASTER OF THE SWORD--ONE WHO COULD STOP A THRUST WITHIN A FRACTION OF AN INCH OF THE SPOT HE SOUGHT.
"THIS YOUNG MASTER WAS A BRAVE, HARDY, AND HANDSOME FIFTEEN YEAR OLD, WITH DEEPLY BRONZED SKIN, TESTIFYING TO HIS RUGGED OUTDOOR LIFE IN THE REMOTE REGIONS OF DERBYSHIRE. HE SPOKE BUT SELDOM, AND WITH A MARKED FRENCH ACCENT.
"LATE AUTUMN, 1255 A.D...."

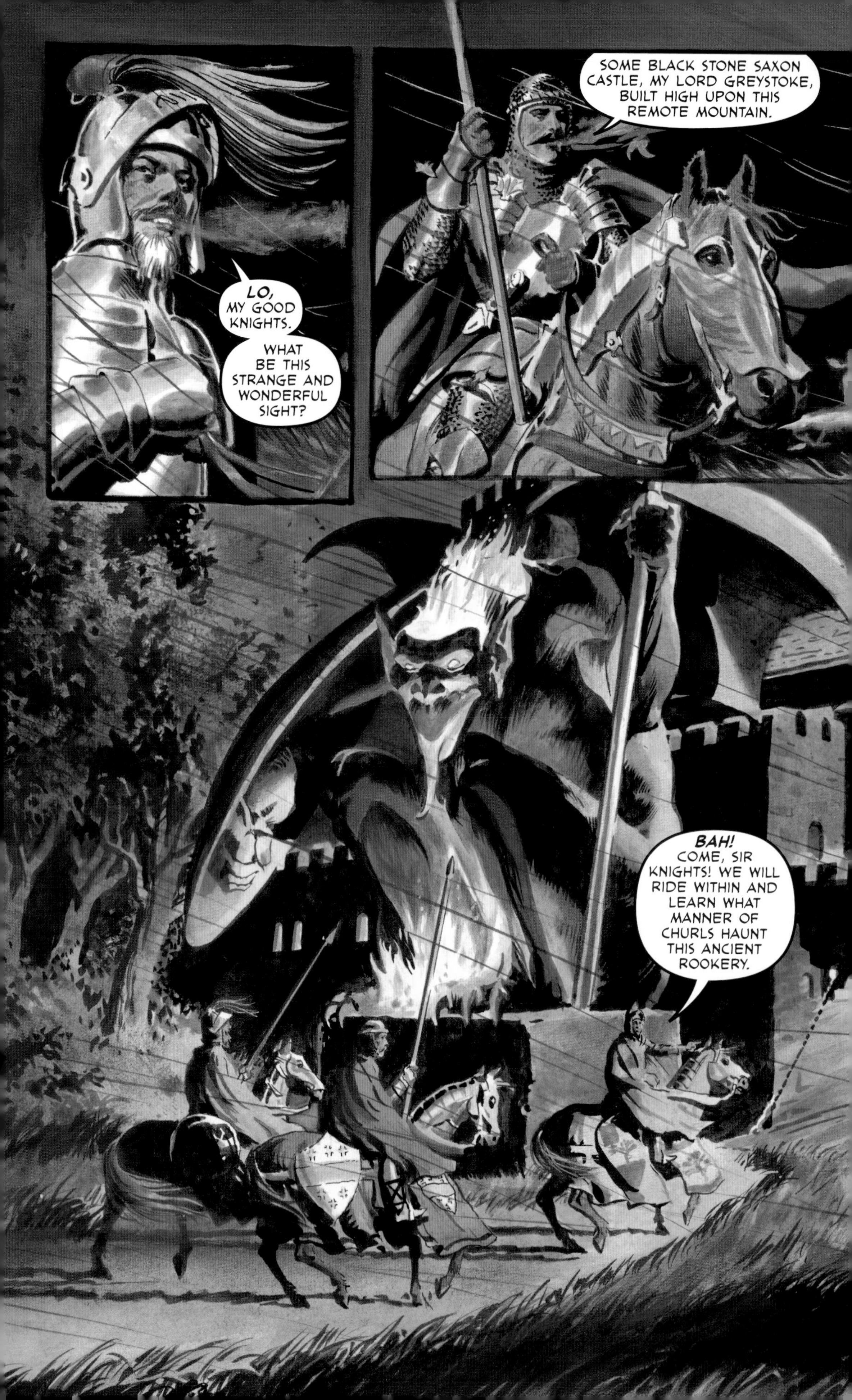
LO, MY GOOD KNIGHTS.
WHAT BE THIS STRANGE AND WONDERFUL SIGHT?
SOME BLACK STONE SAXON CASTLE, MY LORD GREYSTOKE, BUILT HIGH UPON THIS REMOTE MOUNTAIN.
BAH! COME, SIR KNIGHTS! WE WILL RIDE WITHIN AND LEARN WHAT MANNER OF CHURLS HAUNT THIS ANCIENT ROOKERY.

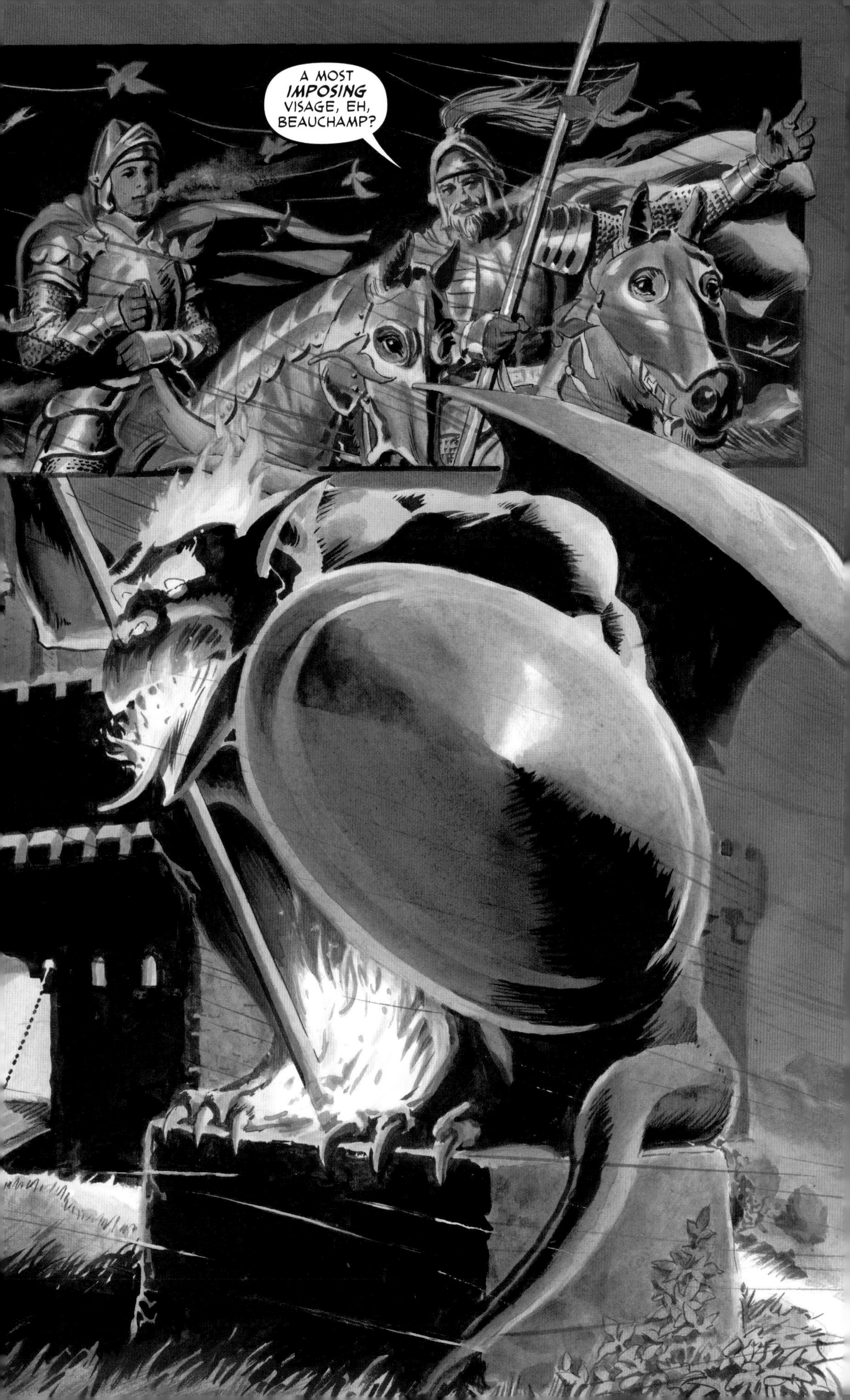
A MOST *IMPOSING* VISAGE, EH, BEAUCHAMP?

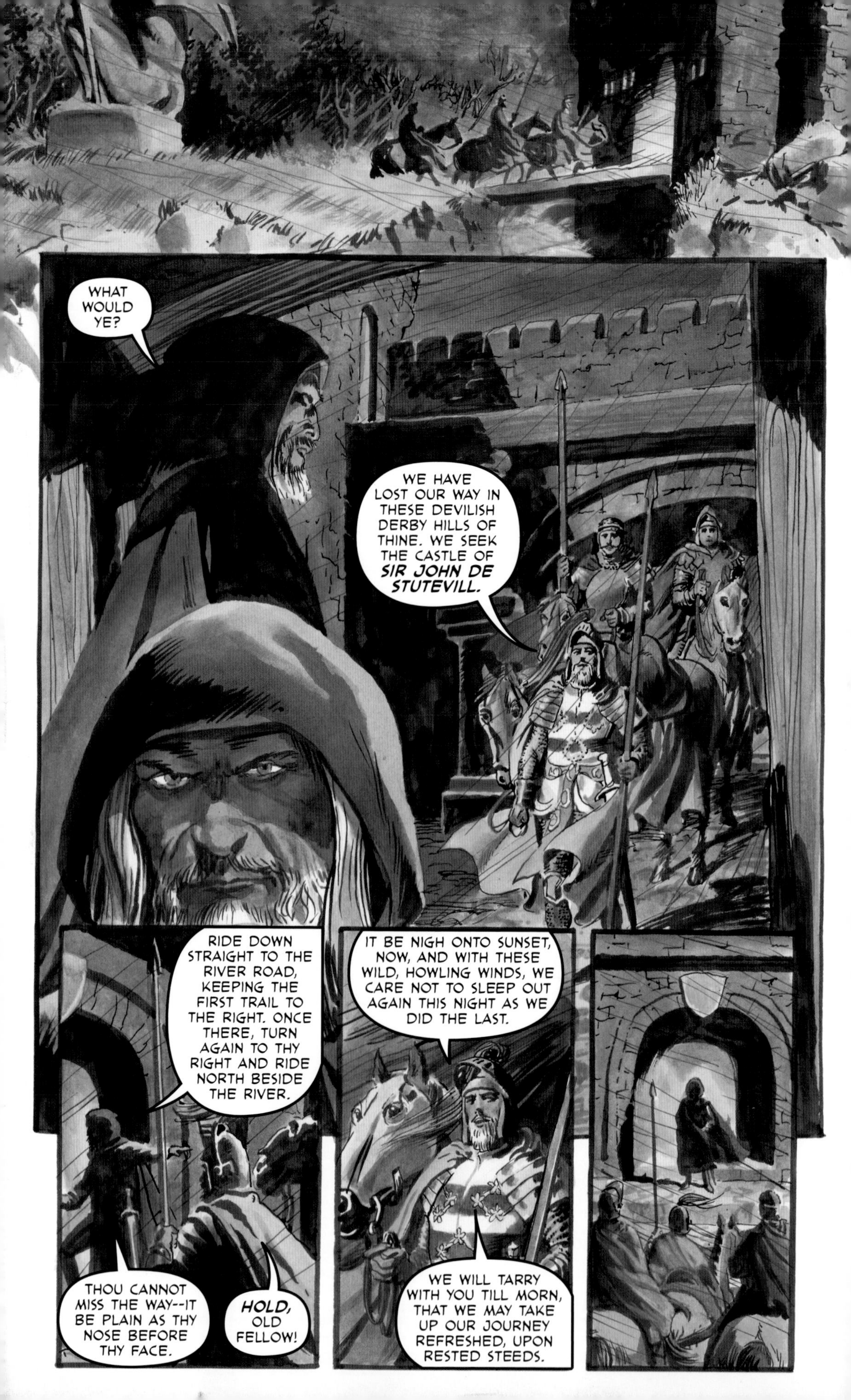
WHAT WOULD YE?
WE HAVE LOST OUR WAY IN THESE DEVILISH DERBY HILLS OF THINE. WE SEEK THE CASTLE OF ***SIR JOHN DE STUTEVILL.***
RIDE DOWN STRAIGHT TO THE RIVER ROAD, KEEPING THE FIRST TRAIL TO THE RIGHT. ONCE THERE, TURN AGAIN TO THY RIGHT AND RIDE NORTH BESIDE THE RIVER.
THOU CANNOT MISS THE WAY--IT BE PLAIN AS THY NOSE BEFORE THY FACE.
HOLD, OLD FELLOW!
IT BE NIGH ONTO SUNSET, NOW, AND WITH THESE WILD, HOWLING WINDS, WE CARE NOT TO SLEEP OUT AGAIN THIS NIGHT AS WE DID THE LAST.
WE WILL TARRY WITH YOU TILL MORN, THAT WE MAY TAKE UP OUR JOURNEY REFRESHED, UPON RESTED STEEDS.

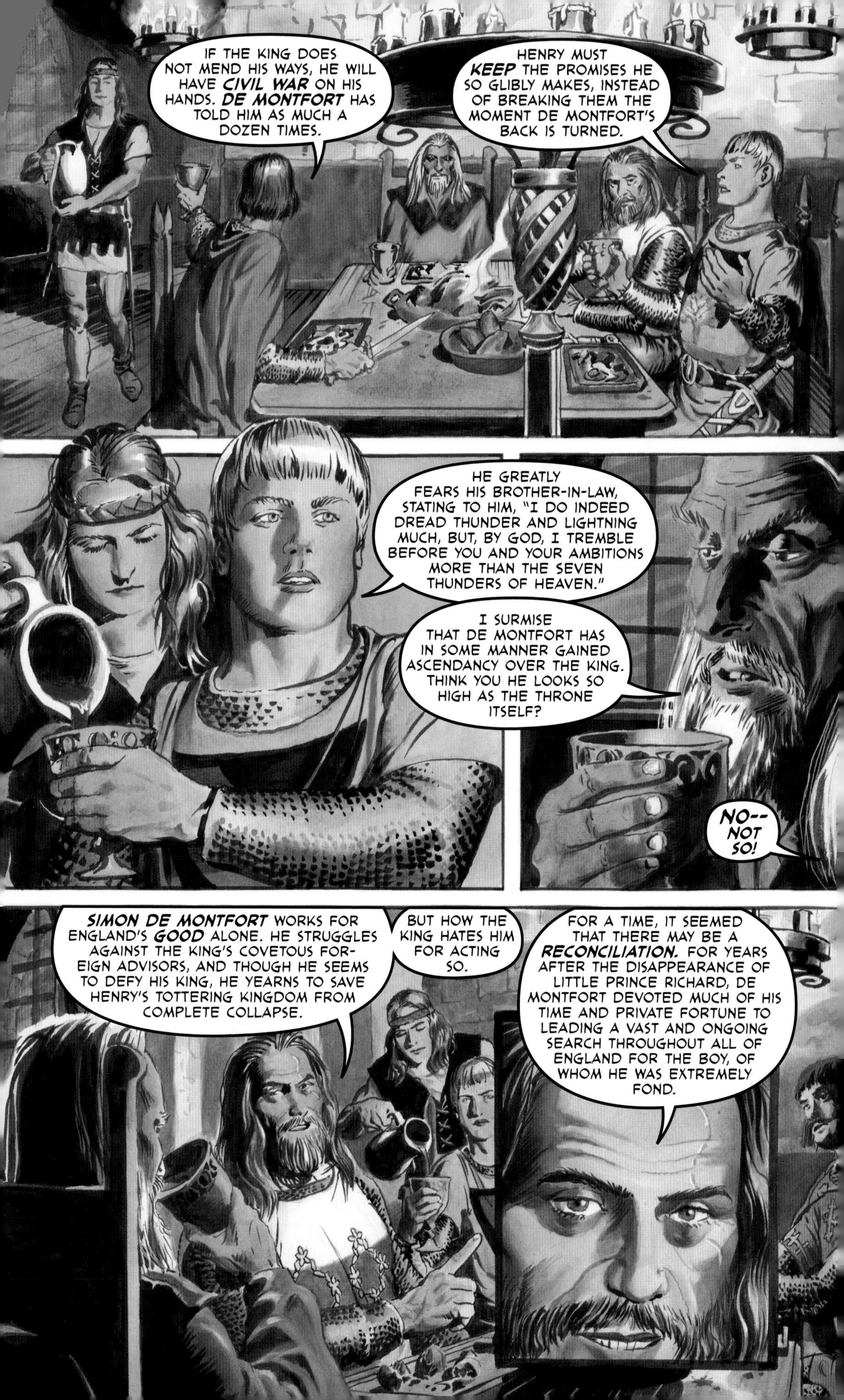
IF THE KING DOES NOT MEND HIS WAYS, HE WILL HAVE CIVIL WAR ON HIS HANDS. DE MONTFORT HAS TOLD HIM AS MUCH A DOZEN TIMES.
HENRY MUST KEEP THE PROMISES HE SO GLIBLY MAKES, INSTEAD OF BREAKING THEM THE MOMENT DE MONTFORT'S BACK IS TURNED.
HE GREATLY FEARS HIS BROTHER-IN-LAW, STATING TO HIM, "I DO INDEED DREAD THUNDER AND LIGHTNING MUCH, BUT, BY GOD, I TREMBLE BEFORE YOU AND YOUR AMBITIONS MORE THAN THE SEVEN THUNDERS OF HEAVEN."
I SURMISE THAT DE MONTFORT HAS IN SOME MANNER GAINED ASCENDANCY OVER THE KING. THINK YOU HE LOOKS SO HIGH AS THE THRONE ITSELF?
NO-- NOT SO!
SIMON DE MONTFORT WORKS FOR ENGLAND'S GOOD ALONE. HE STRUGGLES AGAINST THE KING'S COVETOUS FOREIGN ADVISORS, AND THOUGH HE SEEMS TO DEFY HIS KING, HE YEARNS TO SAVE HENRY'S TOTTERING KINGDOM FROM COMPLETE COLLAPSE.
BUT HOW THE KING HATES HIM FOR ACTING SO.
FOR A TIME, IT SEEMED THAT THERE MAY BE A RECONCILIATION. FOR YEARS AFTER THE DISAPPEARANCE OF LITTLE PRINCE RICHARD, DE MONTFORT DEVOTED MUCH OF HIS TIME AND PRIVATE FORTUNE TO LEADING A VAST AND ONGOING SEARCH THROUGHOUT ALL OF ENGLAND FOR THE BOY, OF WHOM HE WAS EXTREMELY FOND.

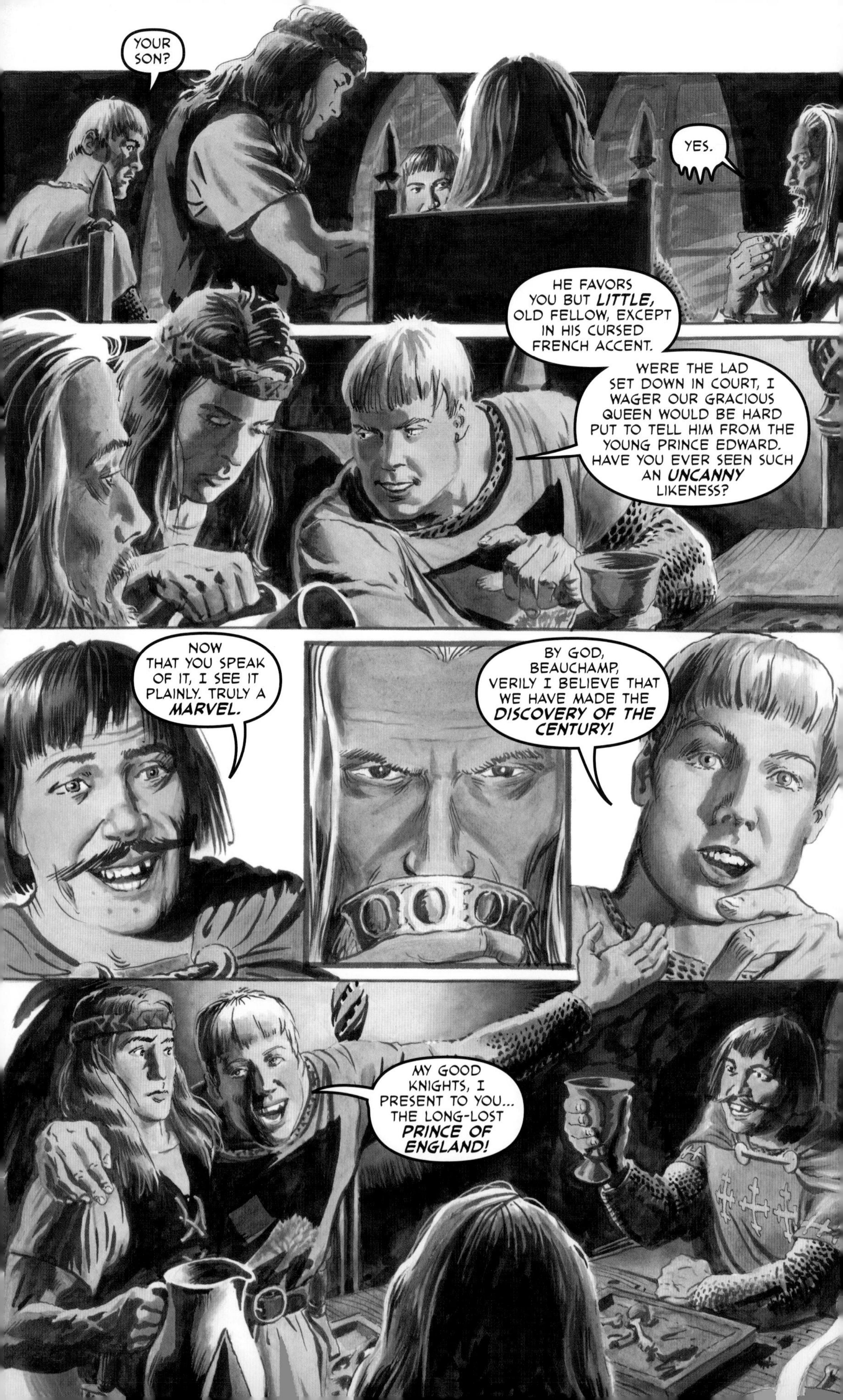
YOUR SON?
YES.
HE FAVORS YOU BUT LITTLE, OLD FELLOW, EXCEPT IN HIS CURSED FRENCH ACCENT.
WERE THE LAD SET DOWN IN COURT, I WAGER OUR GRACIOUS QUEEN WOULD BE HARD PUT TO TELL HIM FROM THE YOUNG PRINCE EDWARD. HAVE YOU EVER SEEN SUCH AN UNCANNY LIKENESS?
NOW THAT YOU SPEAK OF IT, I SEE IT PLAINLY. TRULY A MARVEL.
BY GOD, BEAUCHAMP, VERILY I BELIEVE THAT WE HAVE MADE THE DISCOVERY OF THE CENTURY!
MY GOOD KNIGHTS, I PRESENT TO YOU... THE LONG-LOST PRINCE OF ENGLAND!

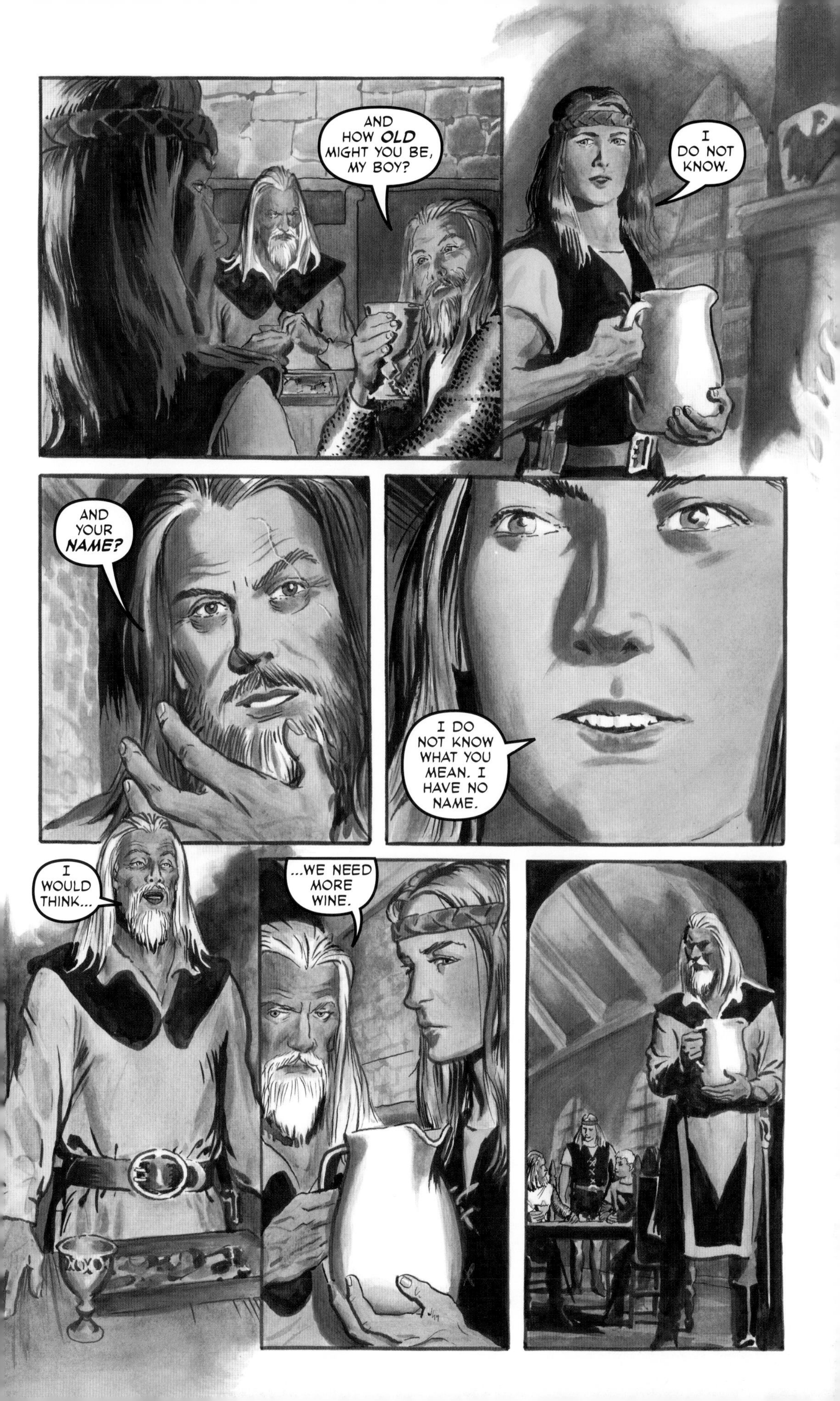
AND HOW *OLD* MIGHT YOU BE, MY BOY?
I DO NOT KNOW.
AND YOUR *NAME?*
I DO NOT KNOW WHAT YOU MEAN. I HAVE NO NAME.
I WOULD THINK...
...WE NEED MORE WINE.

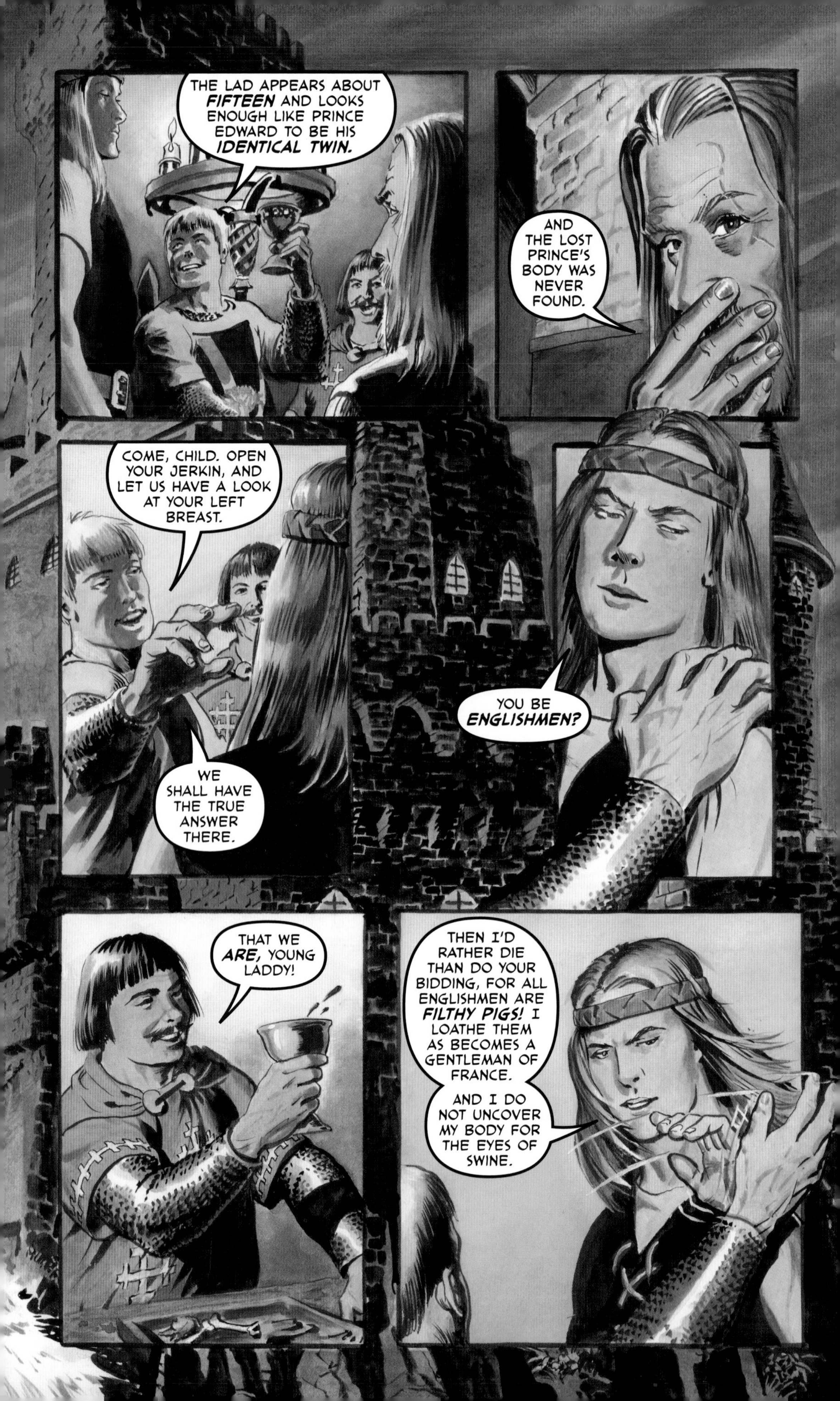
THE LAD APPEARS ABOUT FIFTEEN AND LOOKS ENOUGH LIKE PRINCE EDWARD TO BE HIS IDENTICAL TWIN.
AND THE LOST PRINCE'S BODY WAS NEVER FOUND.
COME, CHILD. OPEN YOUR JERKIN, AND LET US HAVE A LOOK AT YOUR LEFT BREAST.
WE SHALL HAVE THE TRUE ANSWER THERE.
YOU BE ENGLISHMEN?
THAT WE ARE, YOUNG LADDY!
THEN I'D RATHER DIE THAN DO YOUR BIDDING, FOR ALL ENGLISHMEN ARE FILTHY PIGS! I LOATHE THEM AS BECOMES A GENTLEMAN OF FRANCE.
AND I DO NOT UNCOVER MY BODY FOR THE EYES OF SWINE.

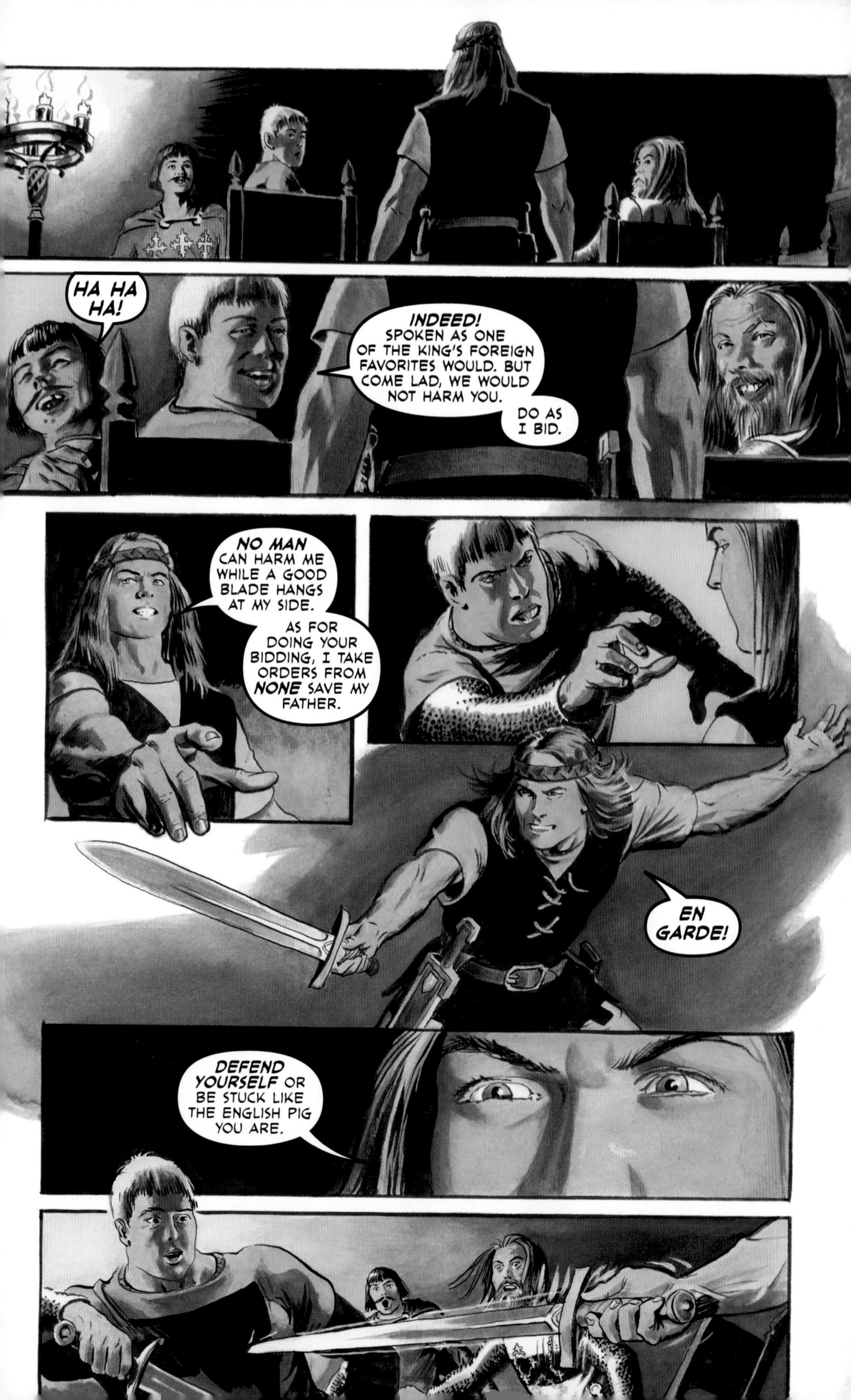
HA HA HA!
INDEED! SPOKEN AS ONE OF THE KING'S FOREIGN FAVORITES WOULD. BUT COME LAD, WE WOULD NOT HARM YOU.
DO AS I BID.
NO MAN CAN HARM ME WHILE A GOOD BLADE HANGS AT MY SIDE.
AS FOR DOING YOUR BIDDING, I TAKE ORDERS FROM NONE SAVE MY FATHER.
EN GARDE!
DEFEND YOURSELF OR BE STUCK LIKE THE ENGLISH PIG YOU ARE.

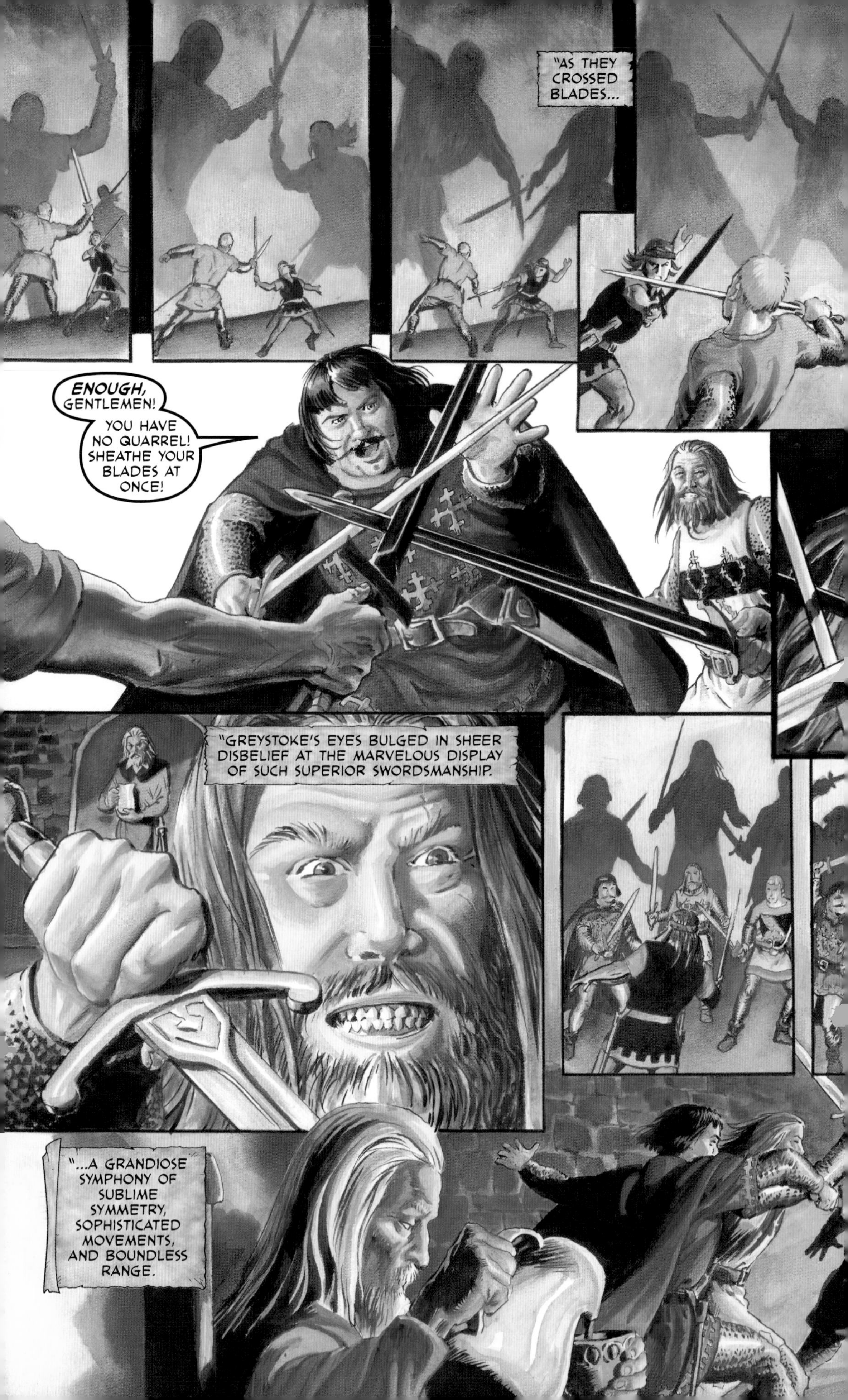
"AS THEY CROSSED BLADES...
ENOUGH, GENTLEMEN!
YOU HAVE NO QUARREL! SHEATHE YOUR BLADES AT ONCE!
"GREYSTOKE'S EYES BULGED IN SHEER DISBELIEF AT THE MARVELOUS DISPLAY OF SUCH SUPERIOR SWORDSMANSHIP.
"...A GRANDIOSE SYMPHONY OF SUBLIME SYMMETRY, SOPHISTICATED MOVEMENTS, AND BOUNDLESS RANGE.

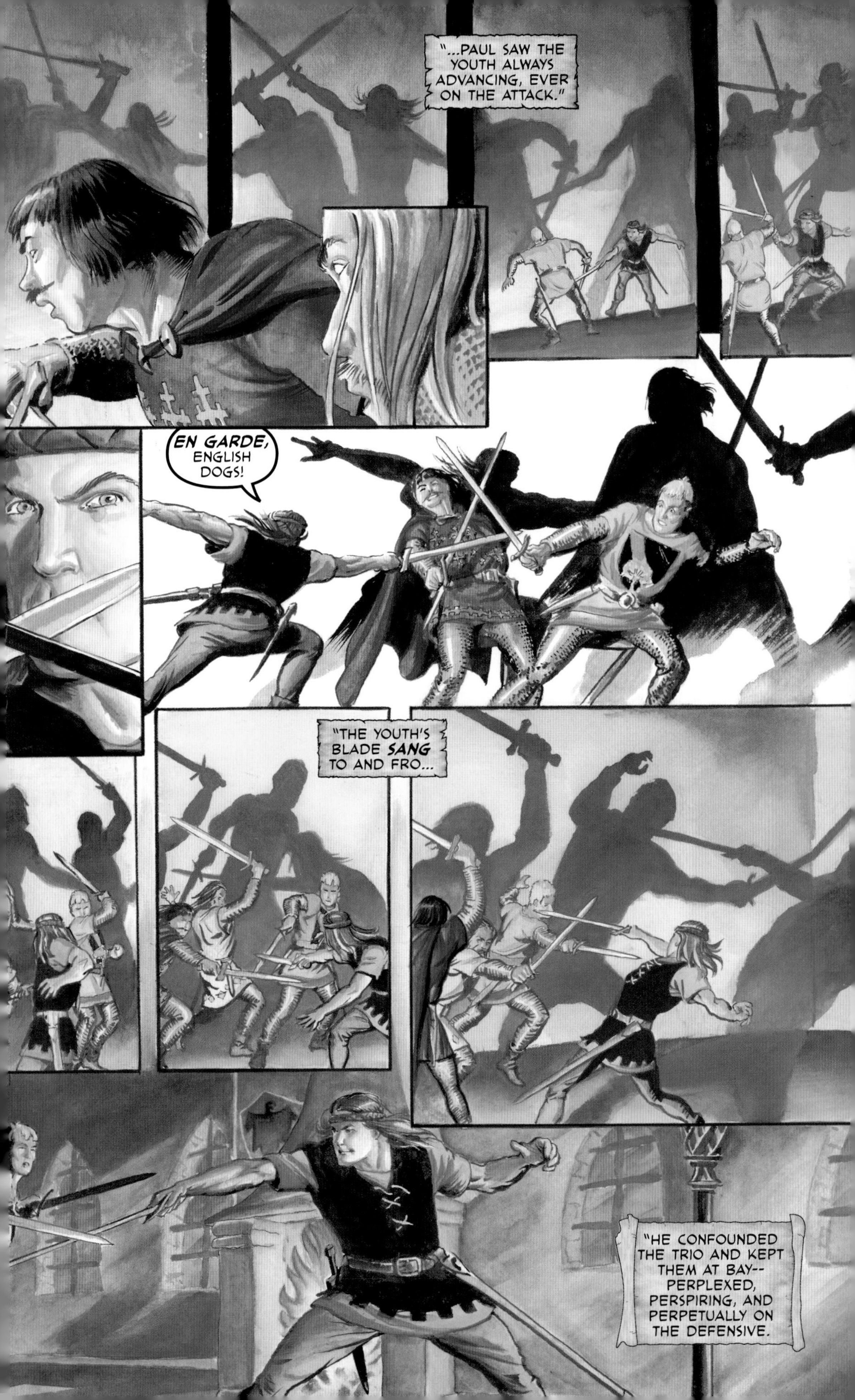
"...PAUL SAW THE YOUTH ALWAYS ADVANCING, EVER ON THE ATTACK."
EN GARDE, ENGLISH DOGS!
"THE YOUTH'S BLADE SANG TO AND FRO...
"HE CONFOUNDED THE TRIO AND KEPT THEM AT BAY-- PERPLEXED, PERSPIRING, AND PERPETUALLY ON THE DEFENSIVE.

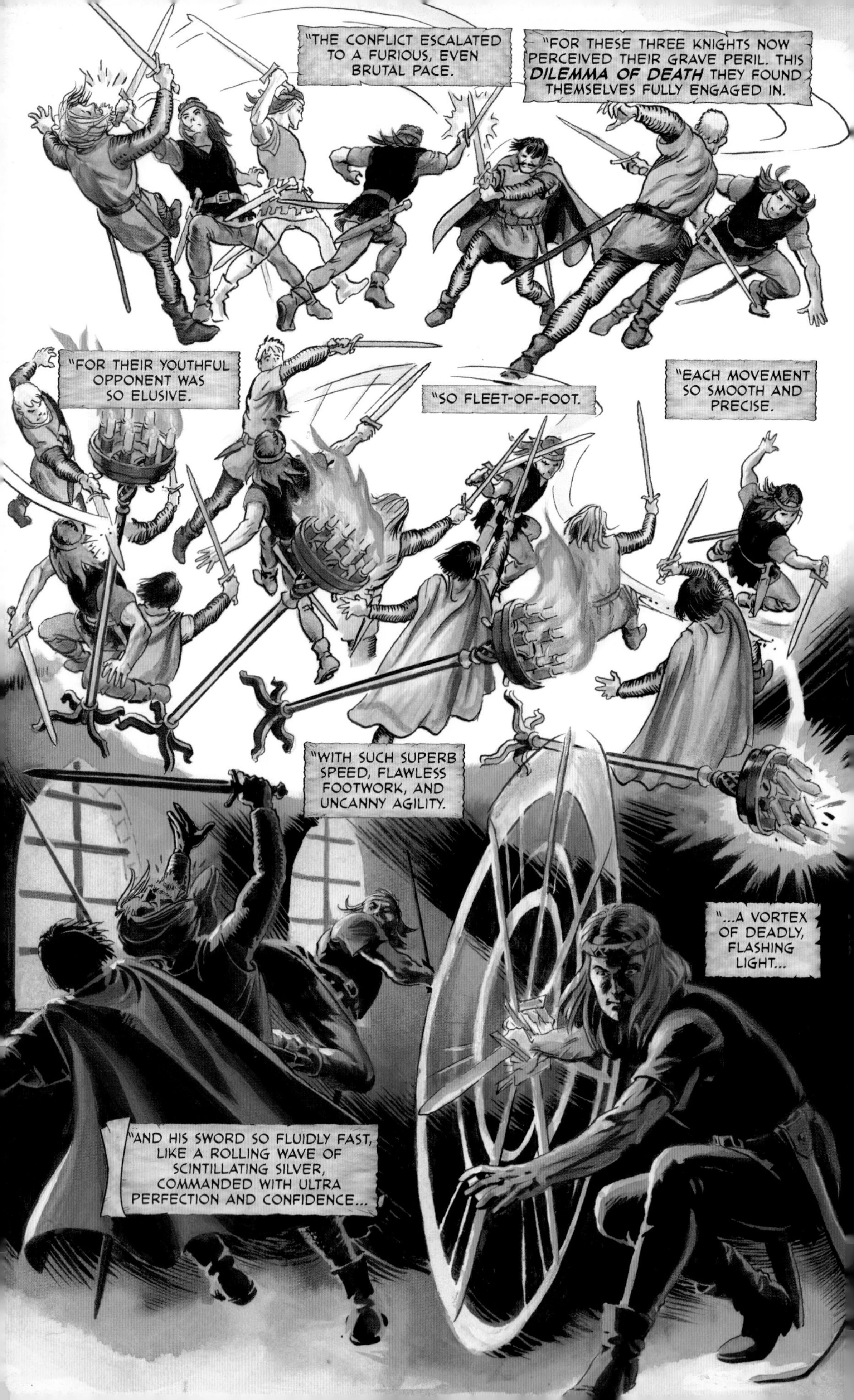
"THE CONFLICT ESCALATED TO A FURIOUS, EVEN BRUTAL PACE.
"FOR THESE THREE KNIGHTS NOW PERCEIVED THEIR GRAVE PERIL. THIS DILEMMA OF DEATH THEY FOUND THEMSELVES FULLY ENGAGED IN.
"FOR THEIR YOUTHFUL OPPONENT WAS SO ELUSIVE.
"SO FLEET-OF-FOOT.
"EACH MOVEMENT SO SMOOTH AND PRECISE.
"WITH SUCH SUPERB SPEED, FLAWLESS FOOTWORK, AND UNCANNY AGILITY.
"...A VORTEX OF DEADLY, FLASHING LIGHT...
"AND HIS SWORD SO FLUIDLY FAST, LIKE A ROLLING WAVE OF SCINTILLATING SILVER, COMMANDED WITH ULTRA PERFECTION AND CONFIDENCE...

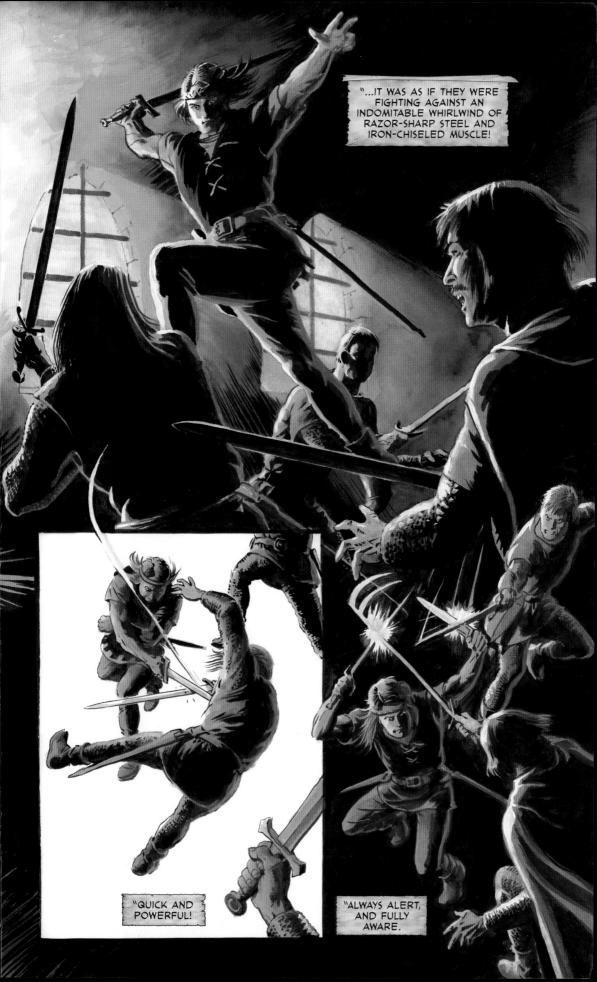

"...IT WAS AS IF THEY WERE FIGHTING AGAINST AN INDOMITABLE WHIRLWIND OF RAZOR-SHARP STEEL AND IRON-CHISELED MUSCLE!

"QUICK AND POWERFUL!

"ALWAYS ALERT, AND FULLY AWARE.

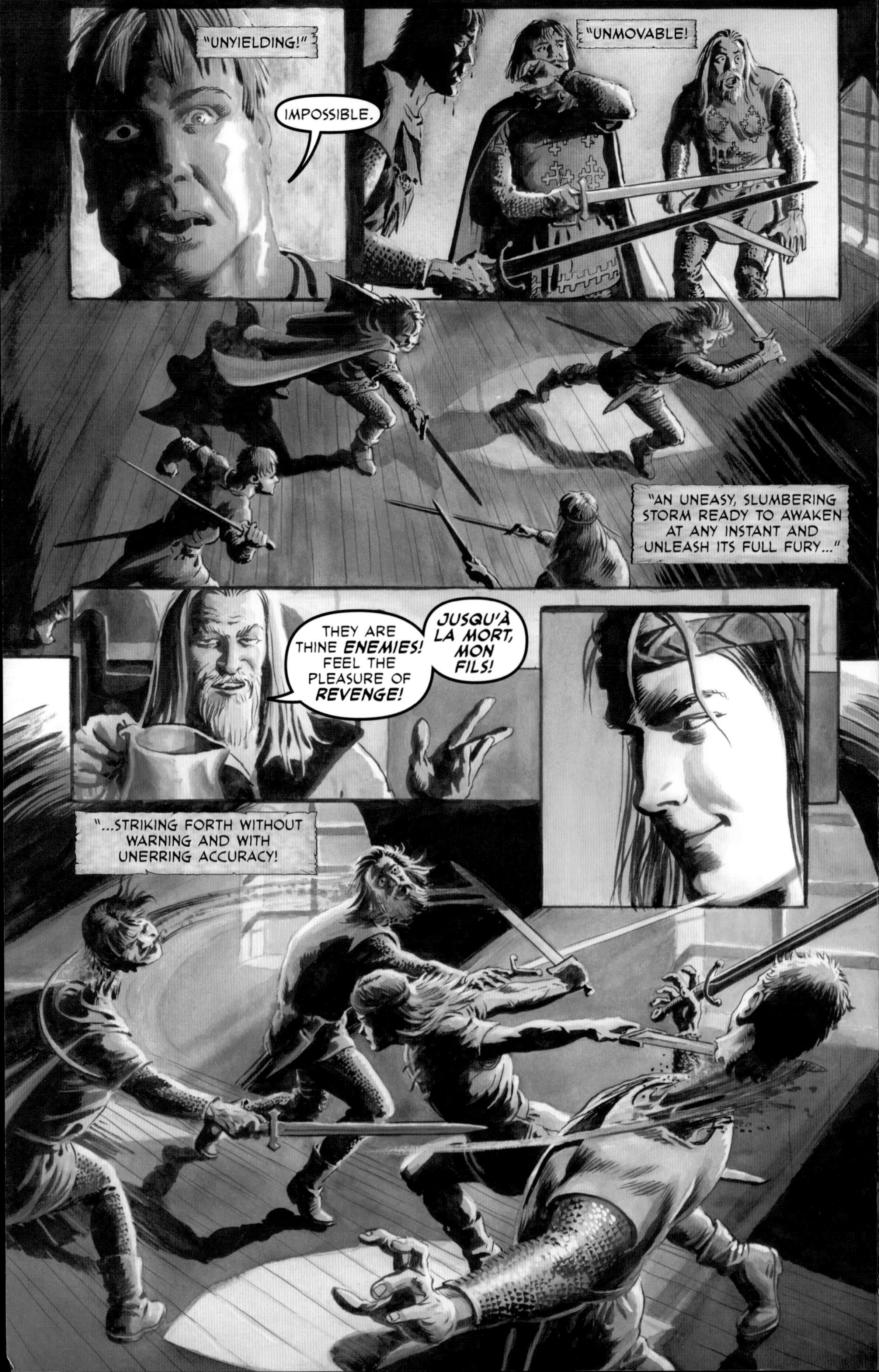
"UNYIELDING!"
IMPOSSIBLE.
"UNMOVABLE!
"AN UNEASY, SLUMBERING STORM READY TO AWAKEN AT ANY INSTANT AND UNLEASH ITS FULL FURY..."
THEY ARE THINE ENEMIES! FEEL THE PLEASURE OF REVENGE!
JUSQU'À LA MORT, MON FILS!
"...STRIKING FORTH WITHOUT WARNING AND WITH UNERRING ACCURACY!

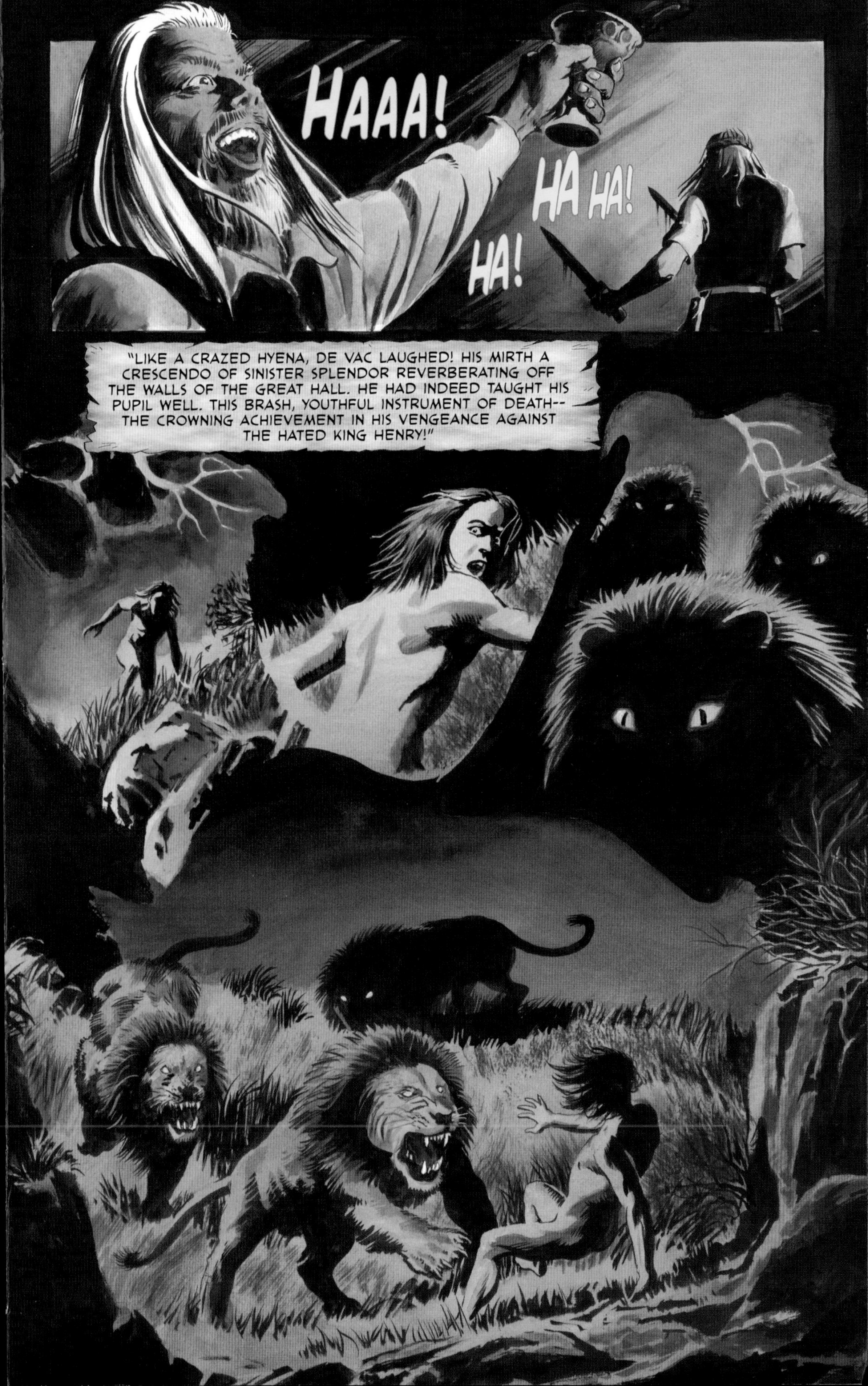
HAAAA!
HA HA!
HA!
"LIKE A CRAZED HYENA, DE VAC LAUGHED! HIS MIRTH A CRESCENDO OF SINISTER SPLENDOR REVERBERATING OFF THE WALLS OF THE GREAT HALL. HE HAD INDEED TAUGHT HIS PUPIL WELL. THIS BRASH, YOUTHFUL INSTRUMENT OF DEATH-- THE CROWNING ACHIEVEMENT IN HIS VENGEANCE AGAINST THE HATED KING HENRY!"

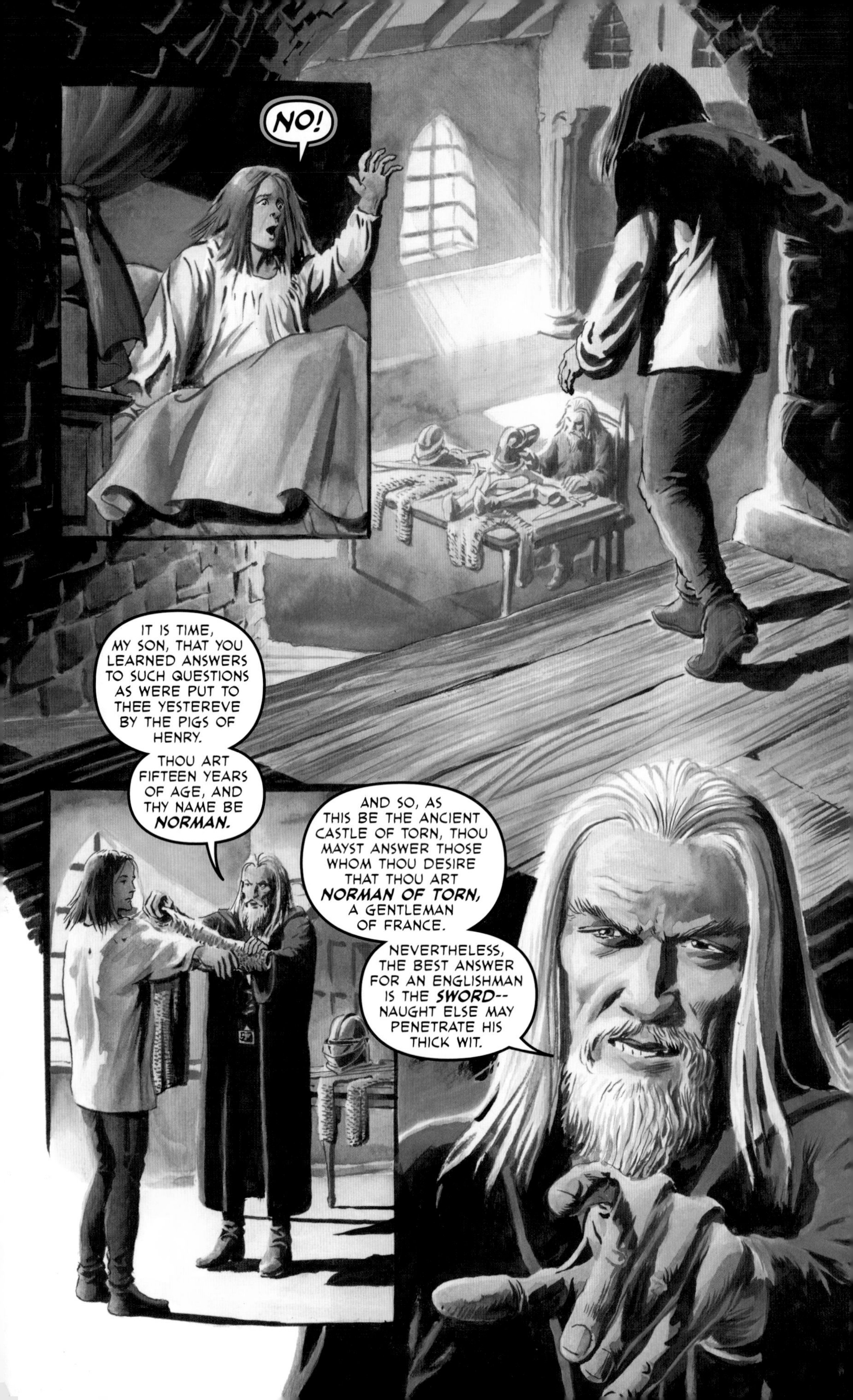
NO!
IT IS TIME, MY SON, THAT YOU LEARNED ANSWERS TO SUCH QUESTIONS AS WERE PUT TO THEE YESTEREVE BY THE PIGS OF HENRY.
THOU ART FIFTEEN YEARS OF AGE, AND THY NAME BE **NORMAN.**
AND SO, AS THIS BE THE ANCIENT CASTLE OF TORN, THOU MAYST ANSWER THOSE WHOM THOU DESIRE THAT THOU ART **NORMAN OF TORN,** A GENTLEMAN OF FRANCE.
NEVERTHELESS, THE BEST ANSWER FOR AN ENGLISHMAN IS THE **SWORD**-- NAUGHT ELSE MAY PENETRATE HIS THICK WIT.

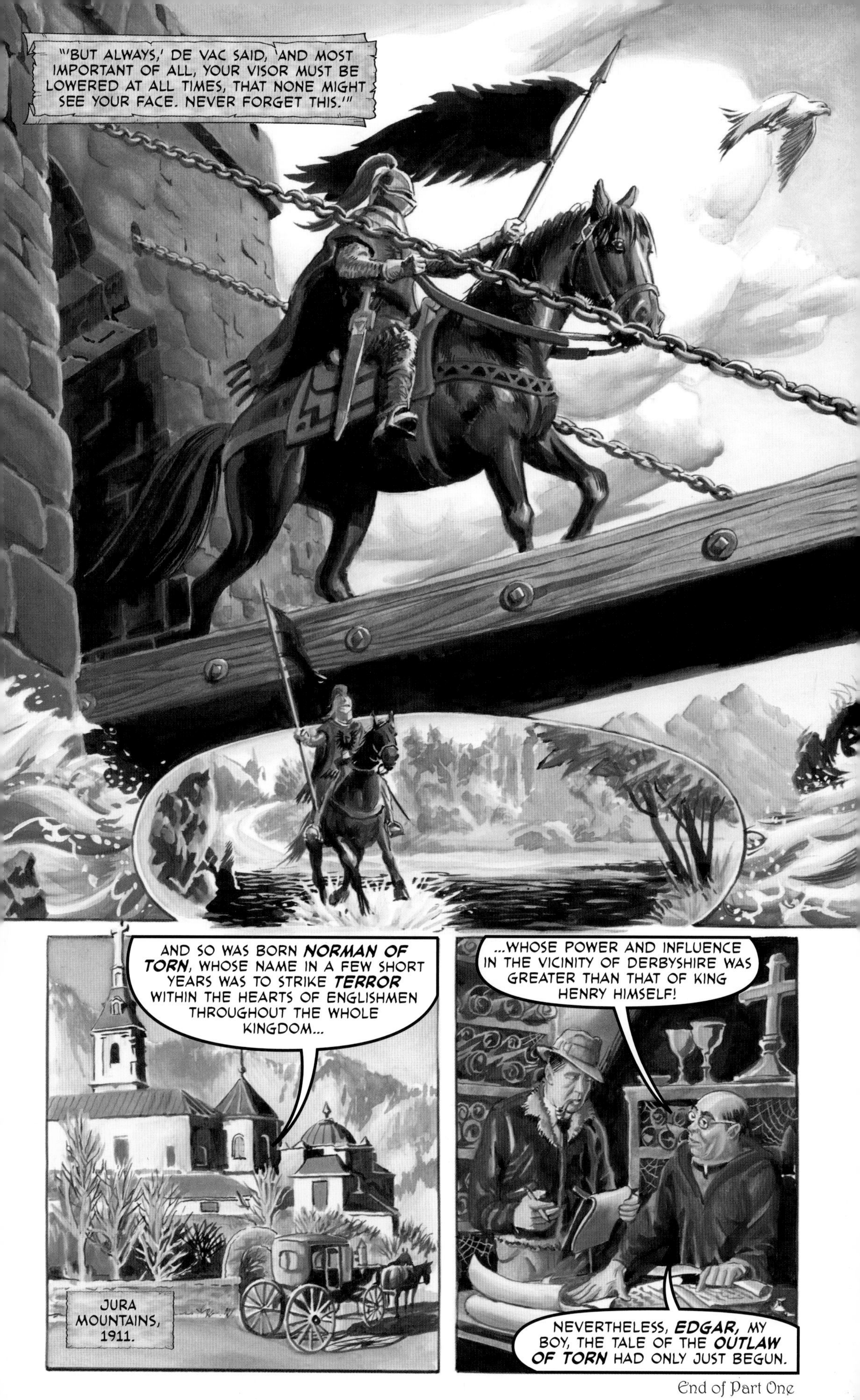
"'BUT ALWAYS,' DE VAC SAID, 'AND MOST IMPORTANT OF ALL, YOUR VISOR MUST BE LOWERED AT ALL TIMES, THAT NONE MIGHT SEE YOUR FACE. NEVER FORGET THIS.'"
AND SO WAS BORN NORMAN OF TORN, WHOSE NAME IN A FEW SHORT YEARS WAS TO STRIKE TERROR WITHIN THE HEARTS OF ENGLISHMEN THROUGHOUT THE WHOLE KINGDOM...
JURA MOUNTAINS, 1911.
...WHOSE POWER AND INFLUENCE IN THE VICINITY OF DERBYSHIRE WAS GREATER THAN THAT OF KING HENRY HIMSELF!
NEVERTHELESS, EDGAR, MY BOY, THE TALE OF THE OUTLAW OF TORN HAD ONLY JUST BEGUN.

End of Part One